When Once Are Not Enough

Adam and Evie

Summer Lake Silver
Book Eight

By SJ McCoy

A Sweet n Steamy Romance

Published by Xenion, Inc

Published by Xenion, Inc.
First paperback edition June 2022
www.sjmccoy.com

Cover Design by Dana Lamothe of Designs by Dana
Editor: Kellie Montgomery
Proofreaders: Aileen Blomberg, Traci Atkinson, Becky Claxon.

ISBN: 978-1-946220-94-3

Dedication

For Sam. Sometimes, life really is too short. Few oxo

Chapter One

Evelyn parked the car as close to the front door as she could get, just as she'd done every night since she'd come to stay here. She left the car running and the headlights on to illuminate the front door, then hurried to unlock it. She reached inside and flipped on the light in the hallway and the one on the porch. Then she ran back, cut the engine, locked the car, and hurried into the house. Once she was inside, she leaned against the door, closing her eyes while she waited for her heart rate to return to normal.

As she stood there, she couldn't help comparing the way her life was now to the way it had been in Chicago. She used to stroll home to her apartment building, stand in the foyer to chat with the doorman for a while, and then ride the elevator up to the twenty-third floor. It wasn't that long ago, but it felt like a different lifetime.

She pushed away from the door and headed for the kitchen. She was hungry; hunger wasn't something she'd been familiar with in her old life, either. It was a constant companion these days. She opened the fridge and took out one of the last two containers of rice and beans. If Taryn could see her now! She could hear her old friend's voice as clearly as if she were here with her. *Rice and beans? Beans and rice, I ask you.*

Taryn's tales of growing up in a family where beans and rice were the staple diet, used to make Evelyn laugh. She hadn't understood, not really. Of course, she knew that Taryn had grown up poor – dirt poor – and Evelyn had understood the concepts of hunger and fear of not having enough, but not the reality. She sighed as she slid the container into the microwave. If it weren't for her friend's stories about her childhood, she didn't know what she'd be eating these days. Taryn might not be here with her, might not be able to ensure that she ate well in the same way that she had in the restaurant, but the stories she told had made sure that Evelyn knew of a food source that she could afford. While it might not be a nutritionally complete diet, it covered the basics and was filling enough.

She sighed as she took the container from the microwave and stirred the uninspiring-looking contents with a fork. She should be grateful, and she was. Just a few short weeks ago she'd been sleeping in her car and hadn't known when she might eat again – or what.

She'd be forever grateful to Russ and Ria. On her lowest day, they'd followed her to her car after she'd failed to find herself a job. Ria had given her a couple of sandwiches and eighty dollars. Russ had given her his card, and a few days later, had given her a job at his gym. Her shoulders relaxed, and she went to get a glass of water from the faucet before she pulled up a stool at the island.

That day had been a turning point. She hadn't known what she was going to do. She'd been down to her last five dollars, and the gas gauge on her car had been pointing at the E for a couple of days. She'd felt as though she was out of options – because she was.

She smiled and started to eat. Regular beans and rice were a sign of progress. Maybe next week she'd buy some cheese to sprinkle over them. She was no longer in such dire straits as she had been, but she was still saving most of the money she was earning at the gym – for when she had to run again.

She froze when she heard a vehicle pull up outside. Her hands started to shake, and the fork fell into the bowl. She wanted to turn the lights out, pretend there was no one here, but it was too late for that. Whoever was out there would have seen the lights already.

She ran up the stairs instead. The small bedroom at the front of the house overlooked the driveway and the front door; she'd be able to see what vehicle was out there and maybe even see who was at the door – if they went to the door.

She tried to catch her breath as she crept along the wall, not wanting whoever was out there to spot movement in the window. She cautiously peeked out and relaxed a little when she recognized Adam's truck. She didn't know why he was here; he'd said that he'd be in Nashville until next week. She wasn't thrilled that she'd have to let him in – it was his house after all. But his truck was a much more welcome sight than what she'd feared she might see out there.

She started back down the stairs when the doorbell rang. Her heart was hammering again – not from fear, not from exertion, but from the thought of seeing Adam. It was stupid and she knew it. Not stupid to find the man attractive, she knew she wasn't the only woman in town who did. But it was stupid for *her*. She wasn't one of the attractive young things who came into the gym to work out. She was a fifty-three-year-old dowdy widow. She might not have been too bad while she still lived in Chicago, but since she'd been in hiding, there was no denying that dowdy was the only word for her.

The doorbell rang again just as she reached the bottom of the stairs. "Evie? Are you okay? I'm coming in."

The door flew open, and Adam came rushing in at the same time that she rushed forward to open it to let him know that she was fine. She rushed right into him and froze when his arms closed around her to steady her.

"Whoa!" He gripped her arms as he stepped back, "I'm sorry. I panicked when you didn't answer the door."

She shook her head. "No, I'm sorry. I was just upstairs, I … I'm sorry." She wasn't sorry that she'd rushed into him like that — only sorry that the brief moment of feeling safe in his arms had ended so quickly. Jeez! She had to stop that kind of thinking.

He gave her a puzzled look. "Are you okay?"

"I'm fine. What are you doing here? I thought you were going to be away until next week."

"I was supposed to be …" He frowned again. "Shit. I'm sorry. I didn't think." He glanced up the stairs. "Do you have someone here?"

"Someone …?"

He pursed his lips. "Do you have *a friend* over? Upstairs?"

It took her a second to figure out what he meant. He thought …? She laughed; she couldn't help it. "No! I don't." She shook her head at the absurdity of the question. "I don't have *any* friends, let alone one I would take upstairs."

He held her gaze for a long moment, and she had to chase away the thought that she'd like to take him upstairs. As if he'd want to take *her* to bed. She imagined that he shared his bed with the kind of girls who came into the gym, and the ones he must meet working security as he did for Clay McAdam. A big star country singer like Clay would have way more groupies than he knew what to do with. She'd guess that plenty of them would set their sights on the singer's sexy, rugged, head of security instead.

She realized that he was still holding her gaze and hadn't responded to her sad confession that she didn't have any friends. He probably wasn't surprised that she had no love life.

"I'm sorry. Come on in. Do you want me to get out now? Now that you're back?" She hurried back to the kitchen.

"Evie?"

She turned around. She didn't even remember when or why he'd started calling her Evie. She'd introduced herself to everyone she met in Summer Lake as Evelyn.

"What?"

He blew out a sigh. "I told you that you can stay here for as long as you like. I don't need the place back."

"But … you need to finish all the work, and you need … you don't need some stray woman here, in your way."

"You're not in my way. Clay wanted to come back to the lake for the weekend. I … wanted to come and see how you were doing. That's all. I'm not here to check up on you, not here to work on the house. I came … to see you."

She frowned. "Why?"

"Because even though you said you don't have any friends, you do; I'd like to think that I'm one."

She just stared at him. He'd been good to her, letting her stay here. The house was still mid-renovation, but the kitchen, bathroom, and main bedroom were already done. The place was livable. Adam had asked her if she wanted to stay here to keep an eye on it for him. She suspected that he – just like Russ and Ria – knew that she'd been living in her car, even though he hadn't asked.

"Why?" she asked eventually. She'd been trying to avoid that question but now, she had to know. Were they all taking pity on her? They were and she knew it, but she was in no position to refuse their charity, and that's what it felt like, all of it – the house, the job, the kindness they'd shown her.

He clasped his hands together and brought them up to rest his chin on them. It was an endearing mannerism that she noticed he did a lot. It didn't hurt that it showed off his muscular arms and ... No. She had to stop that. She hadn't noticed a man in that way in over five years, not since Tom died. She couldn't afford to think about Adam that way; he was ... she didn't know how old, but a good few years younger than her. And even if he were her age, even if he were interested, she had much more important issues to face.

Adam gave her a wry smile. "Well, since you're staying in my house, and we see each other at the gym pretty much every day that I'm here in town, I don't see any reason why we shouldn't be friends. Do you?"

She shook her head slowly. She couldn't think of any reason that she could tell him, anyway. She didn't have any friends anymore because it was safer that way; safer for them and safer for her. She'd only allowed herself to call Taryn occasionally since she left Chicago. And each time she did, she worried that Anatoly might somehow be listening in.

Adam waited, hoping that she might say something. At least she hadn't immediately given him a list of reasons why they couldn't be friends. That was a start. It was more than he'd managed to get from her so far. Although to be fair, he hadn't really tried. She was hiding something, something big. He guessed that she was hiding from someone. And he knew damned well that if he pushed too hard, she'd run.

From the way she'd been living in her car, he believed that she'd been on the run for a while. She probably felt as though she was taking a huge risk by staying in Summer Lake for so long – she'd been here for a few weeks now – and there was no way he wanted to be the reason that she felt she needed to take off again. He'd rather be the reason that she decided to stick around.

It didn't look like she was going to answer his question, so he decided to let it drop – for now. He looked around the kitchen, not surprised to see that it didn't look any different than it had the day she first arrived. She hadn't brought any knick-knacks, there was no clutter, no evidence that she was staying here other than her purse hung over the back of one of the stools and …

"I'm sorry. You were eating?" That was weird. She'd said that she was upstairs when he arrived, and yet there was a glass of water and a bowl of … beans and rice? Yeah, that was it. Shit, she had to be even worse off than he'd thought.

She glanced at the bowl and then back at him and pressed her lips together. "Yes."

He wanted nothing more than to go to her, wrap his arms around and hold her, get her to tell him what the hell it was that she was facing – and let him help. He'd felt drawn to her from the very first time he saw her when she walked into the gym to interview for the job with Russ. But she was so damned skittish that he didn't want to scare her off. And the more time that went by, the more he had to face the fact that she wasn't interested in him that way. She didn't act as though she was the least bit attracted to him. She kept him at arm's length, just as she did with everyone – perhaps more so.

He hadn't been able to resist the desire to come over and check on her this evening, but now he felt like it'd been the wrong move. She was uncomfortable with him being here; he should go.

"I'm sorry. I'll …"

Her phone started to ring, and all the color drained from her face. She looked at her purse as if she thought it might be about to explode.

"Do you need to get that?"

She was shaking visibly as she shook her head.

He waited until the ringing stopped. He'd been about to leave, but there was no way he was going until he knew what was going on.

"I'm sorry." She swallowed as she met his gaze. "I …" She gasped when the phone started to ring again.

Adam raised his eyebrows. "Do you want me to see who it is?"

She shook her head rapidly.

"Tell me what's going on, Evie?"

She turned her back to him and shook her head. He could see that she'd brought her hands up to cover her face, then her shoulders started to shake. That was it. He had no choice. He crossed the space between them in two long strides. He reached for her but stopped himself just in time. Who knew what she'd been through? She didn't need to be manhandled, no matter how much he wanted to hold her.

Instead, he touched her arm. "Talk to me."

She shook her head.

He moved closer.

"Tell me what you're so afraid of."

She shook her head again.

"Are you afraid of me?"

"No!"

"Want to turn around?"

She shook her head again.

The damn phone stopped ringing and then started again. Whoever it was wanted to talk to her and wasn't giving up.

Adam held his breath; this could be a horrible move, but it felt like the right one. He slipped his arms around her waist and pulled her back against him. It killed him to feel the sobs that wracked her body. She was so tense that she felt like she was humming with electricity. A different kind of electricity hummed through him when she relaxed back against him. He tightened his arms around her and held her closer. She wasn't short, she was maybe five-seven, and she fit against him perfectly. He rested his chin on top of her head and just held her. He hoped it was helping her – it felt pretty damned good to him.

Her shaking subsided a little and her breathing slowed.

"Want to turn around now?"

She nodded, and without looking up at him, she turned within the circle of his arms. He cupped the back of her head, and she pressed her cheek into his shoulder.

"I'm sorry."

"Don't be. We just said that we were going to be friends, didn't we? I reckon this is the kind of thing friends do for each other."

She nodded against his shoulder, and he was glad that she didn't seem to be in any hurry to move away from him. This wasn't the way he'd been hoping that he'd get to hold her, but it was what she needed right now.

"You know what else friends do?"

She shook her head.

"They confide in each other, Evie."

She tensed again, and he almost regretted pushing her, but he couldn't regret it. She had problems, big ones by the look of it, and he wanted to help.

She startled when the phone started to ring again.

"Do you want me to answer it – see who it is?"

He felt her suck in a deep breath, and then she did step away from him. "I know who it is. No one has the number for that phone."

He could feel himself frown. Those two statements might not add up to anything that made sense to most people, but in his line of work, he knew what they meant – and they added up to bad news.

She went to her purse and took the phone out with shaking hands. She looked at the screen and then closed her eyes and sank to the floor.

Adam managed to catch her just before she hit her head. He sat cross-legged on the floor and wrapped his arms around her, grateful that she leaned against him and made no attempt to get up. Shit. Whatever was going on, it was bad.

He glanced at the phone that was still ringing where it fell. It was a Chicago area code, but that didn't help him any. He wasn't going to know anything until she talked to him, and after this, she was going to have to talk to him.

She opened her eyes, and his heart clenched in his chest when she looked into his. She was terrified, but she was still trying to be strong, still trying to keep him out. "I'm so sorry. You must think I'm … I don't know what."

He brushed her hair away from her face. "I think you're scared, and I think you're all alone, and I think you've been facing whatever's going on by yourself for way too long. You don't have to anymore."

Tears rolled down her cheeks as she shook her head. "I do."

He gave her a wry smile. "I told you, you've got a friend now."

She visibly pulled herself together. "It's okay, honestly. It's so kind of you, but I'll be fine."

"Come on, Evie."

They both stared at her phone when it began to ring yet again.

He saw a flash of anger on her face as she reached for it. "Hello?"

She turned even paler and started to shake again. Adam couldn't take any more. He held his hand out for the phone, and to his surprise, she handed it over.

"Who is this?"

"Who the fuck are you? Is a better question."

"I'm a friend."

"Think again. Evelyn is my property."

Adam laughed. "Evelyn is nobody's property. She's her own person. You need to think again and stop harassing her."

"Do you know who I am?"

"Some asshole who thinks that women can be property."

"You should ask her, then decide if you think that her friendship is worth it."

The call ended and he set the phone down on the counter.

"Are you okay?"

She let out a short, shaky laugh and scrambled to her feet. "Oh, I'm just great." She grabbed her purse and looked around wildly. "I need to get my things."

"Does he know where you are?" Adam asked as he got up.

"Not yet. But he found my number and I've only had that phone for a couple of weeks – it's not even registered anywhere; it's one of those prepaid ones. It won't take him long. He'll find me. I have to go."

Adam's heart sank. "Where?"

"I don't know! Just … away, away from here, away from you. I knew I shouldn't have stayed here for so long. I got complacent, I …" She shook her head. "You've been so kind. I know you want to help, but it's better – safer – if I just …"

He reached out and touched her arm, hoping to calm her again, but not sure it would work. "Safer for who?"

"For you, of course! If he comes here. If he finds me here …" She shuddered.

"Take a breath." He tightened his grip on her arm, hoping like hell that it wouldn't scare her.

She met his gaze, and he was relieved when she did as he said. Then she took another couple of deep – hopefully, calming – breaths.

"Better?" he asked with a half-smile.

He felt proud of her when she attempted a smile back and nodded, even as she said, "No."

He chuckled. "I didn't think so, but it slowed you down enough to think about the question I'm going to ask you."

"What?"

"Where do you think you're going to go tonight that will be safer than right here?"

She stared into his eyes for a long moment before she shrugged.

"So, stay. I'll stay here, too."

"No! You don't understand, Adam. You don't know what he's like. If he found you with me, he'd …" She shuddered.

"He'd what?" He needed to know what kind of threat she thought this guy was.

"I don't know, and I don't want to find out. I don't want anything to happen to you because of me."

Adam had to smile. "It won't. If I'm what you're worried about, you've got nothing to worry about."

She looked doubtful, but she didn't seem as panicked as she did just a few minutes ago.

"Give me a little credit, would you? Do you think Clay McAdam would have trusted me with his security all these years if I couldn't keep him safe?"

She let out a short laugh. "I don't think crazed middle-aged women present the same kind of threat as this."

"You'd be surprised. Some of those women can be scary." His smile faded. "But seriously, I know how to take care of myself, and I want to take care of you, too."

She still didn't look like she was going to go for it.

"How about you stay here tonight? I'll stay with you. You can tell me all about it. I am a professional – security and risk assessment are what I do. Even if you still want to run in the morning, I'll be able to give you an assessment before you go." He was going to do his best to talk her out of leaving; he didn't want to give her an assessment, he wanted to make one and then put a plan into place and take care of it himself. For now, he was offering the option he thought she was most likely to agree to.

His shoulders relaxed when she finally nodded. "Thanks, Adam." She gave him a small smile. "I wouldn't want to insult you by implying that you can't keep your own home safe for a single night. I'd appreciate your input on what you think I should do from here." Her smile disappeared. "What you think I should do when I leave – in the morning."

Adam nodded. He'd work with what she was giving him for now and then go from there.

Chapter Two

"Do you want a drink?"

Evelyn would love one – she could use something strong right about now. Of course, she had nothing. She felt bad that although this was Adam's house, she was the one who'd been staying here. She should be able to offer him something.

Adam took a step toward her, but she took a step back. She had to. She wanted to feel his arms around her again. When he'd stood behind her and held her, she'd felt truly safe for the first time in months – actually, make that years. She shouldn't have been able to feel that way while her phone was ringing – while she was almost certain that Anatoly had tracked down her phone, if not her whereabouts, yet. But the feel of Adam's broad chest against her back, the sight of his muscular forearms wrapped around her, and his big hands holding her to him, had made her feel not just safe but cared for. She knew that was just her own mind, making stuff up to try and feel better.

Adam was concerned. He was a good guy; he'd care about anyone who was in her situation. She just needed to drag her mind away from the thought – the hope – that he could actually care about her.

"Hey."

She realized that she'd been standing there staring at him and hadn't answered his question.

She shrugged. "I'd love one. But I don't have anything to offer you. I'm sorry." She nodded toward the glass of water sitting next to the forgotten beans and rice and gave him an apologetic smile. "Unless you'd care to join me in a glass of Summer Lake's finest H20; I hear that this year's a great vintage."

She loved the way lines around his eyes crinkled when he laughed. He might be younger than her, but he was no kid.

"I picked up a bottle of Tennessee's most famous if not finest while I was in Nashville. It's in the truck. And I'm guessing that you might need something a bit stronger than H20."

She smiled when she figured it out. "Jack Daniels?"

"Yeah, but if whiskey's not your thing, I was going to order dinner from Giuseppe's. I could get Tino to throw a bottle of wine in with the food." He went to one of the drawers and pulled out Giuseppe's takeout menu. "Since I interrupted your dinner, the least I can do is get you something to replace it."

She looked at the menu but shook her head. She couldn't. It wouldn't be right. She couldn't let him get her dinner. "I … I'm not hungry. Thanks." Her stomach chose that moment to let out a loud rumble.

She tried to laugh to cover up her embarrassment, but it came out as more of a sob, and she brought her hands up to cover her face.

Then Adam was there in front of her again. He closed his arms around her, and she couldn't help it – she buried her face in his chest. After feeling so scared, and so alone, for so long, she just couldn't resist leaning on him, letting him make it all feel better. It'd only be for a few moments. She'd step away again, apologize, but she was going to make the most of this moment while she had it. He was so solid, so reassuring, she felt like she could draw from his strength.

She started to lift her head, but his arms tightened around her. She wasn't going to argue if he was okay with her staying there.

"I've got you."

She closed her eyes. If only!

Goosebumps broke out on her arms when he rubbed his hand up and down her back and held her tighter. "I have, Evie. I've got you. You're okay. And you're going to be okay. I'm going to order us some dinner. We're going to eat, and talk, and drink whatever kind of wine you like best. You're going to tell me what's going on and –"

"No!" She stepped away from him. "The less you know the better, Adam."

He pursed his lips, and she was afraid that he was about to argue, but after a moment, he nodded and held the menu out to her. "First, let's figure out what we're going to eat."

She'd studied this menu many times, dreaming about what she'd order if she could. She knew that the chef's salad was her best bet. It was the least expensive item, and she'd finally get some of the greens she'd been craving.

Adam took his phone out once he was outside. He'd told Evie that he was going to get the whiskey, but he was going to place the order while he was out here, too. If she thought that she was going to get away with just a salad, she was in for a surprise. He planned to order as much food as Tino would deliver. Whatever they didn't eat tonight would go in the fridge for her to eat tomorrow. He frowned. If he could convince her to stay.

After he'd placed the order, he retrieved the bottle of Jack Daniels from the glovebox and headed back to the house.

He could see through the window that Evelyn was pacing the kitchen. He wanted to go to her and hold her again, but he knew he'd pulled that one a couple times too many already. What he needed to do was to get her talking. He was guessing that the Russian-sounding guy on the phone was an ex-boyfriend, but he wouldn't know for sure until she told him.

It was weird. He'd never thought of himself as the possessive kind when it came to women – or to anything else for that matter. He'd had a couple of long-term relationships, but there'd never been anyone he wanted to settle down with. The last woman he'd been involved with for a couple of years had ended their relationship – a couple of months after she'd started seeing someone else. It hadn't bothered him when he found out; he hadn't thought of her as *his* woman, just someone he was seeing.

He pursed his lips as he headed back up to the path to the front door. Was it something about Evie that made men feel that way about her? He felt protective of her. He felt a vested interest in making sure that she was okay – and that she stayed safe. And he couldn't deny that he'd liked having her staying here these last few weeks. She wasn't *his* woman, and he knew it, but having her here in his house, part of him saw her that way. And the guy on the phone had claimed that she was his *property*.

That just pissed Adam off. As far as he was concerned, every single person was their own person. Even if they were in a relationship and became someone's *other half*, they were still their own person, too. And property? No human being should ever be considered property, not in his mind. He knew some people got off on that, but he didn't get it. He didn't think that Evie was the kind of woman who would go for it. She might be in a mess right now, but she still had an air of ... he didn't know what. Sure, she was scared, and she was skittish, but she still had a grace and a strength about her. Going off the few times they'd talked – and tonight was probably the longest time he'd spent with her – he'd guess that in her regular life, she probably had a good sense of humor, too.

He got two glasses down from one of the cabinets and poured them each a drink. "Do you want anything with it? Water? Ice?"

She let out a short laugh. "No, thanks."

He watched as she took the glass and sipped the whiskey.

"Are you not a liquor girl?"

She raised her eyebrows. "Come on, Adam. I'm not a girl – of any variety. I'm a sad old lady." She looked at the glass in her hand. "And I'm only sipping because it's been a long while since I had a drink. I'm taking it slowly because I'm resisting the urge to knock this back and demand that you pour me another."

Adam tipped his glass and drained it before pouring himself a second. "First, I don't mind if you want to knock 'em back. The food should be here in half an hour. Second ..." He was about to say *don't you dare* but thought better of it. "I wish you wouldn't call my friend an old lady."

She gave him a sad smile. "I wish I weren't one, but it's the truth."

He gestured for her to take a seat at the kitchen table and sat down opposite her. He guessed that she was around his age, maybe a couple of years older, but not so much that it made a difference. It struck him that perhaps she was thinking that *he* saw her as a sad old lady. He needed to fix that.

"How old are you?"

She let out a short laugh. "Don't you know you're not supposed to ask a lady that?"

When he held her gaze and smiled, her reaction gave him hope. Her pupils dilated, and a hint of pink touched her cheeks. Interesting. "You're not supposed to ask a lady to stay at your house while you're away or to spend the night with you when you get back either. But …" He shrugged.

She shook her head and smiled. Apparently, thinking that he was just joking. He was, kind of, but if she wanted to take him up on the offer of spending the night with him, he wouldn't mind one bit.

"Okay. Well, since I've already spent several weeks in your house, and it would seem that I'm about to spend the night with you …" She rolled her eyes as she said it, but it didn't stop Adam's interest from stirring at the possibility.

"… I'm fifty-three."

He nodded. That was right around what he'd thought.

She let out a short laugh. "Say something!"

He chuckled. "What do you want me to say? That's not old. We both know it's not."

"No. It isn't. Not really. It's a lot older than you are, though."

Ah! So, maybe that was her problem. "What makes you think that?"

"Because it's the truth. Go on. They say that turnabout's fair play. How old are you?"

"Forty-eight."

She nodded.

"So, if you're calling yourself old, then you're calling me old, too."

She made a face. "Not exactly. You're much younger than I am."

"Only five years – that's hardly any difference at all at our age. It's not even a ten percent difference."

"Ten percent?"

"Yeah. Ten percent of fifty-three is five-point-three – take five-point three away from fifty-three and you get forty-seven-point-seven."

She narrowed her eyes at him, and for some reason, that made his cock stand up and pay even more attention. "Ten percent of forty-eight is four-point eight. Add those two together and you still don't get to fifty-three."

He chuckled. "Nitpicker!"

She laughed with him. "Isn't that what old ladies are known for – being all nitpicky."

"Nope. I'm not buying that you are an old lady. Sorry."

She blew out a sigh, her laughter seemingly forgotten.

"What?"

"Nothing. It was good to laugh for a minute."

"Yeah. You should stick with me. I'll make you laugh – not always intentionally, but ..." He shrugged.

"That's a nice idea, but even apart from the fact that I'm no girl, I need to get out of here in the morning, and I'm hoping you might have some advice for me."

Adam was torn. He wanted to continue trying to persuade her that she should stick with him – in every sense. But he didn't trust that she wouldn't take off the second he wasn't looking, and if she did, he wanted to have helped her as much as he could before she went.

Evelyn set her fork down and leaned back in her chair. She'd promised herself that she wouldn't overeat – not sure that her stomach would be able to take it – but Adam had insisted that she at least try a little bit of everything he'd ordered. She was stuffed.

He smiled and refilled her wine glass, emptying the bottle. If she'd thought that she shouldn't eat too much, she'd *known* that she shouldn't drink too much. Yet, that bottle had gone quickly. She gave him a shame-faced smile. "I'm not sure that I should have any more."

"No?"

He was so damned sexy, the little smirk on his face made her want to kiss him. And that had to be the wine talking. She hadn't kissed a man since Tom died. Her smile faded as she heard his voice echo in her head. *Don't be lonely when I'm gone, Evie. I want you to be happy. Promise me that if you get the chance to love again, you'll take it.* Her eyes pricked with tears, and she brought her hand up to cover her mouth. She'd told him then and she'd believed it since; she didn't want another chance. She only wanted him.

She swallowed when she realized that Adam was watching her closely, waiting for her to answer. She shook her head. "I'm a lightweight. And besides, with everything that's going on, I might get overly emotional." She dabbed at her eyes with her napkin.

His eyes were full of concern as he held her gaze. "So, how about you tell me what's going on?" He looked up at the clock on the wall. "If you're intending to take off in the morning, you need to start talking so that I can help you make a plan."

She narrowed her eyes at him and smiled through pursed lips. "Was this your plan? Ply me with alcohol so that I'd lower my guard and tell you everything?"

He chuckled. "No, but since your guard's down, I do plan to take advantage of it."

A wave of heat coursed through her veins. The thought of him taking advantage? Yes, please! That made her giggle. She really should have taken it easy with the wine.

The little smirk was back on his face as he watched her. "I didn't mean it like that."

"That's a shame!" Her hand flew up to cover her mouth again. Oh, dear Lord, she hadn't said that out loud, had she?

The way he chuckled told her that she had. Her heart started to pound when he spoke again. "I think so, too. But I'd rather wait until you're sober."

She just stared at him. She knew that when she was buzzed like this, she sometimes *said* outrageous things, but she didn't recall ever *hearing* them before.

"What …?"

He clasped his hands together and brought them up to rest his chin on them – his arms might be the sexiest thing she'd ever … Stop! She had to stop that.

"You heard me, Evie. And just so we're straight, I would never take advantage of a woman who's had too much to drink." His smile was sexy, too! "But I would love to revisit this conversation when you're sober."

Her heart raced as she picked up a pen off the table and started to turn it over and over in her hands. She needed to focus. Her mind was spinning. Anatoly had called just a couple of hours ago and told her that he was going to find her soon – she believed him, too. She had to run. She looked back into Adam's big, brown eyes. This gorgeous, sexy man was saying that he would like to … She'd like to as well. But she couldn't – she had to run. She needed to ditch the phone and get on the road. She'd been careful, she'd only used cash since she left Chicago. She had no idea how Anatoly had found the phone. Perhaps he'd been toying with her? Perhaps he knew exactly where she was. Perhaps his goons were on their way here even now.

She shook her head sadly. "I would never tell you this if I were sober, but I'd love to revisit this conversation, too." She blew out a sigh. "It's not going to happen, though. If I were capable of driving, I'd leave right now. I'll be gone first thing in the morning."

Adam nodded. "If that's what you think you need to do."

"I do."

"Tell me about it, though, Evie. Let me help."

She shook her head again. "There's no point, Adam. It's like I said – the less you know, the better. I appreciate the offer, but I can stick with the same plan I had before."

"And what's that?"

She let out a short laugh. "Just drive. My theory was that if I didn't know where I was going to be from one day to the next, there was no way Anatoly or anyone else could either." Damn! She hadn't meant to let his name slip. She needed to be more careful.

"What do you want to do now, then? If you're not going to talk to me."

"I should get some sleep. I'll take off as early as I can."

He nodded. "Okay. Mind if I stay?"

She held his gaze for a long moment. She should tell him to go, just in case. She didn't want him to be here if Anatoly's men were going to come crashing in to get her.

He gave her a rueful smile, apparently misunderstanding her hesitation. "Don't worry, I don't mean *with* you. I just mean here."

"Oh! Of course. It's your house. You should take the bedroom. I … I'll …" There was no place else to sleep. The rest of the house was more like a job site. The kitchen and the bedroom were the only furnished rooms.

His eyebrows drew together. "You'll take the bed, Evie."

"But I couldn't. I …"

"If you're really going to take off again tomorrow, I'm guessing this will be your last night in a bed for a while." He held her gaze, and she nodded.

"You know I was sleeping in the car, then?"

"Yeah. And if you're really going to insist on going back to that, there's no way you're sleeping on the floor here."

"But if I don't, you'll have to."

He shrugged. "It's no big deal."

"But you can't do that, not on my account. I can't let you sleep on the floor in your own house because of me. That's just not right."

"It's only one night. I'll be fine. I'll use all that spare bedding from the closet."

Her heart was pounding in her chest. "This is probably the wine talking. And even so, I wouldn't suggest it if you hadn't already assured me that you'd never take advantage …" She sucked in a deep breath before rushing on. "We could share. We're both adults." She let out a short laugh. "I'm an old lady, after all." She met his gaze.

He looked back into her eyes for a long few moments before he nodded. "If you were an old lady, I wouldn't have any hesitation in saying yes."

He let his gaze travel over her, and she felt her body come to life. Dear sweet lord above! Her nipples tightened and chafed against her bra in the heat of that look.

"You're no old lady." He gave her a tight smile. "But I'm not an asshole. So, we should be fine."

She swallowed, hard. "Okay then."

"Okay. Do you want to go up first while I clean up the kitchen? You can shout for me when you're safely tucked in."

She looked around the kitchen. She should offer to clean up, but she probably wasn't steady enough on her feet to do it without smashing something or making a fool of herself. She simply nodded and headed for the stairs.

Chapter Three

Adam took his time packing the leftovers back into the cartons they came in. He wished he had containers that he could store them in; they'd keep better that way. He checked the ice tray in the freezer and put the arm down so that it'd make more overnight. He had one of those Styrofoam coolers in the truck. If Evie insisted on leaving in the morning, he'd pack as much food as he could in there for her to take.

He scowled to himself. Who was he kidding? He was trying to respect what she was telling him, but he so could not see himself letting her drive away. Just drive – that was her plan? He blew out a sigh, he didn't know how long she'd been following that plan before she arrived in Summer Lake, but he couldn't allow her to go back to it.

He should have made her tell him what was going on. But she'd been so evasive over dinner. She'd asked him about his trip to Nashville and told him what had been going on at the gym but hadn't been keen to answer any of his questions. He still knew that if he pushed too hard, she'd take off.

He shouldn't have bought the wine – or at least, shouldn't have let her drink so much of it. He smiled to himself remembering what she'd said – that it was a shame that he wouldn't take advantage of a woman who'd had too much to drink. Her cheeks had flushed; she'd been surprised at herself. He wanted to get her to stick around so that they could revisit that conversation when she was sober. His smile faded. He'd told her that he wasn't an asshole. So, he needed to stop behaving like one; he shouldn't be thinking about getting her into bed. He should be thinking about how he could persuade her to stay here and let him look out for her.

He refused to listen to the little voice in his head telling him that getting her into bed could be one way to persuade her to stay.

He looked around the kitchen. There was nothing left to do.

"I'm all done!" Evie called.

He sucked in a deep breath and headed for the stairs. He had to stop thinking about getting her into bed. She was already there – and in just a few minutes, he'd join her. But he couldn't lay a finger on her. That would be so wrong. She was trusting him. He was trusting himself, for that matter. Not that it required much trust. As much as he was attracted to her, he had priorities. Her safety was his number one priority.

The bedroom door was halfway open, but he knocked on it anyway before he went in. Seeing her in his bed sent a shockwave through him. Seeing any woman in his bed wasn't something he was used to. He didn't live like a monk by any means, but he preferred to take a woman home rather than bring her back to his place.

Evie's head was the only part of her he could see, but he could make out the shape of her under the covers.

She gave him a tentative smile. "I left the bathroom light on for you."

"Thanks." He went to the closet and reached for a pair of sweatpants from the shelf at the top, grateful that he kept some clothes and toiletries here for when he was working on the house.

When he came out of the bathroom he stopped beside the bed, not sure what to do. Maybe he should get some of the spare bedding out. If he lay on top of the duvet that she was under, he could use another one to cover himself. He'd put the sweatpants on hoping that they'd help hide his attraction for her. Maybe having a whole duvet between them would be better.

His heart started to pound when she threw back the covers with a little laugh. "Go on, get it over with. Just climb on in."

So much for trying to stay away from her. He wasn't about to turn her down and explain why he needed to.

He slid under the covers and lay on his back, trying to stay close to the edge of the bed. This was a horrible idea. He'd probably get more sleep on the floor.

"Thanks, Adam."

"You're welcome." He didn't even know what she was thanking him for.

She blew out a big sigh. "You don't get it, and I know that's mostly because I won't tell you what's going on. But you don't even know me."

He couldn't help smiling to himself, guessing that it was the wine that was making her chatty. "I know that you're a good person and that you need help."

"Yeah, yeah, all of that. But I'm still not going to tell you about it. That wasn't what I was talking about anyway. When I said thank you, I meant … Well, lots of things. I mean thank you for your kindness – for letting me stay here, and for never bringing up before tonight that you knew that I was sleeping in my car. I'm ashamed of that."

"No!" He'd turned to face her before he knew what he was doing.

She was lying on her back, looking up at the ceiling just like he'd been, but when he turned to her, she turned, too. At first, just her head, and she smiled at him. Then she, too, turned onto her side so that she was looking into his eyes.

"I am. If you'd known me in my old life, you'd understand. The Evie who used to be would never have believed that she could end up in a situation like that." She made a face at him. "Homeless!"

"Not homeless. You were on the run. Are you going to tell me what from?"

She gave him a little grin and shook her head. She was so damned cute. She looked like a kid trying to keep a secret. But whatever she was trying to hide, he needed to know so that he could keep her safe.

"Tell me about the Evie who used to be, then?"

Her smile faded. "Yeah. I was married, you know."

Adam tensed at that. He hadn't thought of her as a married woman. Maybe that was just because he didn't want to, but he didn't think that was all. She didn't behave like a woman who had a husband somewhere.

Her hand came up from under the covers and brushed at her eyes. "Tom; you would have liked him. He was a good man. It's been five years since he died."

"I'm sorry." He felt like a shit when he relaxed at that bit of information.

"So am I. It was lung cancer. They did what they could for a few years, but I don't think that's a battle that many people win."

"No."

She gave him a sad smile. "At least we had time to say goodbye. If he'd had a heart attack or something he might have been there one day and gone the next. I imagine that would have been even harder. Not that it wasn't hard to know that we had so little time left."

"I can't imagine how hard it was."

"Sorry." She blew out a sigh. "Before he died, we were fun people. He owned a chain of gyms in the city."

Adam wanted to ask which city, but he let it go. He was guessing Chicago since that was where *Anatoly* had been calling from. Those were the only two bits of information that he had so far, and he hoped that if he let her keep talking without interruption, she'd give more away.

"And I haven't told you this before, but since I'm leaving, I don't suppose it matters now. I am, well I was, a designer."

Adam raised his eyebrows.

"An interior designer. I could have helped you make this place lovely."

"You still can."

She shook her head. "I won't be able to keep in touch with you when I go. I daren't risk it. He found out about that phone somehow. I'm going to throw it out the window once I get away from Summer Lake. I've barely used it and ... well, shoot!"

"What?"

"I'm so stupid! I called Taryn last week. I only call her at the restaurant, never at home, but I'll bet that's how he found the number."

Adam watched her face as she mulled something over.

She met his gaze and held it. "That might be a good thing, don't you think? Maybe he hasn't found me or the phone. Maybe he only found the number from that end – because he's keeping an eye on the restaurant."

Adam nodded. "Yeah. That's the only way I can see him having found the number of a burner phone. He couldn't trace you – but he can keep an eye on anyone you might contact. Who's Taryn?"

"She's my best friend. She's awesome. You'd like her, too. She owns the restaurant. Trattoria Bella Sera. She's the best chef ever." She pursed her lips and gave him another tipsy smile. "She saved me, you know."

"How?"

"Don't look so worried. I don't mean she saved me from … anything bad. I mean the beans and rice. I know you saw what I was eating. It's all I've been eating. Taryn grew up poor, they never had enough to eat. Beans and rice were the staple diet in their house when she was a kid. She used to tell me stories about her childhood." She stopped and blew out a sigh. "I come from quite a wealthy family. Before I met Taryn, I didn't know that beans and rice were considered a meal."

Adam hated that she'd been living the way she had. He had to do something. If she took off tomorrow, she'd be back to eating beans and rice and sleeping in her car.

"What's wrong?"

"Why?"

Her hand came up out of the covers and she traced her finger over his forehead. "You've got big frown lines going."

The feel of her touch on his skin sent shivers racing down his back. He made himself smile. "I'm worried about you, Evie."

"Why, though?"

"Because you're in trouble. Let me help you?"

She searched his face for a long few moments and then she gave him a sad smile. "There is something I'd like to ask you for. I know I shouldn't ask, and you can say no if you don't want to do it, but it would help me more than you know."

"Anything. Just tell me what I can do." Finally, she was letting him in.

She bit down on her bottom lip and looked up into his eyes. "Hold me?"

He swallowed, wondering if his imagination was playing tricks on him.

"I … you know earlier when you put your arms around me? You made me feel safe. I've been so scared for so long. I haven't been able to relax. I always have to be on high alert, ready to run." She looked into his eyes. "I just want to feel safe. But I'm sorry, can you forget I asked? It's dumb. It's bad enough for you that you have to share your bed with the sad, drunk old lady and …"

He couldn't let her carry on talking that kind of shit. He moved closer and curled his arm around her waist, pulling her to him. He had to close his eyes and shift his hips away from her when she snuggled against him.

"Thank you."

"Yeah." His voice was hoarse. So much for making sure he stayed away from her.

He had to close his eyes when she tucked her head under his chin and slid her arm around his waist. He could do this. She was looking for comfort. He could give her that. Then her lips moved against his neck when she spoke again, and he had to clench his jaw to keep in a groan.

"You have no idea how this makes me feel."

He could hardly tell her that she had no idea how it made him feel, but she was likely to find out if he couldn't shift his hips away from her. His cock was hard, aching, eager to get to her.

"It's hard, you know."

He bit down on his bottom lip – he knew only too well!

"It's hard to be alone."

"You're not alone anymore."

He felt her sigh. "I am. I mean, this is nice. I appreciate it more than you know, but this is the first time in nearly six years that I've had a man's arms around me."

She leaned back to look up into his eyes and gave him a wry smile. "Just in case you were wondering, I am not the kind of woman who asks if she can sleep with a guy. This is a first. And I wouldn't have asked you if I thought … if there were any chance that you …"

"That I what?"

"That you might … you know. I'm not one of the girls from the gym. It's not like you're going to want to … You said you're my friend."

Jesus. If she thought that he'd find it harder to resist one of the girls from the gym than he was finding it to resist her, she had no idea. He had to set her straight. He may as well tell her before she felt his aching cock pressing into her stomach. She didn't need to keep fooling herself that he wouldn't want to.

He slid his arm underneath her to hold her closer, then took hold of her chin to make her look up at him.

"What?"

He'd like nothing more than to kiss the puzzled look off her face – to answer her question that way. But it wasn't going to happen. Instead, he smiled. "I'm glad I can make you feel safe, Evie. You are safe with me. You always will be. I want you to relax, I'm glad I can do that for you, too. I'll hold you all night if you want me to. But it's only fair that you should understand something first."

"What's that?"

"I do want to."

She searched his face, then her eyes grew wide as understanding dawned. Then she laughed. "That's too kind of you. You don't need to try to build me up by saying that. I know I'm not …"

He couldn't help it. He slid his hand down to cup her ass and held her against his erection. "Yes, you are, Evie. You're gorgeous. I've thought that since the first time I saw you."

Her cheeks flushed as she met his gaze. "Really?"

"Really." He had to close his eyes as she pressed closer against him. Then, reluctantly, he shifted away. "I meant it when I said that I'd like to revisit that conversation when you're sober." He blew out a sigh. "And unfortunately, I also meant it when I said that I'd never take advantage of a woman who's had too much to drink."

She let out a little chuckle. "Well, damn."

He had to laugh with her, pleased that not only wasn't she horrified, but she was able to joke about it.

Evelyn's head was spinning. She really shouldn't have drunk so much wine. Looking up into Adam's big brown eyes, she wished that she hadn't. She chuckled.

He raised his eyebrows. "What?"

What the heck. She might as well tell him. "I'm glad that you're not the kind of man who would take advantage of a tipsy woman. But that just made me wish that I wasn't tipsy. But then if I weren't, we wouldn't be in bed together – and I certainly wouldn't have dared to ask you to hold me."

She loved his smile. It softened his rugged features. She loved the way his lips lifted just a little bit higher on one side than the other.

She had to close her eyes when he tightened his arms around her. Her head was spinning from the wine, and now her body felt as if it might spin away in a rush of pleasure from the feel of him against her. He'd moved his hips away now, but there'd been no disputing the fact that he was attracted to her; very attracted – in a big way. She pressed her lips together to stop herself from laughing again.

She knew that if she wasn't careful, her laughter would turn to tears. It was only because of the wine, and she knew it. She'd held it together for all this time. Since she'd run from Chicago, she'd mostly managed to keep her emotions in check. Of course, she was scared, and sad, and lonely, but indulging in any of those feelings wouldn't help her, so she'd forced herself to push on, to focus on what she needed to do every day to get through the day.

Now though, lying here like this in Adam's bed, with his arms around her, she wasn't lonely anymore, she didn't even feel so scared – how could she when he was right here with her? Even the sadness receded, replaced by … it wasn't hope, there wasn't anything to hope for, she knew that. But some part of her wine-sodden brain wanted to believe that there was something she *could* hope for with Adam – something that could happen between them.

She blew out a sigh.

"I'm glad you asked me."

She gave him a puzzled look, not remembering what they'd been talking about.

"You said that if you hadn't had too much wine, you wouldn't have asked me to hold you. I'm glad you asked."

She couldn't help it; she tightened her arm around his waist and snuggled closer to him. "I am too. And I'm just drunk enough to take you up on your offer to hold me all night."

He smiled. "It'll be my pleasure."

She chuckled. "It could be our pleasure – if you want." Oh, good lord! She needed to stop it; to go to sleep before she embarrassed them both any further.

She gave him a shamefaced smile. "Can you forget that I just said that?"

He smiled through pursed lips. "I don't think I can, no. I can't take you up on it, but damn, Evie. You can't say that and then expect me to forget it. And just so we're clear. I do want. I want you. I won't take advantage, but if you're still here tomorrow night – and sober – then I reckon it will be our pleasure."

A rush of heat swept through her veins. The thought of any man wanting her was something she'd forgotten. The thought of Adam ... Goosebumps broke out on her skin as she looked up at him.

He looked down into her eyes. He was so handsome! A small smile played on his full lips. "Go to sleep, Evie. We can talk about it in the morning."

"I have to leave in the morning."

He looked deep into her eyes. "I don't want you to go."

Her heart clenched in her chest. She didn't want to go either, but … Her fingers curled against his chest when he lowered his head and brushed his lips over hers. It wasn't a kiss. It was too brief, too fleeting. But the feel of his full, soft lips sliding, however briefly, over hers made her press closer to him. She wanted …

He lifted his head and gave her a rueful smile. "I know I shouldn't have done that, but I have no excuses. Now, *please*, go to sleep."

She chuckled. He was a good guy. The part of her mind that wasn't touched by the alcohol – or perhaps it was just emboldened by it – could appreciate how messed up this situation was from his point of view. If he *was* attracted to her, then she really shouldn't have asked him to share the bed – let alone to hold her! But she couldn't regret it. He felt so good. He was warm and hard, and his arms felt so good, and … her eyes were closing.

And even as she drifted off, she realized that tonight should be the scariest night she'd had since she left Chicago. Anatoly had found her number. She'd heard his voice. He'd told her that he was going to find her and … And none of it seemed nearly so scary now because Adam was here. Instead of feeling even more scared, she felt safe.

She tried to remind herself that she wasn't safe and that she shouldn't be putting Adam in danger. But she couldn't hold on to those thoughts. All she could do was relax into the way he made her feel; his arms around her, his warm body so close to hers, and his breath in her hair. Screw the fear, she was going to savor every moment of this that she could.

Chapter Four

Adam paced the kitchen as he waited for the coffee to brew. It was early, it wasn't even light yet, but he'd had to get up. Letting go of Evie – he'd been true to his word and held her all night – and getting out of bed, had been the last thing he wanted to do. He'd barely gotten any sleep; he'd just lain there, looking at the woman in his arms, holding her closer once she was asleep, loving the feel of her and the smell of her.

About an hour ago, she'd reached her arm up around his neck and pressed herself against him – the full length of her warm, soft body. Her full, soft breasts had been torture against his chest. His cock had throbbed and ached to get closer to her heat, so tantalizingly close through his sweatpants. He'd allowed himself to bury his face in her neck, but the sweet scent of her had only made him harder. His hand may have found its way down to close around her ass and hold her closer against him, but the little sound of pleasure that she'd made had brought him back to his senses in a hurry.

She'd told him that she hadn't been in a man's arms since her husband died five years ago. He imagined that in a half-waking state, any woman would give in to the feel of physical intimacy after going so long without any. It'd be wrong of him to keep holding her – encouraging her to give him more. He couldn't do that to her. And what he couldn't do to himself was get carried away and then have to wonder afterward whether it was because she wanted him, or just because he was a warm body who happened to be there.

He reached for a mug and poured himself a coffee. Once he was settled at the kitchen table with it, he wondered how this morning was going to go. He didn't imagine that Evie was going to feel a hundred percent, but he doubted that would stop her if she'd made her mind up to leave. He was hoping that she hadn't made her mind up – that she'd see the sense in staying here. Running might seem like her best option, but it really wasn't. If she kept running, she only had two options; either Anatoly would find her, or she'd be on the move forever, always looking over her shoulder. That was no way to live.

If he could persuade her to stay here – with him – he could figure out what the deal was, who Anatoly was, why he was after her, and how Adam could put a stop to it. He blew out a sigh and took another sip of his coffee. That was a big if, though. How could he persuade her to stay? What could he say that would make her understand that she was safer here with him? How could he convince her that she needn't worry about putting him in danger? He knew that worried her, and he knew that she was the kind of woman who'd put herself in more danger rather than put him in any.

He didn't know who Anatoly was, or how big of a threat he was, but he did know that he could handle it.

He reached for his phone where it was charging on the windowsill. He smiled when he saw a text from Davin.

Davin: Did you finally get somewhere? I thought you'd be back last night.

He'd told Davin that he'd be back at the guest house. He'd thought that he was only stopping by to check in on Evie.

Adam: I think I'm getting somewhere with getting her to open up and tell me what she's running from. That's all though.

Davin: That's something, right? Are you going to be spending the weekend at your place? I've got everything covered here.

Adam smiled. Davin was a good guy. They'd worked together for a lot of years now. For the last several years they'd been working as Clay McAdam's security team but before that, they'd served together on a Special Forces team. The guys had scattered since then, but he and Davin had stuck together.

Adam: Thanks. I'll let you know in a little while. She wants to run, but I'm trying to convince her to stay.

Davin: What's she running from?

Adam: I still don't know. She thinks the less I know the better.

Davin: Tell her who you are then. Don't let her think that you're just some guy who might get hurt – let her know just how capable of taking care of her you are!

Adam made a face at his phone. He didn't like to broadcast what he used to do. People knew him as a security guy. That was all they needed to know. He wondered though if perhaps Davin was right. Would knowing that he was a former Delta operator help Evie feel safe enough to stick around? He'd tell her if it would.

Davin: Stop thinking about it and do it! I've never known you to get like this over a woman before. I don't know her that well, but I can see why you're so hung up on her. Do us both a favor and do what you can to make her stay. I know you're going to make my life miserable if you let her be the one who got away, and I have to watch you mope.

Adam laughed.

Adam: When have I ever moped over a woman?

Davin: Never! But I've never known you to get this hung up on one. Face it, Evie's not just some chick you want to sleep with. She's a woman who you can see yourself with. This is a first all around. Don't fuck it up and regret it – go for it!

Adam: Thanks, bud. I'm going to.

Davin: Good. I've got things covered here. Give me a shout if you need me.

Adam: Same goes.

He set his phone down and took a big gulp of his coffee. Davin was right. Evie wasn't just some chick who he wanted to sleep with. But was she someone he could see himself with? He wasn't so sure about that. Yeah, he was attracted to her, he liked what he knew about her so far, but that didn't mean … He hadn't been able to see himself with any woman before. Not in the way that Davin meant it, anyway. He knew what Davin meant because that was the way he used to talk about his wife – especially after their divorce. He'd been able to see himself spending the rest of his life with her. That's what he'd wanted, what he'd thought would happen. Adam hadn't thought about any of the women he'd dated that way. He hadn't thought he worked that way.

Now, even though he wasn't sure that he could see himself with Evie in the way that Davin meant, he knew that he wanted to see himself with her for long enough to find out what they might share. He chuckled into his coffee. Was it just that the rest of his life wasn't such a long time as it used to be? In his twenties and thirties, he'd been in the unit. He hadn't wanted to complicate his life by getting involved with a woman.

He shook his head. He didn't need to get ahead of himself, didn't need to get caught up in wondering what could or might happen between Evie and him. The first thing he had to do was convince her that she needed to stay. Not for any personal reasons of his own; simply for her safety. Here, in Summer Lake, she had him, and she was surrounded by people who cared about her – several of whom would also be able to help keep her safe. Summer Lake might be a smalltown backwater, but these days it had a small but growing community of former military and intelligence guys. Even though she'd be staying put in one place, Adam liked her chances a lot better here than he would if she were out on the road by herself again. He scowled – especially living in her car.

~ ~ ~

Evelyn took her time in the shower, hoping that she might be able to wash away the worst of her hangover. What had she been thinking? She hadn't had a drink of anything alcoholic since … she couldn't even remember. She closed her eyes when images of the last night she'd spent at the restaurant with Taryn flooded her mind.

They'd shared a bottle of wine that night after the kitchen had closed. Like so many other nights, Evelyn had gone there for dinner and hung out afterward. Taryn had joined her at the bar, and they'd sat and talked and laughed with the regulars until closing time. She missed her friend. She missed her life.

She let the hot water run down over her, wishing that it could wash away the last several months. It wasn't doing much for her hangover, let alone the disaster that her life had become. She turned the faucet off and got out to dry herself off. She got ready slowly, trying to delay the inevitable embarrassment she was going to have to deal with when she had to face Adam. The poor man!

It had been so good of him to allow her to stay. She finished getting dressed and rubbed a towel through her hair. She didn't remember everything that she'd said to him after they got into bed. A rush of heat coursed through her veins. She remembered all too well that she'd asked him to hold her – and that he had. She wasn't sure if she'd dreamed that he held her against him – against one rather large and very hard part of him. She had to have dreamed that right? Her wine-sodden, sad, lonely mind must have made that part up.

When she couldn't put it off any longer, she stuffed her few clothes and toiletries into her bag and carried it with her down the stairs. She hated not knowing when she'd get to shower again. But she had to leave. This time she'd be wiser. When she left Chicago, she'd stayed in a different motel every night until her cash was running too low. Then she'd had no choice but to sleep in her car. Some of the rest areas on the highway had showers for truckers, and she'd used those a couple of times, but that had been scary. This time she planned to sleep in the car for a few nights, then allow herself the luxury of a motel. Maybe she'd do that once a week.

"Good morning." Adam was standing in the kitchen doorway with a smile on his face.

He made her heart leap in her chest. He was just that handsome. She couldn't help smiling back at him. "Morning."

"Do you want some coffee?"

She gave him a shamefaced smile. "Please. I need it."

She followed him into the kitchen, where he poured a mug for her. "I didn't see any cream or sugar, so I'm guessing that you don't take them."

"Thanks." She wasn't about to tell him that she'd thought she hated black coffee until recently. That would mean explaining that she hadn't wanted to waste any of her money on luxuries. As far as she was concerned, coffee was a necessity, and cream and sugar were luxuries.

He sat down at the table and gestured for her to sit opposite. She hid her face behind her mug, not wanting him to see how embarrassed she was as she spoke.

"Listen, Adam."

He raised his eyebrows and smiled, "Yeah?"

She swallowed. Why was it so sexy the way his lips did that? They lifted higher on one side than the other and it made her want to kiss him. Jeez, did she ever need to get a grip?

"Thanks for last night."

He chuckled, and she felt the heat in her cheeks. "Sorry. I shouldn't laugh. I just wish that we'd done something that we could thank each other for."

Was he serious?

"Do you remember what I said before you went to sleep?"

She frowned. "Which part?" She could think of a few things that he'd said, but she wasn't sure how many of them were just her imagination.

He looked into her eyes, his brown gaze intense. "I said that it would be my pleasure to hold you all night."

Evelyn swallowed. She'd been fairly certain that she'd only imagined that part.

He was still smiling, but there was a question in his eyes. "You said that it could be our pleasure – if I wanted."

Her cheeks were burning now. "I'm pretty sure that I asked if you could forget that I said that."

He smiled through pursed lips. "And I did tell you that I didn't think I could. I couldn't take you up on the offer, but damn, Evie. I told you that I wanted you to be clear. And this morning, I want to make double sure that you are clear – that you understand; I do want you. And like I said, if you're still here tonight – and sober – then I reckon it will be our pleasure."

She set her mug down and looked away. So, she hadn't dreamed any of it? She swallowed, hard.

"Look at me."

He said it gently, it wasn't a command, but she obeyed as if it were. She was relieved to see him smiling.

"I mean it, Evie. I want you to stay here. I want to keep you safe. I want to get to know you."

She stared back at him.

"Don't you want that?"

She let out a short laugh. "You're kidding me, right? You're not seriously asking me if that's what I want?"

"I'm dead serious. I need to know if you want any or all of that. I want all three things; for you to stay, for you to let me keep you safe, and for us to get to know each other." He frowned. "But the first two are most important. If you want to stay and let me help, then don't worry if you're not interested in me. It's not a conditional offer. I can't help the way I feel about you, but I can set that aside if you'd rather."

She rested her elbows on the table and brought her hands up to cover her face.

"You can just say if you're not interested in me, Evie. It's okay."

She laughed again. She couldn't help it. "Do you expect me to believe that you're … interested in me – like that?"

He smiled and reached for her hands, pulling them away from her face and engulfing them in his own – damn, he had big hands! And that so was not what she should be focusing on right now.

"I do expect you to believe me, yes. I thought I made my point last night."

She pressed her lips together, knowing exactly what he meant. He'd closed those big hands around her ass and held her against his – very impressive – erection. She pressed her thighs together as a wave of heat coursed through her veins.

He squeezed her hands and looked at her earnestly. "It's okay if it was just the wine for you. I'm glad I could be the one who was there when you needed someone."

She closed her eyes. If he was being honest, then she needed to be, too. "I didn't need someone, Adam. I wanted you."

He grinned and brushed his thumb back and forth over her knuckles. "*Wanted* – as in, wine-induced? Or *want* – ongoing?"

She stared back at him. What could she say to that? "Let's call it wine-enhanced, shall we? I find you attractive, Adam. I have since we first met. But …"

His smile faded. "But what?"

"But I didn't think … there isn't any point … you're younger than I am. I'm not exactly your type, and apart from anything else, I can't tell you who I am, and I was never going to be here for long anyway."

"What if I say that I think there is a point? I'm not that much younger than you are – it's barely a difference. I don't know what you think my type is – I don't know that I have one. But if I do – you're it. And I know that you think you shouldn't stay, but I think that's exactly what you should do. Stay. Let me keep you safe. Tell me what's going on with you – who you are, who this Anatoly is."

She shook her head and tried to withdraw her hands, but he held on.

"Can you honestly tell me that you think you'll be safer on the road by yourself than you are here – with me?"

"Adam, you don't know him. You don't know what he's capable of. I know security is your thing but … it's not just him. He has men."

Adam shrugged. "I have men, too. There's not just me. You know my partner Davin. And you seem to forget that the guy you work for, Russ, is a former Marine. And Cal, Manny, and Ryan are in the gym pretty much every day. Do you think that, between us, we couldn't keep you safe – if we knew what was going on, and what we need to protect you from?"

She stared back into his eyes. Her heart was pounding. He had a point. Russ had been trying to get her to tell him what was going on with her, and he'd said so many times that he wanted to help her. She felt safer whenever he was around. And she loved it when Cal, Ryan, and Manny came into the gym – because while they were there, she was able to relax.

She bit down on her bottom lip. She didn't relax in the same way when Adam came in – not because he didn't make her feel safe, but because he made her feel other things, too. He made her feel nervous because she didn't want a make a fool of herself.

Was he seriously telling her that she wouldn't be making a fool of herself? She sighed. It was all too much.

"I'm still waiting, Evie."

"Oh, right." He'd asked if she thought that they couldn't keep her safe. "It's not a question of what you guys could do to help. It's a matter of me not wanting to put you in that position. You don't know …" And she wasn't about to tell him, who Anatoly was, or what he was capable of.

"But I keep telling you that I want to know. I want to help. And you can bet that the other guys want to help, too." He gave her a wry smile. "You know they're all working for Dan and his security business? They've had holdup after holdup on their clearances and approvals to get the kinds of government contracts they're after. They'd love to have something to work on while they wait to get up and running. And believe me, Evie, you keep saying that I don't know what this Anatoly's capable of; you have no idea what we're capable of."

She frowned. "What do you mean?"

"I mean, they're all former operators of one kind or another. Manny's the easiest one to explain – he's former FBI. He used to be the SAC – Special Agent in Charge of the Sacramento field office. Cal and Ryan worked together for years – for one of the agencies that shall not be named except in alphabet soup."

Evelyn stared at him. She'd figured that they were all former military of some description. But she didn't know what to say or what to think about the information that Adam had just shared. "Is that supposed to be secret?"

He chuckled. "Nah. You'd be surprised how wrong the movies get that kind of stuff. Intelligence officers can usually talk about who they worked for after they retire. They're not going to tell you about what they used to do, but the employer is no big secret."

She frowned. "Are you saying …? It sounds like you're talking from experience. Are you one of them?"

He laughed. "No. I'm former military, not intelligence." He squeezed her hands, which reminded her that he was still holding onto them. She should have pulled away by now, but it felt good. "Davin told me that if it would help convince you to stay, I should tell you what I used to do."

She held his gaze, wondering what he was going to say next. She was having enough difficulty thinking of the guys at the gym as spies.

"Do you think that I should – tell you?"

She swallowed. "I don't know, Adam. Even if you tell me that there's a whole army here and that you're the commander – or whatever the bigwig is called – I don't know that it'd make me stay. If anything happened to you – or to anyone – because of me, I just wouldn't be able to live with it."

He blew out a sigh and squeezed her hands. "I don't want you to go, Evie. For your sake or for mine. I want you to stay here – with me."

Her heart was pounding in her chest. He looked like he really meant it. He looked … sad!

She hung her head.

"How about you stay for one more week? It'd give you more time to prepare. And if you're going to leave Russ in the lurch at the gym ..."

She frowned. "I don't want to leave him in the lurch."

"I know, and that wasn't fair of me. He'll be fine. I'm just playing on anything that I think might push you toward staying."

She looked up again and met his gaze. She was torn.

He got to his feet and tugged her hand, so she joined him. As soon as she was facing him, he closed his arms around her and looked down into her eyes.

How was she supposed to stay strong and stay brave when he looked at her like that? When he made her feel safe ... and sexy!

His hand ran up her back, and he tangled his fingers in her hair, sending another rush of heat through her veins.

He lowered his head and brushed his lips over hers. It was too much – his closeness, the tenderness in his eyes, it felt as though it might overwhelm her. And yet, it wasn't enough. She wanted to feel his lips for longer, his mouth on hers, his tongue slide against her own, and his body ... She sighed as he crushed her against his hard body. She wanted to know what it would be like to spend another night with him – this time naked and ...

He pressed his lips against hers again before leaning back to look down into her eyes.

"Stay."

She nodded – how the hell could she say no to that?

Chapter Five

"Promise me you'll still be here when I get back?" Adam raised an eyebrow.

Evie blew out a sigh. "I promise."

"Thanks." He was relieved that she'd said she'd stay, but he wasn't convinced that she meant it. "I'll be as quick as I can. And when I get back, you're going to talk to me, right?"

She made a face. "I still think that it's better if …"

He gave her a stern look. "Trust me?"

She held his gaze for a long moment and then nodded before she turned away. He wanted to go to her, to hold her again, and to make her understand that she could trust him, that he would keep her safe. But he felt like he'd already pushed his luck. He'd kissed her – okay, so it was only a brief touching of lips, but he didn't know that he could go near her again without kissing her for real. Yes, he'd held her to make her feel safe, and he wanted to again, but he also wanted a hell of a lot more than that.

"I'll be back." He forced himself out the door. He'd promised her breakfast, and there was nothing in the house, other than last night's leftovers. He called in an order to The

Boathouse before he started the truck. He'd have time to hit the grocery store and stock up first.

He marched up and down the aisles, loading his cart with every staple he could think of. He didn't expect that he'd have to leave for work again for at least another week, but he wanted to stock the fridge and every cabinet in the kitchen so that Evie would have plenty to keep her going.

He brought the cart to an abrupt halt as he rounded the end of the aisle and almost ran into Russ.

"Whoa!" Russ held his hands up and smiled. "It looks like someone's in a hurry." He eyed the loaded cart. "And on a major spree by the look of it. How are you doing, Adam? I thought you were in Nashville till next week."

"We were supposed to be, but Clay wanted to get back here for the weekend – since Marianne wasn't with him this time."

Russ smiled. "Missing his lady, huh? I know how he feels. Ria was back in Napa last week, but she came home two days early."

Adam had to smile. He loved that Russ, who'd been single for as long as he'd known him, was now living with his lady – and they were engaged. "Yeah, there's always the likelihood that the trip will get cut short if Marianne's not with him."

"So, what?" Russ eyed the cart again. "You're making the most of the time at home to stock your kitchen?" He frowned. "No, the guesthouse, right? You and Davin live onsite with Clay while you're working?" He raised his eyebrows. "I know you're not stocking your own kitchen because Evelyn's staying at your place."

Adam dropped his gaze. Russ already knew how he felt about Evie; he'd encouraged him to do something about it. But he didn't know how Russ would feel if he knew that he'd asked her to stay – with him.

Russ chuckled. "Okay. What's going on? Your poker face has abandoned you – you look guilty as hell. Are you finally making progress with her?"

Adam made a face at him. "Not guilty – not yet anyway. But …" He blew out a sigh. "I think I'm finally making progress in finding out what's going on with her."

"What's she told you? She still won't tell me anything – or Ria. Ria takes her out for coffee at least once a week, but she won't say anything about what her deal is. What do you know?"

"Still not much. I told you I thought she was running from someone? Well, she is. I stopped by to see her when I got back last night, and some guy was blowing up her phone trying to get hold of her. All I know is that his name is Anatoly, it was a Chicago number, and she is scared to death of him."

"Why?"

Adam scowled. "She still won't tell me. The fact that he'd found her number – even though she doesn't think he knows where she is yet – was enough to make her want to run again. She was ready to leave last night. I persuaded her to stay until this morning, and now she's agreed to stay for the week."

Russ pursed his lips. "She needs to stick around and let us help her figure it out."

"You don't need to tell me that. But she's so damned scared of him. She keeps saying that it's best if I don't know. She's scared that he or his men might come here – that I might get hurt."

Russ chuckled. "I want to ask if she doesn't know you at all, but if between last night and this morning you managed to get her from staying the night to staying the week, I can only assume that she knows you pretty well by now."

Adam pursed his lips. "Assume away. You'd be wrong."

"Seriously?"

He let out a short laugh. "Seriously. She was scared, and she had a little too much to drink."

Russ nodded. "Okay. Well, what do you need from me?"

"I don't know yet. You've already helped me out without knowing it."

"How so?"

"I may have reminded her that if she just took off, she'd be leaving you in the lurch at the gym."

Russ gave him a wry smile.

"I know, I know! It was low, and I even admitted afterward that I was just saying whatever I thought might convince her to stay."

"And she's going to stay for the week?"

"That's all she agreed to, so far. But I plan to convince her to stay for good."

"I thought as much."

"And since she's more worried about my safety – about the safety of anyone who tries to help her – than she is about her own, I reminded her that there are more than a few guys around here who are capable of keeping her safe – you included."

"Yeah. If ever we decide we need a local militia, we'd have quite a formidable force."

Adam gave him a wry smile. "Yup. Between former Marines, spooks, FBI, and Deltas, she has no need to worry about some small-time crook hunting her down."

Russ raised his eyebrows. "What makes you think that this is some small-time crook? To me, when I hear *Anatoly* and *Chicago*, I think Russian mob."

"Fuck!"

Russ nodded. "Yeah."

Adam looked down at his cart before looking back up at his friend. "Why didn't I make that connection?"

Russ shrugged.

"I'd better get back to her and get her to start talking. When he called last night, I was just so damn angry that he was terrorizing her. I didn't think. He told me she was his property, and I thought he was just some sleazy asshole who thought women could be property. Then he asked if I knew who he was. Told me I should ask her — and decide if I thought her friendship was worth it."

"That doesn't sound like a small-time crook to me."

"Me neither. I need to get back."

"Yeah. Talk to her and give me a call later. Let me know what the deal is. If he is what we think and he tracks her down to Summer Lake, we're going to need to talk to the guys and circle the wagons."

Adam had to smile. He loved that there was no question in Russ's mind that everyone would come together to protect Evie. "Thanks. I'll call you later."

Evelyn sat back in her chair and pushed the plate away. Between last night and this morning, she'd probably eaten more than she had in the last week.

"Do you want anything else?" asked Adam.

She smiled. "Only for you to let me clean up. Thanks, Adam. I needed this."

He nodded. "You need to let me clean up, too."

"No." She got to her feet and started clearing the table. "You stay right there, please. Do you want more coffee?"

She came and refilled his mug. As she was putting the coffee pot back, she stilled when she sensed him behind her.

"Are you going to talk to me now?"

She swallowed.

"Come on, Evie. You can only put it off for so long."

She sucked in a deep breath and turned around to face him before nodding slowly. "I know. I'm just scared, Adam."

"And I don't want you to be. I need you to know that I can help you. I'll keep you safe, but I can't do that if I don't know what it is that you're scared of." He reached for her hand. "Come on, let's sit down."

He led her back to the table but frowned when he reached it. "Damn. I wish I had more furniture. This isn't a conversation we need to have perched at the kitchen table."

It was her turn to frown when he tugged her hand and led her toward the stairs. She stopped when they reached the bottom, and he turned back to her with a rueful smile.

"The bed's the only comfortable place to sit. That's all. I'm not going to …" He gave her a wry smile. "Just so we're clear – I hope that at some point soon, I will get to …" He shrugged. "But right now, all I'm trying to do is make you comfortable while you tell me what the hell is going on with you."

She nodded, and followed him upstairs, glad that she'd thought to make the bed before she came down earlier. She wasn't sure just how comfortable she would feel sitting on the bed with him – not that she'd feel uncomfortable, more like … what? Nervous? It didn't matter. She had to put however she was feeling about Adam aside for now.

When they reached the bedroom, he kicked his shoes off and climbed onto the bed, sitting back against the headboard.

When she hesitated, he patted the space beside him and smiled. "To borrow your words from last night, *Go on, get it over with. Just climb on in.*"

That made her smile and kick her shoes off. When she sat beside him, he wrapped his arm around her shoulders and drew her into his side. It felt good – right. She and Tom used to sit in bed like this on Sunday mornings sometimes. He would read the papers while she read her book.

"Is this okay?"

She nodded.

"Are you sure? You look sad."

"I … it just reminded me of when I was married. Tom and I …" She bit down on her bottom lip. Adam didn't need to hear about her marriage. He'd told her that he was attracted to her – that he wanted her to stay here – with him. If that were really the case, he didn't need to hear about what she and Tom had shared.

His big brown eyes were watching her intently. They were so gentle, they seemed almost out of place in his rugged face, and yet at the same time, the overall effect was to give him a soft, but strong air that she found so very appealing.

"Want to tell me about him?"

"Do you want to know?"

He smiled. "I'd like to. I imagine he must have been a great guy; you love him. And I know that he and I have at least one thing in common."

"What's that?"

His hand came up, and he brushed his thumb over her cheek, sending shivers cascading down her spine. "We share the same taste in women."

She swallowed, still not quite able to believe that he was for real – that a guy like him could be attracted to someone like her.

His smile faded. "I meant everything I said last night, Evie. I want to get to know you, to see what can happen between us."

"You're …" She didn't know what to say. He wasn't that much younger than her. Five years was barely any difference at all at their age or at any age, for that matter. She was just …

"I'm what?"

She shrugged. "Perhaps, it's not you – it's me. I'm just surprised, that's all. That someone like you would see me that way."

He touched her cheek again. "You're a beautiful woman. You don't really believe that old lady stuff you were spouting last night, do you?"

"No. I don't really. Fifty-three isn't old. I know that, of course. It's not even so much about my age, it's just … Well, after losing Tom. I felt like my life was over. That all the good parts had already come and gone. I was getting myself back together. I had a decent life going. It might have taken me five years, but I had my business, and I had Taryn – she's my best friend. And we had the restaurant. It's just. I thought I was living out the last part of my life – the part after my husband died. I know I'm not old, but I feel old compared to you – in terms of the kind of lives we live. We're not that far apart in age, but I suppose I was classing myself as someone who'd passed the part of her life where she was married and classing you as someone who hadn't even made it to that stage in life yet. And as a relatively young guy, I'd expect you to be interested in younger girls." She gave him a rueful smile. "Isn't that the way it usually works? Guys are still considered sexy as they get older while women are put out to pasture."

He chuckled. "Perhaps once upon a time. But not anymore. I don't think it's about *what happens* or *the way it works* so much as how you want it to be – what you decide for yourself and your own life. Sure, there are some folks who are old in their fifties, but there are also plenty of folks who are still young and living full lives in their eighties. There is no one way of looking at it, no one way of being. There's only what we each choose for ourselves."

He smiled. "You can decide that you're old, or you can decide that you're just getting started on the second half of your life. You can decide that you're a sad and lonely widow, or that you're embarking on a new adventure – and that you're open to a new relationship."

She lifted her gaze to meet his.

He winked. "And yes, I mean with me."

Her heart pounded in her chest. How was it possible that she was sitting here in bed with this gorgeous man, and he was suggesting that they might explore a relationship?

His smile faded. "And I'm not going to push you about that. You take whatever time you need to think it over. But I am going push you to finally tell me about Anatoly, about why he thinks that you're his property, and why you're on the run from him."

She nodded. As much as she would like to stick with the subject of what might happen between them, she knew it was time to open up and tell him why she was on the run. She hated the thought that something might happen to him because of her, but she needed to talk about it, needed his input – he was an expert, after all.

She sucked in a deep breath and blew it out slowly. "Okay. You know I told you that Tom owned a chain of gyms in the city?"

Adam nodded.

"Well, he was working his way toward retiring. He'd built the whole business from nothing over the years, and he used to work all the time. Over the last few years, he'd brought in a manager to oversee everything so that he could step back a bit. That turned out to be a godsend after he got sick. Glenn was already in place, and he took over the day-to-day running of everything. He'd been a friend of Tom's for years, so we felt comfortable that we had someone we knew and trusted at the helm." She blew out a sigh. "But we were wrong."

She looked up at Adam; his arm tightened around her shoulders, and his eyes encouraged her to go on, but he didn't interrupt, didn't question her, or try to hurry her.

"He was good at the job, but he had some personal issues. He was a gambler, although we didn't know it back then. In fact, I don't think it was that bad back then. But he took it hard when Tom died and he started drinking more and I guess, gambling more. He got himself deeper and deeper into debt, and he started borrowing from bad people – the kind of people who don't care what they do to get their money back. After we did the taxes last year, I couldn't figure out why the business was barely breaking even. The gyms have always made good money. Glenn fed me all kinds of excuses about the economy and people working out at home, but I knew something was up. I hired an investigative accountant and he found that Glenn had been stealing pretty much all the profits.

"When I confronted him, he broke down and told me everything and begged me to help him." She shrugged. "He was Tom's friend and I wanted to help him. I hated the idea of him being in danger. So, I lent him some of my own money. I told you I come from a wealthy family, and my own business used to do pretty well. I thought that the amount I loaned him would be enough to pay off his debts and that he'd pay me back little by little out of what he made managing the gyms."

She shook her head. "I didn't understand that gambling is like any other addiction. Of course, he spent everything I gave him – he told me afterward that he'd genuinely believed that he could double the money – that he'd be able to pay off his debts and pay me back. Instead, he still had his debts and now he owed me as well. That's when Anatoly's men started showing up at the gyms. They trashed a couple of them and started scaring the members away.

"I was there one night when they came in and I yelled at them. I told them that they weren't going to be able to get the money out of the gyms because Glenn didn't own them; I did. They just laughed in my face, of course. They found it amusing that a woman would scream at them while Glenn just cowered in the corner. I guess they must have told Anatoly about that because the next time I spoke to Glenn, he told me that Anatoly wanted to meet me. I refused at first. It was nothing to do with me. I mean, I knew by reputation who Anatoly was – I don't think you can live in Chicago and not know, but …" She shuddered.

"Glenn was so scared of what they were going to do to him that in the end, I agreed to go with him. When we got there,

Anatoly told Glenn that he would accept me as payment – that all his debts would be forgiven if he just handed me over." She shuddered again and Adam's arm tightened around her shoulders.

"It didn't seem real at first. I mean, that's crazy stuff that happens in mobster movies, right? Or the kind of awful stuff that you hear about in human trafficking stories that happen somewhere on the other side of the world. It's not the kind of thing that I think of as happening in suburban Chicago."

"I thought I must have misunderstood; other than that ridiculous offer, Anatoly acted like a charming businessman. He was civilized and polite. He told us to think his offer over and that he'd be in touch. I even laughed about it afterward, thinking that I had somehow gotten the wrong end of the stick. Glenn didn't laugh, though. And then a couple of days later, he showed up at my apartment – with two of Anatoly's men." Her heart raced as she remembered that night. She'd opened the door and been surprised to see Glenn with two men that she recognized from their visit to Anatoly's house.

Glenn had looked guilty as hell, and the two goons had kept leering at her. She'd led them all through to the family room and offered them drinks. She'd been shaking like a leaf when she went into the kitchen– she just knew that those men planned to take her. So, instead of fixing their drinks, she'd simply slipped quietly out the front door, ridden the elevator down to the garage, gotten into her car, and fled. She'd known that they were there to collect her – to take her to Anatoly, and she had no intention of going. She'd told Taryn about the whole thing, and her friend had assured her that Anatoly was known to take women as payment. That he paraded them around as his new girlfriend whenever he was out in public, but that they all disappeared after a few months – missing, presumed dead.

She looked up at Adam. "I knew that they were there for me – to take me to him. So, I slipped out and ran. I went to my usual ATM and withdrew as much cash as I could. I didn't want to be using cards or my phone. I swung by the restaurant to see Taryn and told her everything and then I headed out of Chicago. I was on the road for a couple of months before I ended up in Summer Lake."

She gave him a wry smile. "And you know everything that's happened since I arrived here."

Adam took hold of her hand and brushed his thumb over her knuckles. "You were smart to run."

She let out a short laugh. "It didn't take much to figure that out."

"And when he called you last night, is that the first you've heard from him?"

"No. Well, the first I've heard directly from him, yes. But his people were going by the restaurant for the first few weeks."

"Did they threaten your friend?"

"No. Thank God! Taryn has connections of her own."

Adam raised an eyebrow.

"She's friendly with a … let's call him a competitor of Anatoly's. Anatoly knows that if any harm comes to her, he'll be facing a war."

Adam held her gaze, and she didn't see any harm in explaining.

"There are some families in the city that you just don't mess with. When she was younger, Taryn was married to a man in one of those families. He died young, but his brother is now the head of the family, and he still considers Taryn to be under his protection."

Adam nodded.

"Until this whole thing came up with Glenn, I didn't take any of the mob stuff seriously. I thought it was just urban legend, you know? I thought Taryn was teasing me because … well, because I suppose that compared to her, I'm a little naïve."

Adan hugged her closer. "Not naïve, Evie. You just don't have any experience with those kinds of people – that kind of life."

"I didn't have, but I do now. Now, I don't know how my life will ever be my own. Anatoly has sworn that he won't give up until he finds me. I know it's not so much about me as the fact that he doesn't like not getting his own way. He decided that I would be his, and he won't stop until I am."

Adam pressed a kiss to her forehead. "He will, sweetheart. I'm going to make sure of it."

When she looked up into his eyes, there was nothing soft there, just a steely determination. It was the kind of look that she'd seen in Anatoly's eyes when he'd told her that he was going to make her his woman. Coming from Anatoly it had made her blood run cold, but from Adam, it made her feel safe.

Chapter Six

.

Adam couldn't resist squeezing Evie's hand before he got out of his truck. "Just sit tight, I'll only be a few minutes."

She looked nervous but nodded and didn't argue. He climbed out of the truck and headed into the airport building.

After everything that she'd told him this morning, there were a dozen things that he wanted to get to work on. He didn't have any connections in Chicago, but he didn't doubt that he'd be able to figure something out. Between his old teammates and a couple of other groups of guys who worked security in different guises, he was hopeful that he'd be able to make Evie's problem go away. Between himself and the guys he knew here in town, he was confident that he'd be able to keep her safe.

The first step in keeping her safe was the reason that they'd come over to the airport. He didn't know if Anatoly had traced her phone – yet. But he didn't want to take any chances. He'd called Smoke, who ran the airport and a charter company based here, to see if he had any flights leaving today. He'd been happy to hear that Diego's son, Zack, was flying him down to Colombia for a family event. When Adam had called him to explain the situation, Diego had been happy to take Evie's phone with him – and to leave it on. Diego might not be former military, but Adam knew that he'd worked with Manny down in Colombia years ago. Whatever his background might be, he was someone Adam would want on his side if the shit hit the fan.

As soon as he entered the building, Diego and his lady, Izzy, greeted him. Izzy gave him a big smile.

"Where is she?"

"She's outside, waiting in the truck."

Izzy made a face at him, but Diego chuckled. "Perhaps she preferred to wait out there, *mi amor*. I don't know Evelyn very well, but I don't think she's as outgoing as you are."

Adam smiled at them. "Yeah, with everything that she's had going on, she's felt safer keeping to herself. I'm hoping that will change once we figure this thing out, though."

Diego's smile faded and he nodded, looking much more serious. "I'm happy to take the phone. We're making a stop in Orange County, so I'll turn it on when we land there, and I'll make sure that it ends up someplace where people will think twice before wanting to follow it."

"Thanks." Adam handed the phone over.

"What else can I do, *mi amigo*?"

Adam shrugged. "I don't know yet. She only told me the full story this morning. I'm going to see what I can dig up, then I'll put together a game plan."

Diego nodded. "Anything I can do to help, you let me know, okay? We'll be gone for the next few days, but we plan to be home on Wednesday."

"Thanks."

Diego gripped his shoulder. "I wasn't always a banker. I know you have your military guys here in town, and elsewhere, I'm sure. But ..." a cold expression crossed his face, "... I lost a cousin years ago – she disappeared, and we never found her, but we all knew she was taken by human traffickers. It used to be commonplace down there back then." He shook his head. "I'm sure it still is." He smiled again. "My point is that if you can use me – or my resources – for anything, I want to help."

"Thanks." Adam didn't know Diego all that well, but he'd always liked the guy. Now, he liked him even more and looked forward to getting to know him better. "For now, taking Evie's phone is huge."

Izzy grinned at him. "Evie, huh?"

Adam laughed. He'd always liked Izzy, too. She was no shrinking violet, but she was good people. "Yeah."

She gave him a knowing look. "Well. Give her my number. I'd say that I'll come see her when we get back, but I don't want to be too pushy." She shot a look at Diego when he laughed. "Tell her that she can call me anytime, and I'll try to hold off, but I'm there for her if she wants me."

"Thanks, Izzy."

"Hey, guys."

They all turned to see Zack and his fiancée, Maria, walking toward them. Zack was carrying a sleeping infant in a car seat. "Are we ready?"

Diego squatted down, smiling at the baby. "We are, now that our grandson's here."

He took the car seat and leaned down to kiss Maria's cheek.

Adam grinned at them and nodded. "I hope you have a great trip and thanks again."

He left them to it and hurried back out to the truck. He knew how much family meant to Diego, and he was happy for the man, but he couldn't imagine taking a family trip like that. He'd rather take off for a tropical island to hang out on the beach with his lady – if he had a lady – than spend a vacation meeting up with relatives.

He smiled as he approached the truck. Seeing Evie sitting there in his passenger seat, he wanted to make her his lady. First, though, he had to make her safe, and in order to do that, he had to get Anatoly off her back.

"Do you want a glass of wine?" Adam asked.

Evelyn smiled through pursed lips. "I should probably stick with water."

He laughed. "Just one glass is all I'm offering; I'm not trying to get you drunk."

She had to laugh with him. "Honestly. I don't know which is worse. If I say that I shouldn't drink too much …" She stopped. She'd been about to remind him of what he'd said last night – that he'd never take advantage if she'd had too much to drink. She could feel the heat in her cheeks. She could hardly tell him that she didn't want to drink too much if that would put him off!

He smiled. "It's okay. Come on, sit down."

She wasn't sure what he thought was okay, but she was glad to leave the subject behind and slid into the seat opposite him.

She was glad that he'd given in when she insisted that he should let her make dinner. It was the least she could do after everything he'd done for her. And besides, it'd been months since she'd cooked a decent meal. Between all the time she'd spent on the road, and then the last few weeks that she'd been staying here, eating beans and rice, she was eager to cook again. Adam had bought enough groceries to get them through the apocalypse. The fridge was crammed full, as were all the cabinets. She'd laughed when he returned from the grocery store this morning and made trip after trip back to his truck to bring everything in.

He poured them each a glass of wine, and she promised herself that she wouldn't overdo it tonight. He raised his glass to her with a smile.

"Here's to putting all of this behind you."

She clinked her glass against his. "I'll drink to that. Thanks, Adam, for everything."

He smiled. "Thank you for telling me about it, and for letting me help. I haven't done anything yet, but we'll get this taken care of, Evie. I promise."

"Don't say that you haven't done anything. Just giving Diego and Izzy my phone to take with them is a huge weight off my mind."

"Yeah. I don't know if Anatoly had or could trace it, but now, if he does, he'll have people chasing off to Colombia instead of coming here."

"Yeah."

"What's wrong?"

"Nothing."

"No, don't say nothing; tell me."

"It's just … I tried so hard to be careful. I've been living the way I have because I don't want to access any of my accounts. I was eating beans and rice and sleeping in my car because I didn't want to give him any way to trace me. I have plenty of money, Adam, and I'll pay you back for everything just as soon as I can."

He frowned, but she held her hand up. "I will. I guess I just feel stupid that despite all the precautions I've taken, I just couldn't resist calling Taryn. She's my best friend. She's been so worried, and I miss her so much. I should have known better though. I gave him an open door by calling her … just like you said."

"No. You can't beat yourself up. You've isolated yourself from everything – everyone. It's not like you felt able to talk to anyone here. You've been all alone. It's understandable that you'd want to talk to your friend." He smiled. "Hopefully with your phone winging its way to Colombia, it won't be an issue. And now you have a friend here that you can talk to – me."

She smiled back at him. "Thanks, Adam. You've been amazing. You really have. And I love that I have you to talk to now. I guess I'll just have to hope that Taryn won't worry too much. I want to call her one last time to let her know that I'm okay, even though I know I shouldn't call her anymore."

Adam frowned. "We'll set something up. You can call her at the restaurant. I'll talk to the guys. I'm sure we'll be able to route a call so that it can't be traced."

"That'd be so good. I just want to let her know that I'm okay. And I need to know that she's okay, too. If Anatoly found my number by going through her phone records at the restaurant …" Her hands started to shake. "Oh, god! Do you think that he might go after her? Try to get her to tell him where I am? She can't of course, she doesn't know but …"

Adam held her gaze for a long moment. "I don't know, Evie. I hope not, but I'll call Dan after we've eaten, and ask him the best way to make an untraceable call. But you did say that he probably won't want to mess with her – given her connections."

Evelyn blew out a sigh. "You're right. I'm just getting panicky. Sorry."

"There's nothing to apologize for."

After they'd eaten, and Adam had cleaned up the kitchen, he turned to where Evie was sitting at the little table. He really needed to get some furniture. He needed to get the work finished on the house first, though. He'd bought the place several months ago, but he hadn't been in any hurry to finish the renovations. He'd bought the place because he'd finally been feeling the urge to have a home of his own. But between the fact that he was gone so much of the time, traveling with Clay, and that he felt at home living in Clay's guest house with Davin whenever they were here at the lake, getting the house finished hadn't been high on his priority list. He hadn't wanted to intrude on Evie too much since she'd been staying here, but now – now that they were here together, finishing the house was one of his top priorities.

He hated that the only choices they had were either to sit here at the little kitchen table or to go upstairs and sit on the bed. He didn't hate the idea of being in bed with her – far from it. But he was hoping that when they got there it would be the beginning of something. He didn't want to put her off by rushing her.

"Are you okay?" she asked with a worried look.

"I'm fine – why?"

"You look irritated. You don't need to stick around here with me, you know."

He squatted down in front of her, resting his hands on her knees. "I want to. Unless … are you saying that you'd rather be by yourself?" If that's what she wanted, he wasn't going to force his company on her, although he might be the one sleeping in his vehicle if she wanted him to leave. There was no way he'd just go back to Clay's place and forget about her. If she wanted him to leave, he'd bunk down in his truck outside.

A rush of warmth filled his chest when she covered his hand with hers. "No. I don't want to be by myself. I like you being here."

His heart started to hammer as he looked into her eyes.

"I just don't want to impose on you," she continued. "I don't want you to feel like you have to stay here and look out for me. It's Saturday night; I'm sure you have better things to do than hang out here with me. Don't you usually go to The Boathouse with everyone?"

"Sometimes I do. But I have no interest in going there tonight." He frowned. "Have you ever been?"

"No. I didn't think it was wise to go out in public unless I had to." She let out a short laugh. "And besides, I was saving my money for beans and rice."

He made a face at her. "When we go out in the future, you won't need to spend a penny. I'll take care of it."

"Oh, I didn't mean …"

"I know. I'm just saying. That's what a guy does when he takes his lady out."

She raised her eyebrows. "His lady?"

He grinned at her. "That's what I want. That's what I'm working toward here. Of course, I'm going to keep you safe and get Anatoly off your back – whether you have any interest in me or not. But totally apart from all of that, I've admired you from afar for long enough. Now that we've finally broken the ice, you should know what my intentions are."

Her cheeks were slightly flushed, but she smiled. "Okay, then."

"Is it?" Adam cocked an eyebrow. "Is it okay?"

She nodded slowly. "It is. I have no idea how to play games. I was married for nearly twenty-five years. I haven't dated anyone since Tom died. I don't know how the whole dating thing goes anymore."

Adam grinned. "You don't need to know. All you need to know is if you're interested in me – interested in us getting to know each other better and seeing where things can go between us."

She nodded. "I am."

"Great." He chuckled.

"What's so funny?"

He smiled through pursed lips. "Just that the only options I can offer you right now are either taking you to bed or going out for a drive somewhere. I think you're right to not want to go out in public too much yet. I'm hoping that one of the guys I called this afternoon will be able to get back to me tomorrow and we should know if Anatoly figured out where you are, but until we know for sure, I think you're best lying low."

"I do, too."

"So, which is it to be? Want to go and sit upstairs or would you rather go out for a drive?"

Taking her out driving around didn't feel like the wisest option – not until he knew for sure that there wasn't going to be anyone waiting to ambush them. But he had to give her the choice. It wasn't like he was asking her to go upstairs with him in the traditional sense, but still – it'd be tempting while they were there, and he didn't want her to feel uncomfortable.

He started to feel a little uncomfortable himself when she ran her tongue over her bottom lip nervously.

"I'd rather not go out, if you don't mind. I'm still a bit jittery. I …" She let out a short laugh. "I'm nervous about going upstairs with you, too, but in a whole different way."

He smiled and got to his feet. "There's nothing to be nervous about, Evie. Yes, I'm attracted to you. Yes, I hope that we'll get to that point someday soon, but I would never do anything that you weren't comfortable with – you have to know that, right?"

She laughed again. "Oh, I do. I trust you completely." The twinkle in her eyes as she got to her feet to join him made him stick his hands in his pockets to give himself more room. His cock pressed uncomfortably against his zipper when she added, "It's me that I'm not sure I can trust."

He smiled through pursed lips. "Well, that puts a whole different spin on things. I trust you to do whatever you're comfortable with – and believe me, I'll be happy with whatever that is."

He took hold of her hand and led her toward the stairs. He couldn't help watching her ass as she went up ahead of him. Maybe she was just joking, but it hadn't sounded like it. He'd wanted to take things slowly in the bedroom, but if she wanted to go there, he was hardly going to turn her down.

Chapter Seven

Evelyn felt unsure of herself again as she watched Adam kick his shoes off and climb onto the bed. It was only the same thing as he'd done this morning, but now they'd talked about it – about their attraction for each other – and about the possibility of what might happen between them.

Once he'd piled the pillows up against the headboard and settled back against them, he held his hand out to her with a smile.

"Come on. We don't need to make this awkward or anything. We're just two friends finding a comfortable place to sit and talk."

He looked so earnest, the poor guy was trying to reassure her and that was sweet of him – although the unmistakable bulge in the front of his jeans that he kept trying to adjust was much more reassuring to her. She might not have thought about sex much since Tom died, but there was no denying that it felt good to see the effect she was having on Adam.

She climbed up beside him and leaned back against the pillows. He turned to smile at her and then surprised her by rolling off the bed. "I forgot. I have a TV and an old DVD player in the closet in the spare room. I'll set them up and we can watch a movie."

It was crazy that she felt disappointed at that. She'd been thinking about other ways they could occupy their time than watching a movie. But bless him, Adam was doing his best to not go there. "That'll be great."

Ten minutes later, he had the TV and DVD player hooked up and handed her a stack of movies to look through.

"Sorry, I should have thought of this before. I could have hooked it up for you. I don't have cable or anything yet, but you could have watched movies while you've been staying here."

She smiled. "It's fine. I have a little radio and I listen to the news. And I have my E-reader with all my books on it."

Adam nodded. "Still, I'll get cable and internet hooked up next week. Do you see anything there that you might want to watch?"

She chuckled. "I think I should let you choose."

He rolled his eyes at her. "Okay, so my taste runs mostly to action movies, what can I say? I'm a guy."

She nodded happily, liking that he was such a guy. He was very much a man's man from what she knew of him. He was big and strong, very much a protector – he was just what she needed right now. She smiled to herself at the thought that he was also what she wanted. Thank goodness she'd stopped after one glass of wine tonight. She wasn't going to go blurting that out.

"So, educate me? I don't know much about action movies."

Adam cocked his head to the side. "Tom didn't watch them?"

She loved that he asked about Tom. She hadn't wanted to say too much about him, but Adam seemed keen to know. "No. I guess, given that he owned a string of gyms, you might expect him to be into action movies and that kind of thing, but he wasn't. He preferred to read, and to spend time in the garden."

Adam nodded.

For some reason, describing Tom that way made her feel disloyal somehow. "He could kick some ass, though. I wouldn't have had to worry about Anatoly if Tom were still here."

Adam nodded and climbed back onto the bed beside her. "I don't doubt it. You don't mind me asking about him, do you?"

"No! I just … it feels strange. I don't want to harp on about my dead husband."

He took hold of her hand. "I don't see it that way."

"How do you see it?"

He looked into her eyes. "You shared most of your life with him. You loved him. He's a part of you – even though he's not here anymore. The more I learn about Tom, the more I learn about you. And I remember with my mom after my dad died, she always wanted to talk about him – she said that talking about him kept him around."

"Yeah. It is nice to talk about him, but I don't want to make you uncomfortable."

"It doesn't."

"Okay, then."

"Okay."

She smiled. "Are you going to put a movie on then and educate me about action heroes?"

He chuckled and hit the button on the remote. "Step one complete, the movie is playing. As for step two – educating you …?" He let his words trail off and gave her a mischievous smile. "We'll have to see about that."

All the muscles in her stomach and lower tightened in anticipation. She pressed her thighs together against the unexpected heat that pooled between them. She might not have thought about sex much since Tom had died, but as Adam rested his arm around her shoulders, and she tried to focus on the movie, she couldn't think about anything else.

~ ~ ~

Adam forced himself to stare at the screen. He'd only just managed to stop himself from saying that he could educate her about action heroes. How freaking cheesy would that have sounded? He needed to get a grip.

He tightened his arm around Evie's shoulders, refusing to allow himself to think about how it would feel to grip her hips in his hands as he … nope. Focus on the damn movie!

It wasn't working. He kept trailing his fingers over her arm without even realizing that he was doing it until she shivered against him. He felt like a damn teenager at the movies with his first girlfriend, wondering when or even if he should make a move.

Evie was leaning against him, seemingly engrossed in the movie – although he didn't think it was the kind of thing that would normally capture her attention. He looked back at the screen again, watching a team of guys getting ready to storm a shack in the jungle. If he wanted to educate Evie about such things, he'd point out how the first three men were asking to be shot. But he didn't think she'd be interested in hearing how Hollywood so often got it wrong, and he didn't want to sound like the asshole who thought he knew better than the writers and directors. He did know better – but she didn't know that about him yet.

She turned to look up at him just as he was stealing a glance at her. Their noses were only inches apart. He heard her breath catch and leaned back a little to give her space.

She frowned.

"What's up?"

"It's just … I mean, I don't know how these things work, but wouldn't those first three men get themselves shot to pieces if they went in like that? It seems stupid to me."

Adam chuckled. "Yep. You're absolutely right. They would. Hollywood doesn't always get it right."

She shook her head and glanced at the screen before turning back to him. "What about you? I know you were in the military – like Russ and so many of the others were. What did you do?"

He held her gaze for a moment before he answered. "I was Special Forces."

She raised her eyebrows and smiled. "Does that mean that if you tell me you'll have to shoot me?"

He laughed. "No. I was a Delta operator."

She gave him a puzzled look. "You mean Delta Force – like the men in black who you see on the news going in to rescue hostages? The ones you don't see but you hear about taking down terrorist leaders?"

He nodded.

"Wow."

Adam chuckled and waited for her to elaborate.

She turned and looked up into his eyes. "I had no idea. But it does explain a few things."

"What kind of things?"

She smiled. "You make me feel safe. And I suppose that's only logical since you spent your career making sure that people were safe."

"Yeah. I told you, I can take care of you."

Her hazel eyes seemed to shimmer with the reflected light from the TV. She was so damn beautiful.

He couldn't resist, he leaned in closer but managed to stop with his mouth an inch from hers. He knew he wasn't going to be satisfied with a simple brushing of lips this time, but he didn't know if she felt the same way.

He felt the tension leave his shoulders when she reached up and rested her hand on his chest. She had to be able to feel his heart thundering. It thundered even harder when she moved in to close the final distance between them.

Her lips were full and soft. He managed to keep it gentle to start with, brushing his lips over hers like he'd done last night. But that brought back the memory of holding her in his arms, of the way her soft warm body had felt pressed against his.

He curled his arm around her waist, drawing her to him as he ran his tongue over the seam of her lips. He groaned when she opened for him, and his tongue slid against hers. She let out a little moan that had him harder than steel.

He ran his hand up and down her side, allowing his thumb to graze the side of her breast, and capturing her gasp as she shivered against him.

Her hand came up to grasp at his shoulder as he deepened the kiss. She tasted like the wine they drank earlier and something sweet, something that was just simply Evie.

He shifted onto his back, pulling her with him so that she was straddling him. His cock throbbed inside his jeans, aching to get closer to her.

She whimpered as he ran his hands down her back and then allowed himself to grasp her ass, pulling her down onto him as he rocked his hips. She gripped his T-shirt at his shoulders and kissed him back with an urgency that surprised him. He'd wanted to take things slowly, had thought that she might be nervous, but the way she was rocking against him, allowing his tongue to explore her mouth, she might just be as eager as he was.

He wasn't going to assume anything, though. He gentled the kiss before finally pulling back and smiling up at her.

"Damn, Evie."

She nodded breathlessly and smiled back at him. "Damn is right! It's been a long time for me and …" She closed her eyes, and when she opened them again, she shook her head in wonder. "And I'm hoping it won't be too much longer."

He smiled back at her. "What are you saying?"

She narrowed her eyes at him. "Are you going to make me say it?"

"Not if you don't want to." He grinned. "How about if I say a few things that I think you might mean, and all you need to say is yes or no?"

"Okay."

His hands caressed her hips without him making any conscious effort to do so. "Are you saying that it'd be okay if we get into bed now?"

"Yes."

"Are you saying that it'd be okay if I undress you?"

Her cheeks flushed a little at that, but she nodded. "Yes."

He took hold of the hem of her T-shirt and pulled it up and off over her head. His breath came out in a rush at the sight of her breasts. His hands came up and hovered close to them as he smiled. "Are you saying that it'd be okay if I …?"

"Please," she breathed.

He closed his hands around them, but then reached around to unhook her bra before sliding the straps down her arms and off.

"You're so beautiful," he breathed before ducking his head. He kissed each taut peak before he looked back up at her.

"Are you saying that you'd be okay if I got naked with you?"

She rolled off him with a smile. "I am."

He pulled his own T-shirt off and then rolled off the bed to make quick work of getting rid of his jeans, pulling his boxers down and off with them.

His erection sprung free and pointed straight at her when he turned back around. He held still for a moment, loving the way she let her gaze travel over him. He was in decent shape, he'd had to be in his career, and he'd kept up with his physical fitness since he got out.

He swallowed at the sight of her running her tongue over her bottom lip. "You're quite a specimen, aren't you?"

That broke the moment, and he had to laugh. "A specimen? You make me sound like a bug in a jar."

"Oh, sorry!" Her cheeks flushed a deep red as she looked up at him. "I'm so sorry. I told you, I don't know how to play this game. I've only … I …"

"Hey." He climbed back onto the bed beside her and wrapped her up in his arms. "I was only joking with you. It's all good."

She nodded against his shoulder. "The view's definitely good."

He chuckled. "I like it better from where I'm sitting. And I'm going to like it even more when we get rid of the rest of your clothes."

She unfastened her jeans and pushed them down over her hips. He helped out, tugging them down her legs and off, taking her panties with them. He bit down on his bottom lip when she sat naked before him. She was beautiful.

She met his gaze shyly. "This is where I get self-conscious, and can't help thinking that I won't compare too well with the kind of women you usually …"

He shook his head and curled his arm around her. "You're gorgeous, Evie. Don't doubt it for a minute."

She still looked unsure, but then she smiled when he closed his hand around his aching cock. "This guy doesn't stand to attention for just anyone, you know."

She let out a short laugh. "When you put it that way, it's hard to deny that he seems kind of interested."

Adam laughed. "Kind of interested? It's a bit more than that. So, I'm going to need you to keep guiding me with yeses and noes, okay?"

"Okay."

He took hold of her hips and pulled her further down the bed so that she was lying on her back, and he was leaning over her. He let his hand slide up over her ribcage, and hover just under her breast. "Do you want me to …"

"Yes!"

He closed his hand around her full breast and then teased her nipple with his fingers before ducking his head to take it into his mouth. He loved the sound she made when he sucked hard on the taut bud, loved the way she writhed beneath him.

He kissed his way down over her stomach, nibbling at her hips and then parting her thighs so that he could get between them. He looked up at her with a smile, loving that the flush on her cheeks spread over her neck and breasts. "Are you saying that it would be okay if I …?" He traced his fingers over her slick entrance, and she let out another little sound as she nodded rapidly.

The noises she was making made him want to know how she'd sound when he finally buried himself inside her. But he planned to take his time before he got there.

Evie grabbed two fistfuls of the sheet as he ducked his head between her legs. Her heart was pounding, and she moaned when he opened her up with his thumbs and sank his tongue inside.

"Adam!"

He lifted his head and grinned up at her. "This okay?"

"Oh God, yes!" She closed her eyes as he slowly pressed a finger inside and she felt herself tighten around him.

When she opened her eyes again, he met her gaze and held it as he slid his finger in and out. All she could do was stare back into his eyes. Perhaps she should feel embarrassed; she didn't know him that well, but it felt like she did. It didn't feel like he was just some guy, she trusted him. By staying here, she was trusting him with her life, and by sharing his bed like this, she was trusting him with her body and with her heart.

Well, not her heart. She shouldn't get carried away. They weren't talking about hearts here. She closed her eyes when he dropped his head. The feel of his mouth on her, the way he added a second finger, made it impossible to focus on anything except the pleasure he was giving her. His fingers pumped in a steady rhythm, and his lips and tongue teased her until she was panting, rocking her hips in time with him.

He glanced up and her and smiled. "Do you want to come for me?"

She nodded, and her breath caught in her chest as he thrust his fingers deeper and she felt herself tighten around them, then he closed his mouth around her, and she came apart. She gripped the sheet beneath her as wave after wave of pleasure crashed over her. Her orgasm hit hard, and she saw stars behind her eyes as Adam drew every last breath of pleasure out of her.

When she finally stilled, he came up to lie beside her and closed his arms around her with a smile.

She smiled back at him. He was wonderful! She blew out a big happy sigh. "Thank you! Give me a minute, and I'll return the favor." She reached down to curl her fingers around him. He was so hot and hard. She loved that he'd taken care of her pleasure first, but she didn't want him to have to wait much longer.

His smile faded.

"What's wrong?"

He smiled again. "Nothing's wrong. That was amazing. I love that you gave yourself to me like that – that you trusted me. But I'm not seeing it as a favor that you need to return."

"No?"

"No." He winked at her. "I'm seeing it as a warm-up."

"A warm-up?" She raised her eyebrows.

He dropped a kiss on her lips. "Yeah. The second I got you naked, I wanted nothing more than to cover your body with mine and bury myself so deep inside you that we can't tell where you end, and I begin."

Her breath caught in her chest as his words made her press her thighs together at the rush of heat between them.

He kissed her again. "But you said that you haven't been with anyone since Tom. So, I wanted to make sure that you're … warmed up." He trailed his fingers up and down over her ribs. "I'm not looking for an *I'll do you a favor and you do me one* kind of deal. I was just trying to make sure that you're comfortable first." He met her gaze, looking more serious. "Yeah, physically, but emotionally, too. I need to know that you're okay with it, with this … with me."

She reached up and wrapped her arms around his neck, pulling him down into a kiss before she leaned back so that she could look into his eyes. "Thank you."

He shrugged and gave her that lopsided grin she was starting to love. "I still don't see it as something to say thank you for."

She laughed. "I don't mean for the orgasm – although, it was kind of breathtaking. I mean, thank you for being so … considerate."

He nodded. "I just wanted you to have the chance to see how you felt afterward. I'd hate to make love to you and then have you regret it … for both our sakes."

She cupped his cheek in her hand. "I won't regret it, Adam." She pressed a kiss to his lips and used her arms to guide him over her. "I want you."

He pressed her down into the mattress as he settled his weight over her. "I want you, too, Evie."

She clung to him as he used his knees to spread her legs wider. Her heart was racing now, desperate for the moment when he'd do what he just said and bury himself deep inside her.

He still wasn't in any hurry, though. He looked down into her eyes and chuckled. "We probably should have talked about this sooner, but you don't have any worries about contraception with me. I had a vasectomy years ago."

"Oh!" She nodded. "Now, I feel dumb. You don't have any worries with me either, or you wouldn't even if you needed to." She let out a short, embarrassed laugh. "I mean, I'm past all that. And you already know that I haven't been with anyone in years. I'm clean." She rolled her eyes at him. "I told you I didn't know how this dating thing goes anymore."

He dropped a kiss on her lips. "You don't need to know how the dating thing goes, all you need to know is that I'm clean, too."

She gave him a puzzled look, wondering all of a sudden if he meant that he wasn't interested in dating her – just in having sex.

He gave her a stern look. "You don't need to worry about the dating thing because you're with me now – if you want to be?"

She stared back into his eyes for a long moment. His hot, hard head was pressing at her entrance, his big, brown eyes were looking steadily back into hers, and a small smile played on his lips.

He rocked his hips, and she caught her breath as he pressed a little way inside and then held still again. "Do you want me, Evie?"

She wasn't sure which question he was asking; did she want to be with him, or did she want him to make love to her. Either way, her answer was the same. "Yes."

His shoulders relaxed and he nodded. "I want you, too." His breath came out on a low growl as he thrust hard until, just like he'd said, she didn't know where she ended, and he began. "I want to make love to you, and I want to be with you," he breathed.

She nodded, unable to form words as their bodies started to move together. He drove deeper and harder, making her feel as though he was becoming a part of her as they carried each other higher and higher. He felt so good, so right. She clung to him as each thrust pushed her closer to the edge until he took her over and she gasped his name. She felt him grow impossibly harder and then he tensed and held deep as they carried each other away. She felt as though she was flying, high above the clouds, and at the same time, deeply and solidly connected to reality. Even if this – being with Adam – was a new and unfamiliar reality, it was one that she wouldn't mind getting used to.

When they finally stilled, Adam propped himself up on his elbows and looked down into her eyes. He dropped a kiss on her lips, and she wrapped her arms around his shoulders. She didn't have words. But then she didn't feel as though she needed them. His eyes told her that he felt the same way she did. They'd just shared something big, something real.

He held her gaze for a long moment before he nodded. "I'm glad you want me, Evie. Because after that? You've got me."

He pressed his face into her neck and nibbled, sending aftershocks racing through her.

"You've got me, too, Adam."

"I know," he whispered into her hair.

Chapter Eight

"So, I take it you had a good weekend?" Davin greeted Adam with a smile when he let himself into the guest house at Clay's place on Monday morning.

Adam nodded happily. "I did. How about you? Is there anything going on here?"

"Nope. All's quiet. Clay came down here on Saturday afternoon, asking about you."

"What did you tell him?"

"Just that you were spending the weekend at your house." Davin chuckled. "That you were getting busy over there."

Adam let out a short laugh and shook his head at his friend.

"What? Clay assumed that I meant you were getting busy with the work on the house." Davin cocked an eyebrow. "Are you going to tell me that I was wrong to assume something else?"

Adam shrugged. Part of him wanted to tell Davin all about it – not the details, but about how happy he was. About how close he felt to Evie after this weekend, and how …

Davin gave him a puzzled look. "What? Am I wrong? Are you going to tell me that you didn't get anywhere with the lovely Evie?"

"No! You're right to assume something else." Adam gave him a wry smile. "We had a good time together. But … it's not just about that. It's …" He shrugged. "I want to tell you all about it, but I don't want to tell you too much because …" He chuckled. "It doesn't seem right to kiss and tell. I know that's the way it usually works – we catch each other up on our conquests over the weekend but …"

Davin grasped his shoulder. "It's okay. I get it. Evie's not just some conquest. I already knew that. I shouldn't have put it the way I did. I was only yanking your chain, talking about getting busy. Evie's a lady and you're right not to go talking about her like that." He gave Adam an apologetic shrug. "All I can say in my defense is that I'm not used to you being with a lady."

Adam had to laugh. "Yeah. You're right. You don't need to apologize. I just … this is new to me."

Davin grinned. "It might be new, but it suits you. I've had the feeling ever since we first met Evie that something was going to happen between the two of you."

"You have?"

"Yeah." Davin laughed. "I mean, come on. Even your names say that you're meant to be."

Adam rolled his eyes.

"What? I thought that was why you called her Evie when everyone else calls her Evelyn."

"No. It's just … even from the first time I saw her, and Russ told me her name was Evelyn, she didn't look like an Evelyn. That seems like too formal a name for her."

Davin laughed. "Whatever you say. Anyway, what are you doing here?"

"Err, showing up for work. It is Monday morning."

"Yeah, but there's nothing going on. Clay's treating the rest of the week as a vacation. Since he got everything wrapped up early in Nashville, he's calling this time off."

"I know, he always does that when we get back early. But even though there's not much going on, it doesn't mean that I'm going to leave you by yourself the whole time."

"It's all good. I've got nothing else to do. Nowhere else I'd rather be so …" Davin shrugged. "I've got a handle on everything. You go back to your place if you like."

"Nah. I'd rather hang out with you."

"Do you want to go over the details for next month's travels?"

"Actually, what I really want to do is figure out how I can put a stop to Evie's problems."

"Oh, shit. Sorry, man. I didn't think. What have you found out? What's going on with her? What are we going to do about it?"

Adam smiled, loving that Davin automatically assumed that he'd be helping out with whatever he planned to do. It was hardly surprising though; they'd been teammates of one kind or another for almost thirty years. Just because the current situation involved a woman – Adam's woman – Davin didn't see it any differently. Then again, if the tables were turned, if Davin were the one who'd met a woman who needed help, Adam would feel the same way.

"Well, if you're in with me on this, I have a whole list I need to work my way down. We got rid of her phone. I need to get rid of her car as quickly as possible." He shook his head. Evie had been sleeping in her car and living on beans and rice because she didn't want to access her accounts – because she was afraid that Anatoly would be able to trace her that way. But it hadn't occurred to her that her vehicle would be another quick and easy way to track her down.

Davin made a face. "Want me to make some calls? I can probably have it on a transport before the end of the day."

Adam sighed. "Can you make it tomorrow? I haven't actually brought it up with her yet."

"Okay, but the sooner the better."

Adam held his hands up. "I know! But I need to be gentle about it. Her car's the only thing she has left of her own. And it's not just transport – she was living in the damned thing for a while there. Plus, she's still skittish. I know she's not going to like the thought that she can't just take off if she panics and feels the need to hit the road."

"Yeah. But you're going to get her something else, aren't you?"

"You know it. In fact, what do think? Do you want to start checking the classifieds, see what you can find? I want to call Dan before I do anything else, and then I need to call my buddy in Milwaukee – see if he has any contacts in Chicago."

"Sure." Davin went to sit at the computer. "What kind of vehicle are we looking for?"

Adam shrugged. "I dunno. See what's available."

Davin nodded. "And how much are we looking to spend?"

"Whatever it takes to get her something she'll be comfortable with. Price isn't the issue. I'd buy her something new but ..."

"I know. If we buy from a dealership, it'll be registered faster. If it's a private sale, it'll take a while longer."

Adam grinned at him. "True, but I think I'll register it in my name, just to be safer."

Davin held his gaze for a moment. "We can register it in mine if you like – then it's two steps removed."

Adam grasped his shoulder as he pulled his phone out of his back pocket. "Thanks, bud."

"You bet. No worries."

~ ~ ~

Evelyn felt her cheeks flush when Russ came in through the front door of the gym and grinned at her. "Morning. Did you have a good weekend?"

She nodded, not sure if he knew that Adam had stayed with her. She knew that the two of them were friendly, and Adam had said that he'd seen Russ in the grocery store. But even if Russ knew that Adam had stayed at the house, she hoped that he wouldn't know – wouldn't have guessed; she doubted that Adam would have told him – that she was now sharing his bed, not just his house.

Russ came and rested his elbows on the front desk where she was sitting and leaned over it with a worried look. "Is everything okay?"

"Yes. Fine. Everything's great. Thanks. How about you? Is Ria not with you this morning?"

She knew that asking about Ria would distract him. He was a man in love if ever she'd seen one.

Russ smiled. "She'll be here in a little while. She had a video meeting with Bentley and Willow this morning. They're setting up some big new media campaign."

Evelyn nodded. "I love that she still gets to work with them, even though she's here with you now."

Russ grinned. "Not as much as I love it. For a while there, I thought she was going to go back to living in Napa so that she could keep up with her work. It's worked out for the best all-around. Bentley and Willow get to run things their way, but Ria's only a phone call – or a mouse click – away when they need her input."

"Yeah. And she can still play as big a role as she wants to in her business." Evelyn was happy for Ria that things had worked out like that for her. But she couldn't help comparing.

She'd had to walk – or run – away from her own business. Of course, her interior design company was nothing like Ria's business. Ria owned and ran DuPont Wineries, one of the biggest wine growers and distributors in the country. But still, even though Evelyn didn't run a huge business like that, it'd hurt to have to just leave her clients hanging.

The first time she'd called Taryn, her friend had told her that she'd called Carrie, Evelyn's assistant, and told her that she'd had to go out of town for a family emergency. Carrie had dealt with everything she could by herself. But it was still a horrible mess. If Evelyn was ever able to go home, she wouldn't have a business left. That was a small price to pay, though – since it meant that she'd escaped Anatoly and whatever future would have awaited her with him. From what Taryn had told her, the women he'd taken as his own in the past spent a few short months being shown off as his latest companion, before they disappeared. She shuddered.

"Are you okay?" Russ was watching her with a puzzled look.

She forced a smile. "Yeah. Sorry. I was just …" She shrugged.

"Are you ready to tell me what's going on with you?"

She met his gaze. "I … don't know. What did Adam tell you?"

"Not much. He said that he'd managed to talk you into staying when you were ready to run again." Russ smiled. "And I told him that I want to do whatever it takes to help. And that I'm sure the guys will too."

He turned and nodded at Cal, who had just emerged from the locker room. Cal nodded in their direction and then came over with a puzzled look on his face.

"What's up?" he asked.

"Nothing," Evelyn answered quickly. She liked the idea that Cal and the others might be prepared to help her out. But she hated the thought that something could happen to them because of her.

Russ smiled at him. "Nothing's up. We were just saying how nice it is to know that there's a whole group of guys in town who'd be happy to help out if ever anyone needed them."

Cal frowned at him, but his expression softened when he looked at Evelyn. "Ah, right. Yeah." He smiled. "That's right. If ever anyone needed help, they'd have a whole team of us at their back. I mean, there's Manny, Ryan, and me, there's this guy, and of course, there's Adam, and Davin, too." He smiled. "In fact, if someone needed help, I'd say that Summer Lake's a pretty good place for them to be." He held her gaze for a moment and gave her a brief nod. "But anyway, I need to get going."

"Are you busy at work now?" asked Russ.

"No. Not yet. I think that'll change very soon – finally. But I don't work Mondays anyway. Terry and I are going up to Stanton Falls today. I just came to get a quick workout in while she takes her time over her coffee." He checked his watch. "But she'll probably be ready by now. I'll see you guys tomorrow."

After he'd gone, Evelyn blew out a sigh. "Does he know? Have you told him?"

Russ laughed. "No. How could I tell him what's going on with you when you haven't told me? He's a smart guy; he figured out what I meant, that's all."

"Yeah. Thanks, Russ. I'm sorry."

"You don't need to apologize. I get it. You've been used to keeping everything to yourself. But I hope that's going to change now. Now that you've told Adam what you're running from, I hope you're going to be okay with telling the rest of us." He smiled. "That's the kind of information that'll help us keep you safe."

She nodded. "Thanks. I just … I didn't want to land my problems on you. It's not that I don't trust you. I do. It's just that you don't need the kind of trouble that I could bring to your door. That's all."

"I get it. But in case you haven't figured it out already, we want to do whatever we can to help. The guys around here aren't worried about trouble coming to our door, we're more interested in keeping you safe behind the door while we stand out front and face down the trouble for you."

She had to smile. "So I'm starting to see."

"Anyway. Do you want a coffee? I'm going to make myself one."

"Please."

She watched him make his way into the breakroom next to the office. He was one of life's good guys, no question about it. And she had to admit that Cal was right. Of all the places that she could have landed as she ran from Anatoly, Summer Lake had to be the best one.

~ ~ ~

Adam frowned at the sight of the empty driveway when he got home. He'd pulled Evie's car into the garage on Saturday. If Anatoly hadn't found it yet, then he wasn't sure that it made any difference now. But he wasn't taking any chances. He wanted to get rid of it. Davin had found a transporter headed for the East Coast that he could get it on tomorrow. Adam just hoped that she would agree to let it go. He wasn't going to strong-arm her into doing anything she wasn't happy about, but he hoped that she'd understand the need.

It was weird though, he was glad that her car was safely out of sight, but it felt wrong not to see it sitting on his driveway. He'd grown used to it being there. Since she'd been staying here, he'd driven past the house whenever he got back to town

– just to make sure that she was still around. He smiled. He
hadn't stopped to check on her until Friday night, hadn't
wanted to impose on her, or more like he hadn't wanted her to
feel uncomfortable, hadn't wanted to do anything that might
make her run again. He'd kept telling himself that letting her
stay at his house was only about giving her a safe place. But it
had been more than that right from the beginning. He'd been
attracted to her the first time he saw her.

He made himself get out of the truck. If she looked out and
saw him sitting there, she'd wonder what he was up to. He
hesitated when he got to the front door and knocked before he
let himself in. He didn't want to scare her.

"Evie? Are you home?" He'd said that he'd pick her up from
the gym after work since he'd given her a ride in this morning.
But she'd called him earlier and said that she was going for
coffee with Ria at the end of the day, and Ria had offered to
drop her off.

He liked that she'd made at least one friend – and that friend
was Russ's lady. He shouldn't be letting his mind go there, but
he liked the idea that the two of them might become one of
the couples in town – the couples who all hung out together.

"Are you here?" he called again when she didn't answer.

"Sorry. I'm upstairs."

He was halfway up, taking the stairs two at a time before he
even realized what he was doing.

"Are you …?" he asked as he pushed the bedroom door
open. The sight of her made him forget the question. She was
standing there in nothing but a towel. Little drops of water still
shone on her shoulders.

The way she smiled made his heart beat faster. "I'm fine. I
just needed a shower when I got in. I didn't think you'd be
back yet."

He grinned and prowled around the bed toward her. "I would have been here earlier if I'd known I'd find you naked in the bedroom."

She laughed, but her cheeks flushed, and she held the towel a little tighter. He needed to cool it. They might have enjoyed each other in bed the last couple of nights, but whatever was happening between them was still new. She was into him, he knew that, but she wasn't completely sure of him yet – or of herself for that matter.

When he reached her, instead of pulling the towel away as he'd planned to, he closed his arms around her and hugged her to his chest.

She didn't immediately relax against him, so he loosened his hold, ready to step away. "Sorry."

"No!" She tightened her arms around his waist. "It's not that I don't like it. It's just I'm worried I'll get you wet."

He couldn't help chuckling at that. "I wouldn't worry about that. I was thinking the opposite – I'm hoping that I might get you wet."

Her cheeks flushed again, and he loved the way it spread down over her neck and chest. "Adam!" She was embarrassed, but her eyes shone as they looked up into his.

He laughed. "Yes, Evie! I hadn't even thought about it until today, but if we're Adam and Eve then aren't we supposed to …?" He cupped her ass and held her against his cock, which had stood to attention the moment he saw her in that towel.

She laughed with him and smacked his arm. "I think Adam and Eve were all about procreation, and we've already established that that's not in the cards for us – thankfully."

He chuckled. "Yeah. I guess. But you can't deny that Adam and Eve were made for each other."

Her eyes widened as she looked into his.

He shrugged. He was hoping that she might feel the same way, but it was different for her. She had a whole lot on her plate to worry about – just little things like her life and her business and everything that she'd given up to go on the run, and the fact that her life was in danger. He shouldn't be pressuring her, and he knew it. First, he needed to take care of Anatoly – to eliminate that threat in whatever way it took. Only then would it be fair to ask her to think about her future – with him.

He dropped a kiss on her lips. "Sure seemed like we were made for each other last night," he said with a smile, trying to lighten things up again. He kissed her bare shoulder, resisting the urge to lick off the drops of water. Then he ran his nose up her neck until he was just behind her ear. He loved the way she shivered as he spoke against her skin. "I'll make you dinner first, but after that, I think we should try again – let me prove to you that I'm made for you."

The way she pressed her hips against his told him that she was thinking that he meant he was made to fit inside her. He did, partly. He'd just have to give her time to understand that he meant he was made to be in her life too.

He stepped away from her. "I'll go see what I can get started for dinner while you finish off up here." While he was at it, he should probably take a minute to see what the hell he was thinking anyway. Just a couple days ago he'd been questioning Davin's assertion that Evie was someone he could see himself with. Was he really ready to start trying to persuade her that they were made for each other?

Chapter Nine

Evelyn felt silly as she swallowed the lump in her throat and dabbed at her eyes. She knew that Adam was right – it was for the best that he'd found someone to take her car away. But she couldn't help wishing that it didn't have to go.

He came out into the garage where she was standing and put a hand on her shoulder. "You'll be able to get it back once this is all behind us."

She turned to look over her shoulder at him. "I know. Thank you. It's so good of you – and Davin – to arrange this, to think of it even. I feel pretty stupid that it didn't occur to me that my car would be as traceable as anything else."

He came closer and closed his arms around her, pulling her back against his chest. "Don't be hard on yourself. You did well – knowing not to use your phone or your cards. Most people wouldn't have thought of that. And it seems that Anatoly didn't think to try finding your car. So, it's all good. Maybe it's overkill, maybe I'm being too cautious, but I think this is for the best, for now."

"It is. Thank you. It's just that … I know it's only a car, but …" She shook her head. "It's been good to me. It kept me safe. It was my home – my entire world for a while there."

He dropped a kiss on the top of her head. "I know. And that's understandable. Davin would have found a way to get it out of town yesterday, but I knew you'd feel this way. That's why I asked him to wait until today. I wouldn't just get rid of it without talking to you about it, and I had a feeling that you'd want to say goodbye."

She turned around within the circle of his arms and rolled up on her tiptoes to press a kiss to his lips. "Thanks, Adam."

He nodded. "Not a problem. I told you; I'm going to take care of you. And that means in every way – not just put a stop to Anatoly."

She searched his face for a moment. He was so sincere. She knew how lucky she was that he'd decided to step up for her. He was a good man. He might have a bit of a hero complex going, and she was going to have to watch herself with that. It'd be far too easy for her to get carried away with all of this – to start seeing him as her savior, her hero. And he was both. But she was under no illusions. She fully expected that when – if – they managed to stop Anatoly, and what that could even look like, she didn't know, but if they managed to resolve the situation, Adam would move on. He'd have done what he set out to, which was to protect a woman in danger. She couldn't go letting herself believe that anything more would happen between them.

She smiled against his shoulder as he held her head there. He'd told her that he felt like they were made for each other – and he proved his point in bed, too! But she was going to have to keep reminding herself, when he said stuff like that, that he only meant physically. They were good together in bed, he wasn't wrong about that. But she couldn't let herself think or hope that he thought they were made for each other in life. She'd be forever grateful to him, and not just for taking her under his protection and for deciding that he was going to help her deal with Anatoly somehow. She'd be forever grateful that he'd reminded her that she was a woman – and shown her just how good a woman could feel. She'd demoted herself to the role of a lonely widow after Tom died. But Adam had shown her that she was wrong about that. He'd taught her that her life was opening up to another chapter – and it was a chapter where she could love again.

She sighed against his shoulder as he held her, realizing that he probably thought she was still sad about the car. He couldn't know that what she was sad about right now was knowing that even if she found love again, it wouldn't be with him. He'd be the catalyst, but she knew better than to hope that a man like him would be happy to settle for someone like her.

~ ~ ~

"Knock, knock?"

"Hey, Clay!" Adam looked up from the computer, surprised to see Clay letting himself into the guest house. "Is everything okay?"

Clay nodded as he came in and took a seat in one of the armchairs on the other side of the room. Adam and Davin had this room set up as an office, and Adam was sitting at one of the computers. From here, he had a good view of all the security screens that displayed images of the property, though he hadn't been focused on them – he'd been emailing with one of his old Delta buddies who had a friend in Chicago.

"Everything's good with me," said Clay. "And with Marianne – she said to say hi, by the way." He raised an eyebrow.

Adam knew what he was getting at. He rarely went more than a couple days without seeing Marianne. He was usually up at the house for one thing or another when they were here. It wasn't as though Clay had any active threats against him at the moment – he hadn't had for a couple years now, but he and Marianne had become friends to Adam and Davin. It wasn't just about work – he liked them. They'd all become a part of each other's lives.

"Yeah, sorry. Davin's been carrying the load around here. I've been … distracted." He knew that wasn't the best thing for a security guy to admit but he'd always been honest with Clay, and he wasn't about to change that now.

"I figured. Is everything okay with you?"

"Yeah. It's …" He met Clay's gaze and let out a short laugh. "I … have you met Evelyn?"

"The woman who's been staying in your house?"

"Yeah."

"Only briefly. I've been wondering what the deal was. Marianne said that she was in some kind of trouble, and that you'd offered her your place out of the goodness of your heart."

Adam chuckled. "Yeah."

"And?" Clay laughed with him. "What's the rest of the story?"

"I'm sure you can guess."

"I kind of figured that your motive for letting a woman stay in your house might not be purely altruistic?"

"You could say that. She …" What the hell. He'd always been straight up with Clay, and he imagined that more than a few people already knew what Evie's situation had been before Russ had hired her to work at the gym. "She had some troubles. She's been on the run for a while, and she was living in her car. When I found that out, and I had a house sitting empty …"

"What kind of trouble? What's she running from?"

"Some asshole in Chicago – where she's from, decided that he would take her as payment for some other asshole's gambling debts."

Clay scowled. "Her husband?"

"No. He died a few years back. The asshole with the gambling debts is the guy who her husband brought in to manage his business after he got sick. Evie only discovered what was going on when the business stopped showing a profit. He'd spent all his own money and was gambling hers. Then he borrowed from the wrong people. They wanted the debt paid, and when he couldn't give them the money, they wanted to take her."

"Shit! That sounds like a mafia movie."

Adam nodded. "Almost, Russian mob by the sound of it. The guy who wants Evie as payment is named Anatoly."

Clay shook his head. "So, what are we going to do about it?"

Adam smiled. "You don't need to do a damned thing. And I promise you, even though I've been a bit distracted this week, I won't let it interfere with my work here. Davin's on the ball."

Clay waved a hand at him. "I'm not worried about that. I'm fine." He winked. "If I didn't like you and Davin so much, I'd go without security these days. There are no threats on my horizon."

Adam frowned. "You can't ever know that – and I'm not just saying that because I like working for you. You can never be too careful in your position."

"Yeah, I know. But this – what you have going on with … Evie? I thought her name was Evelyn."

Adam smirked. "It is."

"Okay. And that answers the next few questions I want to ask. But most importantly, I'm happy for you to take whatever time you need to figure out her situation. Whatever time, and whatever else. If you need the plane, take it. All I ask is that you give the pilots as much notice as you can – you know Luke and Zack love being back here with their women."

"Thanks, Clay. But I don't …"

"Don't dismiss it out of hand. All I'm saying is that if you want to get her out of here, you can use the plane. If you think that she'd be safer in Nashville, take her there. I know you don't have an apartment there anymore, but you can take her to the house. Stay there with her."

Adam gave him a grateful smile. "Have I ever told you how much I like working for you?"

Clay laughed. "No, and I've never told you how much I appreciate you – and let's keep it that way, can we? I'm more comfortable with you giving me shit, and me driving you nuts when I won't follow orders."

Adam laughed with him. "Okay. Let's stick with that then."

Clay nodded. "Are you going to bring her out with everyone?"

Adam's smile faded. "I don't know. Not until I know a bit more. Right now, I have no idea if there's some Russian goon lurking around, ready to snatch her – or worse. I've got a couple old Army buddies up in the Chicago area trying to find out what they can, but until I know more, I'd rather keep her off the radar."

"Okay. In the meantime, if you want to bring her over here, or if she's getting stir crazy, you know Marianne would love to meet her."

"Thanks. She's not just hiding at the house, though. She's working at the gym. Like I said, she was living in her car before; she needed the money."

Clay scowled. "Do you need …"

"No. Thanks. I've got it covered. It's not like she's destitute, she has money, she's just been scared to access her accounts."

"Okay. Well, I imagine Marianne might find her way into the gym after I tell her about this."

"She doesn't need to."

Clay laughed. "We both know she doesn't need to – but we also know what she's like. Do you want to be the one to tell her not to try and take Evie under her wing? Because I sure as hell don't."

Adam had to laugh with him. Marianne was an awesome lady. She was perfect for Clay. They might not have met until their late fifties, but it was obvious to everyone that they were made for each other. And that thought took him back to Evie again. He'd had her agreeing with him – loudly – in bed, that he was perfect for her, but he was hoping that, once this was all behind them, they might walk the same path that Clay and Marianne had.

~ ~ ~

Evelyn's stride faltered when she came out of the office and saw Adam standing at the front desk with Russ and Ria. He'd said that he'd pick her up after work, but she'd thought that he'd wait outside in his truck – not come inside. She made herself smile and walk toward them. It was silly of her to be surprised. He was in here all the time; there was no reason that he shouldn't come in to get her.

Ria smiled at her as she reached them. "I'm going home now. I was going to suggest we meet for coffee at the bakery in the morning, but from what Adam was just saying, I think I'll pick up our order and bring it in here."

Evelyn looked from her to Adam and back. Had he told them what was going on? And why did she think it was a problem if he had?

He smiled at her. "I was just telling these two that I'm being overprotective with you these days."

She raised an eyebrow, but Ria didn't give her the chance to speak. She laughed. "I think you might as well get used to it, too, Evie."

Evelyn turned to her, but she just lifted one elegant shoulder. "If you'd like, I can give you guidance on how to deal with an overprotective military man who goes around shortening your name, but I'm afraid I can't help with you trying to change them."

Russ slung his arm around her shoulders and drew her into his side with a smile. "That's because there is no changing us." He looked down at Ria. "And you should probably admit that you don't really want to, anyway."

Adam raised his eyebrows at Evie, and she relaxed. If she was honest, she wouldn't want to change a thing about Adam, either. She felt so much safer now that she had him looking out for her, and she loved that he'd started calling her Evie almost as soon as they met. It'd felt like he knew her better than anyone else here, since she thought of herself as Evie, and they only knew her as Evelyn. Now, it was true – he really did know her better than anyone else here – better almost anyone anywhere ever had. Of course, he didn't know her as well as Taryn did, and he certainly didn't know her like Tom had – and no way could she allow herself to hope that one day he might. She needed to rein herself in with that kind of thinking. She could enjoy what they shared while it lasted, but she couldn't set herself up for disappointment. If he managed to make Anatoly forget about her somehow, that would be the end of things – it'd be the end of her problems and the end of her friendship with Adam. She just had to keep reminding herself of that.

"Anyway, *Evie*." Russ grinned at her. "We're going to head home, but we'll see you tomorrow."

Ria reached out and patted her arm. "I hope you like being called Evie because it looks as though you're going to have to get used to it. If it's any consolation, it's not so bad – in my experience, changing your name opens up the opportunity to change your life." She shot a look at Adam before adding, "For the better."

When they reached the truck, Adam came and opened the passenger door for her. "Are you okay?" he asked.

She had to smile. He looked so worried. He was probably concerned that she was bothered by what Russ and Ria had said. "I'm fine. Are you?"

He nodded and closed the door. When he got into the driver's side, he turned to face her before he started the engine. He reached for her hand and held her gaze for a long moment before he spoke.

Her heart started to pound. Whatever he was about to say, he looked like it was something serious.

"What is it?" she asked when she couldn't wait any longer.

He smiled. "I just want to say that I hope … I hope your life will change for the better now."

"Aww. Thanks, Adam." He was such a good guy.

He leaned across the console, and she met him in the middle. He brushed his lips over hers the way he had that first night he stayed with her. It was too brief, too fleeting, she wanted more. As he sat back and started the engine, she tried to pull herself together. She'd do well to heed those kisses as a reminder about his presence in her life – it too would be too brief, too fleeting; and she had no doubt that once this was all over, she'd want more. But she'd just have to be grateful for the time she got with him. From everything he'd told her about himself and the connections he had, she hoped that he would somehow be able to convince Anatoly to leave her alone. And that would be wonderful. It was crazy, and she knew it, but she was hoping that he didn't pull it off too quickly. Of course, she wanted her life back, but she knew her life would never be the same after him. Her life wouldn't be the same because she wasn't the same; he'd already changed her – for the better.

Chapter Ten

Adam looked down at the phone in his hand and then back up at Dan. "Thanks, man, I appreciate it. What do I owe …?"

Dan frowned and waved a hand at him. "Nothing! She can keep it. I'm just sorry it took me this long to set it up for you. And it's up to you – and Evelyn, of course – but if you want to throw off anyone who's listening in, you can select a location before she makes the call and then back it up with whatever she says."

Dan took the phone back and held it up as he showed Adam the list of locations that he'd programmed in. "If she wants to tell her friend that she's in Florida, she can choose either Orlando or Miami before she makes the call. It'll ping off any of a dozen preselected towers so that, to anyone attempting to trace the call, it'll look as though she really is wherever she says. And like I said, don't worry if she forgets. If she doesn't select a location from the list before she makes the call, the program will select one at random."

Dan smiled. "In fact, that might work in her favor, too. If she's telling her friend that she's in Miami but her phone shows that she's in Philadelphia, they're going to think that the phone is giving her away. She's managed to stay off their radar for all this time, so they might just think that they're onto a lucky break – and go to Philly to look for her there."

Adam smiled. "That's amazing. Thanks so much, Dan."

"I'm happy to help. And anything else you need, you let me know, okay?" Dan grinned when Manny, Cal, and Ryan came out of Cal's office and headed down the hallway toward them. "I can't help you with kicking ass in the same way that these guys can, but I've got you covered on the tech side."

Cal gave them a puzzled look. "Whose ass needs kicking?"

Adam held his gaze for a moment. He hadn't told them Evie's whole story yet, but he knew that Cal would be willing to help if he was needed – and that the others would, too.

"Hopefully, no one's. At least, not here in town."

Cal cocked an eyebrow. "What kind of trouble is Evelyn running from?"

It didn't surprise Adam that he'd already figured out that much.

"Russ didn't give me any details, but when I talked to him and Evelyn the other morning, it sounded like she might need some back up at some point."

"If she does, you can count me in," said Manny.

"And me," Ryan added. "I've wondered what her deal is."

"Thanks, guys. She had some trouble back in Chicago – that's where she's from. A guy who works for her racked up some bad gambling debts and the asshole he borrowed the money from wants to take Evie as payment."

"Shit!" Cal rubbed his hand over the back of his neck.

Manny crossed his arms across his chest and scowled. "Do we know who this asshole is?"

Adam blew out a sigh. "I've had some feelers out up there this week, and it's not looking good. The guy's name is Anatoly Petrov."

"Jesus!" Ryan exclaimed as he exchanged a glance with Cal. "Do you think it's the same guy?"

Manny let out a short laugh. "I hope so. I had so many investigations that led back to him. We could never pin enough on him to take him down. He always had someone else take the fall for him."

Adam cocked an eyebrow. "He's not just some small-time loan shark then?"

Manny shook his head grimly. "Nope. He's smart. He's the head of a large organization. Has been for years." He narrowed his eyes. "And he's set his sights on Evelyn?"

Adam nodded. He didn't like this. If these guys all knew who Anatoly was, then he had to be a major league player. "Yeah."

"I hope you've covered her tracks? That guy doesn't fuck around."

"She pretty much covered them herself. She went off the radar the second she left Chicago. She took out all the money she could get from her usual ATM and hasn't touched her cards or her accounts since. I just got rid of her car, and …" he held up the phone, "Dan just gave me this. She had a burner, but she called her friend who owns a restaurant from it, and Anatoly got hold of the number. I'm guessing that he didn't locate it."

"Where's the phone now?" asked Cal.

Adam smiled. "Diego took it to Colombia with him."

Manny chuckled. "And I'll bet that if anyone manages to track it down there, they'll find themselves in a world of hurt if they try to go after it."

"Yeah, he gave me that impression."

Cal nodded and blew out a sigh. "So, we've got her covered here as best as we can tell. What's the plan to put an end to this?"

Adam loved that all three of them looked at him eagerly, as if awaiting orders. "I hate to say it, but I don't have one yet. It's taken me until now to figure out who he is. I've got a buddy up there trying to gather as much intel as he can. But until I know who I'm dealing with, I can't start to …"

Cal nodded. "Well, you know now. You have your target, and you have your team." He smiled at Manny and Ryan. "Right, guys?"

They both nodded.

Adam smiled at them gratefully. "Thanks, guys." He checked his watch. "Right now, I need to get to the gym to pick her up from work. My only plan for the weekend is to lay low while I get more information. But if you guys …"

"Want to all meet up here tomorrow?" asked Dan.

Cal nodded. "Yeah. I need to go and collect Teresa. We're headed home before we come back out tonight."

"Same here," said Manny.

Ryan grinned. "I'm just hanging around here waiting for Leanne."

"Are you bringing Evelyn – Evie out tonight?" Manny asked.

"No. Like I said, she's been lying low. It's been a week since he found her number and called her. I reckon if he knew where she was, he'd have done something about it by now. But at the same time, going to The Boathouse doesn't seem like the wisest move we could make."

"Have you taken her out at all yet?" asked Ryan. "I'm guessing from the fact that she's staying with you, and the way you keep calling her Evie, that you two are together."

Adam gave him a wry smile. "Kind of, almost, I'm hoping but ..."

Cal grasped his shoulder. "So, how about you bring her out tonight? Take her mind off it. If you're going to get where you're hoping, you need to start dating her, not just keeping her hidden away in the house while you guard her."

Adam blew out a sigh. "I know but ... don't you think ...?"

Manny shook his head. "I'm not sure I'd take her to The Boathouse if I were you either; I get it. But we're not going there tonight. We're going to Giuseppe's. It's quieter there – and a more easily contained environment. I reckon she'd be as safe there with the four of us as she would be at home with just you."

Adam smiled. He liked that idea. "Okay, thanks, guys. I'll ask her if she wants to go."

Cal looked at his watch. "Let me know if you're coming. I can swing by your place on the way there."

Adam wasn't so sure that Evie would go for that. She knew Cal from the gym, but he wasn't sure how well she knew Teresa – or how comfortable she'd be with them picking them up.

Cal laughed. "I'm not offering you a ride; I'm not even inviting you to join us all for dinner. I mean, I am if you want to, but I was thinking I can swing past your place so we can drive in convoy. When we get there you two are on your own, you can have the evening to yourselves – but we'll all be there in case you need backup."

Adam grinned. "Thanks. That'd be great – if she wants to go. I'll give you a call later."

Evelyn couldn't help but notice how different it felt to arrive back at the house with Adam. This time last week, she'd gone through her routine of leaving the car running while she unlocked the door and flipped the lights on. Now, he was here with her, and he came around to the passenger side of the truck and accompanied her to the door. Even while he unlocked it, he kept her in front of him. There was no denying that he made her feel safe. There was no denying that he made her feel other things, too.

Once they were inside, and he'd locked the door behind them, he smiled. She knew that he must have something up his sleeve – it was that lopsided smile that he got when he was particularly pleased about something. Now that she came to think of it, she mostly got to see it in bed. She wasn't allowing herself to question what was going on between the two of them. There'd been a few times over the last week when she'd woken in the middle of the night and thought that he was Tom. Only because she'd spent almost half of her life sleeping next to Tom. But even when she remembered where she was, and whose bed she was in, she hadn't been sad that he wasn't Tom. Of course, she wished her husband was still alive, wished that he could be the one lying next to her. But she'd come to terms with her grief over the last five years. She'd grown used to his absence. It didn't feel like Adam was taking his place – more like he was filling the empty space that Tom had left. She almost wanted to feel guilty about it, but she didn't. She knew that it simply meant that she was moving on with her life in a healthy way.

"Sorry." She realized that they were still standing there in the hallway and Adam was still watching her with that mysterious smile on his face. "What is it? You look pleased with yourself."

He chuckled. "I am. I have something for you that I'm sure is going to make you happy. And I also have a suggestion to make that I hope you'll like."

She smiled back at him. "Want to tell me?"

He took her hand and led her to the kitchen. "I do. Take a seat." He took her coat and hung it on the rack by the back door with his own while she sat on one of the chairs at the kitchen table.

He gave her a wry smile. "What do you say this weekend we go online and order some furniture? It'd be nice to have a sofa to sit on to have a conversation."

"If you like, I can furnish the whole place for you." Her smile faded. "I was going to say that I can do that as a thank you, but what do you think – am I safe to use my accounts?"

"No! I appreciate the offer, but I'm only asking for your design eye. I can buy the stuff, but maybe you can make the place nice if you choose the stuff. I don't want you paying for anything – and I wouldn't, even if it were safe for you to access your accounts."

He came and squatted down in front of her and rested his hands on her knees – she loved the way he did that. "We'll figure out what we're going to do for furniture tomorrow. We're going to be too busy to think about that tonight."

She raised an eyebrow at him. "We are?"

He laughed. "We are – but not in the way that smile tells me that you think I mean." He squeezed her thigh. "At least not until later, not until we get home."

"Home? From where?"

"Do you want to go to Giuseppe's for dinner?"

"I …" She was about to automatically say no. But Adam was just as aware as she was of all the reasons that she shouldn't go out in public any more than she needed to.

He raised his eyebrows as he waited. "This is me asking you on a date."

A rush of warmth flooded her chest. She loved that idea. But she still had to know why he thought it would be okay. "I would love to go on a date with you. That's not why I'm hesitating. And I'm not going to insult you by asking if you think that it's safe – you obviously do, or you wouldn't be suggesting it. So, perhaps a better question is, why do you think it's safe?"

He bobbed up and pressed a quick kiss to her lips. "Thank you."

"What for?"

"For having faith in me – and for not immediately saying no. If you don't feel safe, then I don't want to go. But I think it'll be fine because all the guys will be there tonight. I don't think there's much likelihood of there being anyone around who's waiting to grab you. But even if there were, they wouldn't stand a chance with Cal, Manny, and Ryan there, as well as me."

She nodded slowly.

"And if you think about it, you go to work at the gym every day. It's not as though we're exposing you to some new risk by going out at night. I get why you didn't want to go out when you were by yourself. But you're not on your own anymore." He held her gaze, his brown eyes boring into hers. "You've got me now."

She loved the way that sounded. She loved the way it felt, knowing that she did have him. He was there for her, watching over her, taking care of her. He made her feel safe – and cared for. What she had to keep reminding herself of was that she only had him for now. And since that was the case, she wanted to take the chance to go out on a date with him. She had a feeling that if she lived to be an old lady, she'd look back on this time here with him as one of the most important periods in her life. Of course, she'd look back on it as the time that she was running for her life from Anatoly, but she'd also remember it fondly as the time that she got to spend with the wonderful man in front of her.

She rested her hands on top of his and leaned down to press a kiss to his lips. "I would love to go out on a date with you, Adam. Thank you. And I do feel safe. How could I not with you around?"

The way he smiled back at her made her heart happy. It might just be that he was the kind of guy who had some kind of knight-in-shining-armor complex. He might just be happy that he was getting to do what he was best at and protect someone who needed his help. But the way his eyes shone, it looked like he was happy to take her out on a date – and she was going to enjoy that feeling, while it lasted.

~ ~ ~

Adam grinned at himself in the mirror when he got out of the shower. Evie was still in a shitty situation, but he felt like it was under control for now and that he'd be able to bring an end to it fairly quickly. He'd spoken with his friend up there and he'd told him that he had a contact in Chicago who might have some useful information for him. The contact, a guy named Dalton, was going to call Adam over the weekend.

With what he hoped was progress on that end and with Cal, Manny, and Ryan, in addition to Russ and Davin having his back here in town, he felt good. He felt even better about taking Evie out on their first date. He knew she liked the food at Giuseppe's; they'd eaten takeout from there before, and her friend owned an Italian restaurant, too, from what she'd said. But more than hoping that she'd like the place and the food, he was hoping that she'd enjoy spending the evening with him. He'd stayed here with her since he arrived last Friday night but sitting in the kitchen or sitting on the bed watching movies wasn't the same as going out together. He was looking forward to it.

He cocked his head to one side as he toweled himself off. Evie was talking to her friend downstairs. She'd been so thrilled when he'd given her the phone; the way she'd smiled at him and the way she'd pressed a kiss to his lips as she thanked him had made him feel ten feet tall. He went to the closet and pulled out a pair of jeans and his favorite shirt – this was a date after all. He'd brought a bunch of his clothes and stuff over here from the guest house at Clay's place earlier in the week. It was weird to see his things hanging next to Evie's. Weird in a good way. He'd always been the guy who avoided *the talk* with women – the talk about where things were going between them. He liked his life; he liked his freedom. He hadn't wanted to get too close to anyone while he was still in the unit. That life hadn't been conducive to a long-term relationship. In the years since then, he'd always had his job as his excuse. He couldn't move in with a woman because he lived on site with his employer most of the time. Yeah, he'd had his own apartment as well but ... he just hadn't wanted to share his life in that way.

Now, looking at Evie's few clothes hanging in the closet next to his, he couldn't imagine her leaving. He hated the thought that, once it was safe, she might want to go back to Chicago. She might want to pick up her life where she'd left it.

He blew out a sigh and went to check himself out in the mirror before he went back downstairs. He felt bad for her that she'd had to leave her life and her business. But he couldn't help hoping that it might make it easier for her to make a new life here – with him.

He raised his eyebrows at the guy in the mirror, and the guy shrugged and grinned – anything was possible. All he could do was his best to make her want to stay.

Chapter Eleven

Evie loved Giuseppe's. She felt some of the tension leave her shoulders as soon as they stepped inside.

Manny and Nina were already sitting at a big table in the corner. She liked them, but she was glad that Adam had told her they wouldn't be joining them. She used to be very sociable but after having spent so much time alone over the last few months, she didn't feel comfortable at the thought of being out with a group. And besides, she was looking forward to an evening alone with Adam.

He finished thanking Cal for driving over here with them and turned to her with a smile. He didn't get the chance to speak before Teresa came past him and hugged Evie.

"Hey! I'm so glad to see you out. Especially with this guy." She grinned at Adam. "And you know, if you're ready to start getting out more now, you're always welcome to hang out with Nina and me."

"Thanks." Evie didn't know Teresa very well. She came into the gym a couple of nights a week to work out with Russ, and she was always friendly, but she was usually in a rush to go once she'd finished her session. Evie tried to hide a smile—who could blame her for wanting to rush home to Cal?!

Teresa gave her a puzzled look. "Is that a thanks but no thanks? And honestly, don't worry if it is. I know I can be a bit much and ..."

"Oh! No! Sorry, I just ..." She was grateful for the offer, but she couldn't see herself getting out and about town much. Not yet. "I'd love to, really, I would. It's just ..."

Cal came and stood beside Teresa and took hold of her hand. "Give it a bit more time, and I bet you'll be able to talk Evie into joining in your lunches and girls' nights."

Teresa gave him a puzzled look. "What ... How?"

Cal chuckled. "Come on. Nina and Manny are waiting, and I just saw Ryan's truck pull in. Let's go and sit down." He nodded at Adam and Evie. "You guys have a good night. Just let me know when you're ready to leave and we can do the same thing going home."

"Thanks," said Adam. "Will do."

Teresa laughed and rolled her eyes at Evie. "I guess we women are just supposed to do as the big men say, huh? Don't worry, if I see you go to the ladies' room I'll follow, and we can exchange numbers while they're not there to boss us around."

Evie had to laugh when Cal frowned at Teresa. "You know I'm not ..."

Teresa put her hand on his arm. "Of course, I do. Let's go, big guy. Whatever's going on, you'll tell me what you can, and I'll trust you on the rest."

Adam smiled at Evie as they watched them go, but he didn't get the chance to say anything before the hostess came and showed them to their table.

Once they had their drinks and had ordered their food, Adam reached across the table for her hand. Evie placed hers in it with a smile.

"Thank you, Adam."

"Thank you for wanting to come."

"Oh, I did, this is lovely. But I meant thank you for everything. For being so good to me. For letting me stay in your house before you knew what was going on and then for everything that you've done – that you're doing – since I told you."

He nodded. "I want to help. I'd want to help anyone who found themselves in your situation." He squeezed her hand. "But I especially want to help you."

"Thank you." She wasn't sure what else she should say to that. She wanted to believe that he felt the same way about her that she was starting to feel about him, but she could only hope that she wasn't setting herself up for a big disappointment. He was going to help her out – and she would be forever grateful to him. But she probably shouldn't allow herself to hope that she might become as special to him as he already was to her.

He smiled, seeming to sense her discomfort. "What did your friend have to say? Sorry I didn't get the chance to ask before we came out."

She had to laugh. "She was thrilled to hear from me. And I was thrilled to talk to her. I know you set the phone so that it would look like I was calling from Florida, but I didn't say anything about where I am. I ... it's probably silly and maybe at some point I'll get the hang of it, but I didn't want to lie to her and tell her that I'm somewhere I'm not. Even if it might help to put Anatoly's people on the wrong track."

"That's okay. It doesn't matter. The phone's doing its job."

She nodded. She didn't know how any of that stuff worked. It was only what she'd seen in movies that had made her think that she shouldn't use her own phone.

"So, how is she?" Adam asked. "Is she okay? Has she had any fallout from you calling her?"

"No. She said that Anatoly had been in the restaurant to eat last week." She shuddered. "And that I might perhaps be okay for a while because he had a new woman with him. The poor thing, Adam. Even if it's not the same circumstances, I can't imagine any woman choosing to be with him of her own free will. He might not have taken her as payment for a debt, but I doubt she's happy … and who knows what will happen to her when he tires of her?"

"Yeah." Adam shook his head. "I need to try to speed things up. I've only been focused on you." He met her gaze. "You're what matters. You're most important to me, but I'd hate to think that some other woman might get hurt or worse before I figure out a way to put an end to him."

Evie swallowed. The way he said it sounded as though he wanted to put an end to Anatoly, not just to what he was doing. The world would no doubt be a better place if Anatoly were no longer in it, but it was strange to think of Adam being the one to … kill him. He couldn't mean that, though. Could he?

He smiled at her and raised his glass. "Anyway, we're here to forget about all that for a while." He held his glass out to her and she clinked hers against it, wondering what they were drinking to.

He winked at her and said, "Here's to us."

Wow! Her heart leaped into her mouth. Tom had said those exact words so many times. He'd said them when he toasted her at their wedding, and on every anniversary that she could remember after that. She had to swallow, and her eyes filled with tears.

Adam's smile disappeared. "I'm sorry. I …"

She shook her head and smiled. "Don't be. It's just … that's the toast that Tom always used to …"

"Damn. I'm sorry, Evie. I didn't know."

"And how could you? It's okay. It just caught me off guard. I don't mind. I like it. I like that, for some reason, you chose the exact same words that he always used to."

Adam nodded. "Yeah. I like that, too. That's another thing that he and I have in common. It's not just words, though, Evie."

She closed her eyes and nodded. She knew that it wasn't just words when Tom used to say it, and she believed that it wasn't just words to Adam. What she didn't know was what *us* meant to him.

She was relieved when the server appeared with their food. It looked great and smelled wonderful. It transported her back to the restaurant, to all the evenings she'd spent there with Taryn.

"Are you okay?"

"I am. Sorry. I was just …" She looked around. "Taryn would love this place."

"I hope she will."

Evie raised her eyebrows.

"Once this whole business is behind us, we should get her down here to visit."

Evie nodded, even though she wasn't sure that she understood what he meant again. Was he saying that once she

was free to go home, she should come back to visit and bring
Taryn with her?

She didn't get the chance to ask. Tino, who owned the place,
appeared at their table with a big smile on his face.

"Adam, it's good to see you in here. And, Evelyn, isn't it?"

"Evie," Adam shot her a smile as he corrected her name.

"Evie. Sorry," said Tino. "I'm glad you've come to see us.
You were only here the once, no?"

Adam gave her a puzzled look, but she nodded. "That's
right. I came when Russ and Ria got engaged."

"Well, I'm glad to see you back, and especially with this guy."

"Thanks. It's good to be here – especially with this guy." It
was true, and she didn't see any reason not to say so.

They both grinned at her.

"We were just talking about Evie's friend, who owns an
Italian restaurant," Adam said.

"Really?" Tino's eyes lit up. "Where?"

Evie opened her mouth, but Adam answered before she
could. It was so unlike him, it surprised her until she heard
what he said, "Back in Florida, where she's from."

She didn't think that he'd have a problem with Tino knowing
where she was from, but she knew how gossip spread in small
towns, and in restaurants in particular. There was nothing
malicious about it, but it was probably better that, if people
were going to talk about seeing Adam out with a woman, they
wouldn't be able to give away that she was from Chicago.

Still, she didn't feel comfortable reinforcing the lie so instead,
she told Tino about the restaurant – she was sure there were
plenty that shared the same name. "It's called Trattoria Bella
Sera. She's not Italian, she's a Southern girl, but she's an
amazing cook."

"We were just saying that we should get her out here to visit," said Adam. "I bet the two of you could trade some tales."

"I'd like that," said Tino. "But for now, I'll leave you to your meal. I hope you enjoy it." He smiled at Evie. "I'll check with you later to see if I can come close to your friend's food."

"I'm sure you will. It looks wonderful, thank you."

As soon as he'd gone, Adam smiled. "I hope you didn't mind me saying you're from Florida?"

"No. I get it. And I hope it was okay to tell him the name of the restaurant?"

"Yeah. It'll be fine." He didn't look thrilled.

"It's a very common name from what I understand."

He smiled. "It's okay. Like I said, it'll be fine."

~ ~ ~

When they got back to the house, Adam turned his truck into the driveway and waved over his shoulder as he watched Cal's Suburban pull away. Evie waved out the window at Teresa, and Adam couldn't help laughing when he saw Teresa waving back.

"I hope she wasn't too much?" he asked. He hadn't been surprised when Teresa had been true to her word and followed Evie when she went to the bathroom.

Evie chuckled. "No. She's nice. I like her. And she wasn't pushy at all. She just told me that Cal had explained that I have some stuff going on and she wanted me to have her number."

Adam smiled. "She's good people. But I don't want you to feel like you're under any kind of pressure."

"I don't. I don't see it that way. Honestly, it's nice to feel that I have someone here I could turn to. I haven't had that. And even though that's been my choice, it has been kind of lonely."

Adam nodded as he pulled the truck into the garage and waited for the door to close behind them. "I can see that, but I hope you know that you're not on your own. You've got me now."

He cut the engine and turned to face her, reaching for her hand across the console. He loved that she didn't hesitate to put her hand in his. He held her gaze and looked into her eyes. "You don't need to feel lonely anymore."

Her eyes widened, and her grip on his fingers tightened. "I don't. I... Honestly, Adam, I just don't want to get too used to this."

He cocked his head to the side, not understanding.

She let out a short laugh. "Don't get me wrong, I appreciate everything that you're doing for me. It's just... Not so long ago, all I could picture for myself was a life on the run from Anatoly. Now, now that I have you on my side, I believe that there will be an end to all of this, that I'll get to go back to my life. I couldn't be more grateful to you for that... But I'm trying not to get too used to this."

Adam's heart was thundering in his chest. Of course, she wanted to go back to her life, and of course, he wanted to make that possible for her. But he'd also been thinking about her becoming part of his life. But while his life was here, hers was in Chicago.

He could feel himself frowning. He'd thought that she was starting to feel the same way about him as he felt for her, but from the way she said that she didn't want to let herself get too used to this, it looked like he'd have to rethink that.

He squeezed her hand and made himself smile. His first instinct was to back off, to agree with her that she shouldn't get used to life at the lake. But for once, he didn't want to go with his instincts. His instincts had served him well in his career, they kept him alive, but they hadn't led him into the kind of life that he now knew he wanted — the kind of life he could have with Evie. Well, the kind of life he could have with Evie if she wanted it. He didn't know that she would want it, but he'd never know if he didn't ask her, if they didn't talk about it.

"What if I told you that I want you to get carried away with this?"

She bit down on her bottom lip, looking worried.

"Don't, Evie. Don't look so worried. I get it. I'm going to help you through this, I'm going to get this asshole off your back, no matter what happens. If that's all you want me for, that's fine. All I'm saying... All I want to say... Shit!" He scrubbed his hand over his face then rested his chin between his thumb and forefinger. "What I'm trying to say here is that I can handle it if you don't want me. You don't need to worry about that. I'm going to help you anyway. But I want to lay all my cards on the table for you. I need you to know that I'd love for you to stay here... With me."

Her eyes were huge as she stared back at him.

"I'm sorry. Maybe we should just forget that I said any of that. No pressure, no nothing. If you don't want —"

"Adam," she breathed his name.

He held his breath and waited. He wanted to reassure her again that he wasn't trying to put her under any pressure. But he made himself wait for her to speak.

"You really mean that?"

His breath came out in a rush. "Yeah, Evie, I really mean that. I don't go around saying shit like that to women for the fun of it. In fact, I've never said that or even anything like it to a woman before. I'm usually the guy who doesn't stick around, the one who does what he can to help and then rides off into the sunset."

"So, I wasn't wrong then." She gave him a sad smile. "I've kept trying to tell myself that no matter how much I … like you, like what's going on between us, I shouldn't let myself hope for anything more."

"But, Evie, that's what I'm telling you. I'm saying that that's how I *usually* feel, that's how I've *always* felt with women in the past. But it's *not* how I feel about you. I'm saying that I like you, that I like what's going on between us. That, in fact, I like it so much that I want to see where this thing between us can go. But maybe I'm just being selfish. You can't know how you feel about anything until you know that Anatoly is taken care of, that he's not going to come after you. I guess I can't ask you to make any decisions about your life until this business is taken care of. But when it is, when you're free to choose between going back to your old life and staying here with me, then I'll ask you to choose. How does that sound?"

His heart was pounding in his chest as she held his gaze. Way to lay everything on the table at once! He told her he wasn't going to put her under any pressure and yet that's exactly what he'd done.

"Sorry, Evie, I shouldn't…"

"Don't be sorry, Adam. Please. I might be struggling to believe what you just said, but it's not something that you need to apologize for."

Hope surged in his chest, but he waited for her to continue, not wanting to make any assumptions.

"I want to say that…" She shook her head and met his gaze. "But I probably shouldn't say too much of anything at all yet, right?"

"That depends." He gave her a wry smile. "If you want to say that yes, you've already figured it out, and you already know that you want to stay here with me then you could say that." He winked at her. "But I know you're not ready to say that yet. So, how about instead of sitting out here in the garage, we go inside? You know how I feel, you know what I want, I don't think we need to dwell on it. Just keep it in the back of your mind and when this is all over then you can decide. And don't feel bad if what you decide is that you want to go back to your life."

When they were back inside the house, and Adam had locked all the doors behind them, he felt less sure of himself than he had in the whole time that he'd been here with her. He was mad at himself. He shouldn't have put her on the spot like that.

She smiled as she got two glasses down from the cabinet. "Thanks for this evening, Adam. I really enjoyed it. Do you want a drink?"

He nodded and went to get the bottle of Jack Daniels. He needed a drink. He felt like he'd messed up. He poured two glasses and handed one to her.

"Listen, Evie, can we just forget…"

She came to him and put her hand on his arm. "If it's okay with you, I'd rather not forget. I …" She let out a short laugh. "It's only fair that I should be as honest with you as you have been with me. And I can tell you honestly that what you said took me by surprise." She held her hand up when he started to speak.

"Please, let me say this before I lose my nerve. You took me by surprise in a good way. I've been thinking that … That once this is all over, you'll send me on my way back to Chicago and not give me another thought." She raised her hand again. "Don't take this wrong, but I thought that your interest was mostly in doing what you do, being who you are. I thought that you were all about saving the woman who needed help. I … I won't deny that I've started to develop feelings for you. But I didn't want to fool myself into thinking that you might have feelings for me, too."

Her cheeks were red when she finished talking, but she held his gaze and shrugged. "I mean, come on, you're the sexy action hero and I'm the sad old widow."

He frowned and took a step toward her but stopped himself before he reached her. He wanted to close his arms around her but thought it better to let her decide if that was what *she* wanted. He held his arms out to the sides and relaxed when she stepped into them, resting her head against his shoulder. He curled one arm around her waist and brought the other up to cup her head, loving the feel of her breath on his neck.

"I think I've asked you before not to call my friend an old lady," he said with a smile. "And I think, even with the mess I've made of things tonight, that you know I want to call you more than my friend."

She lifted her head and looked up into his eyes. "I've made a mess of this as well, Adam. But I need you to know that I'd like for us to be more than friends, too. I don't want to put you under any pressure though, either. So, how about we say that for now, we'll just take things day by day? I trust you and I know that if anyone can make Anatoly leave me alone, it's you. But who knows how you'll feel by the time this is all over? I might drive you nuts in the meantime. You might be glad to see the back of me by then." She gave him a small smile. "You might be desperate to send me back to Chicago."

He pressed a kiss to the tip of her nose. "I know what you're saying, and you're probably right. We should take this day by day, make the most of this time that we have together." He kissed the tip of her nose again, amazed at himself for doing it. He didn't think of himself as the kind of guy who would do shit like that. But with Evie, it just felt right. "But I have to tell you that I already know … I know that when you're free to decide, when it's just as safe for you to go back to Chicago as it is for you to stay here, I'll still be hoping that you choose to stay here because you want to — because you want me."

She held his gaze for a long moment before she nodded.

Adam nodded back. They'd said what they needed to for now. All he could do was solve the Anatoly problem for her and then hope that she discovered that she wanted him as much as he wanted her

Chapter Twelve

Evie looked up at the sound of a knock on the office door. She'd been working back here this morning because Russ had asked her to help with the roster and with scheduling classes. She didn't mind, it was easy work. She'd done it all for years for Tom back in the early days. Still, it felt strange to be sitting back here with the door closed when she'd been used to sitting out at the front desk. She wanted to believe that Russ genuinely needed her help with the admin work, but she couldn't help wondering if Adam had asked him to keep her back here.

"Come in," she called when the knock came again.

The door opened, and Ria stood there smiling at her. "Hi, how are you doing today?"

"I'm doing fine, thanks. How are you?"

Ria came in and closed the door behind her. "I'm great. I spent the morning on the phone with the children and now I'm ready for some lunch. I came to see if you'd like to join me?"

Evie pursed her lips. She'd love to go to the bakery. She'd come to enjoy having lunch there with the woman she'd come to think of as her new friend. But she was feeling less sure of herself lately. Adam was watching her much more closely. And she didn't know but she guessed that Cal, Manny, and Ryan were coming into the gym separately so that at least one of them was there most of the time.

"It's okay if you're too busy," said Ria with a smile.

"No, it's not that. I'd love to go with you. It's just..."

"Oh!" Ria nodded. "I'm sorry. I should have realized. If you like, I can go and get us something and bring it back here."

Evie got to her feet. "You know what? I'm tired of being cooped up back here. I could use some fresh air and we'll get that on the walk over there. And it'd be nice to have a change of scenery." She looked around with a smile. "These four walls might be as sick of me as I am of them."

Ria arched one perfectly groomed brow. "I understand your feeling that way, but do you think we should check in with Russ first?"

Evie nodded and pulled her phone out of her purse. "Yes, we'll talk to him before we go, and ... I'm going to check in with Adam too." She rolled her eyes. "This feels strange. Part of me wants to rebel against it but that poor man is doing so much to keep me safe. I owe it to him to check in with him before I go gallivanting around town."

Ria chuckled. "I understand. I understand both sides. I don't think either of us is comfortable with the idea that we need to get a man's permission before we go anywhere. But at the same time, you're not asking permission."

Evie shook her head rapidly. "Oh, my goodness, no! It's not that. It's more out of respect for him and deference to his knowledge and experience." She couldn't help a small chuckle. "That man is doing everything within his power to keep me safe. I really don't want to let him down by being one of those too stupid to live women who goes off and gets herself in trouble despite everyone's efforts to help her."

Ria nodded. "You're far from stupid. Why don't you give him a call while I go and check with Russ?"

Evie stared at her phone for a moment. It felt strange to call Adam. He was at work this morning. He'd told her that Clay didn't have any travel plans looming, but she knew that Adam's job entailed more than traveling with him. Adam, and his colleague, Davin, were Clay's full-time security team. She felt bad that Adam had spent most of his time providing her with security recently.

Adam had reassured her repeatedly that Clay knew about her situation and that he had no problem with her being Adam's main focus. Still, Adam had told her that he was going to work today, and she was torn about disturbing him there.

She hit the call button and waited, and all her worries evaporated when he answered.

"Hey, Evie." She could hear the smile in his voice. "Is everything okay?"

"Everything's fine, and I'm sorry to disturb you at work."

"You're not disturbing me. I've told you; you can call me anytime you want to."

She could feel herself smiling. He had told her that, repeatedly. "Thanks, Adam. The reason I'm calling is that Ria just asked if I want to go for lunch at the bakery." She let out an embarrassed laugh. "I feel a little silly, like I'm calling to ask for permission. But at the same time, I wanted to check in with you before I went. What do you think, is it safe?"

He didn't answer immediately, and for a moment, she hoped he wasn't annoyed that she was bothering him at work. But she knew better than that; that was just her own insecurities coming into play. He confirmed it when he finally spoke.

"I think you'll be fine. But I have to tell you... It means more than you know that you called to check with me first."

Evie felt a rush of warmth in her chest. She was glad that she called and even more pleased with his answer.

"You still there?"

"Yes," she said with a smile. "I don't mind telling you that I struggled with calling you."

"Why?"

"Well, for one thing, I'm not the kind of woman who does well with having to ask a man's permission for anything. And for another, I didn't want you to think that I was pestering you at work."

Adam chuckled. "I think we both know that this isn't about you asking my permission. And I hope you know that I'm no more comfortable with that idea than you are. I hope you also know that I don't see this as pestering. I like it."

"I like it too." She rolled her eyes and looked up at the ceiling. She might be trying not to behave like one of those women who was too stupid to live but she couldn't deny that she was behaving like a dumb girl with a crush.

Adam didn't seem to mind, though. She could hear the smile in his voice when he spoke again. "Good. You call me anytime you like. Especially if you're not sure about anything to do with your safety. I think you've already noticed that I err on the side of caution when it comes to you. But since there's been no sign that anyone's around here looking for you, and it seems that Anatoly is occupied with someone else at the moment, I think a quick lunch at the bakery will be okay."

"Thanks, Adam. If you like, I'll pick us up something for dessert while I'm there."

He was quiet for a few moments.

"Are you still there?" she asked.

"I'm still here. I was just thinking …"

"What?"

He chuckled. "I was thinking about what I'd like for dessert, and it doesn't come from the bakery."

Evie pressed her thighs together against the rush of warmth between them that his words caused. She laughed with him. "Okay, and maybe we can have cake first."

"Or afterward," he said. "Hang on a minute, Evie. Yeah? Okay, hang on. Listen, Evie. If you're okay, I need to go. Do me a favor and let me know when you get back from the bakery?"

"Okay, but I don't want to keep disturbing your day. I'll just shoot you a quick text."

"Thanks, sweetheart. I'll see you later."

Evie stood there smiling at her phone for a moment after the call had ended. *Sweetheart?* She liked that.

~ ~ ~

Adam scowled as he went outside to see what Davin wanted. "What's up?"

Davin gave him a puzzled look. "I could ask you the same thing. What's with the attitude?"

Adam sucked in a deep breath and relaxed his shoulders as he let it out. "Sorry, man. I was on the phone with Evie."

Davin smiled through pursed lips "Why didn't you just say so?"

It was a good question. One that Adam didn't know the answer to.

Davin laughed. "Jesus, Adam! You know I don't have a problem with it. I'm not going to give you any shit. You could have just said." His smile faded. "Is she okay?"

"Yeah, she's okay. I wouldn't have ended the call if she wasn't. I just ... I feel ..." He scrubbed his hand over his face. "I feel kind of dumb! I'm not used to this."

"Looks to me like you'd better get used to it." Davin smiled. "Looks to me like you're making progress."

"What do you mean?"

"I mean, if she's okay and she's calling you just to say hi then I guess that things are progressing between the two of you."

Adam nodded slowly. "Things are progressing. But... She wasn't just calling to say hi."

Davin stood up straighter and folded his arms across his chest. "She wasn't? I thought you said she's okay? What's going on?"

Adam had to smile, loving that his friend was as concerned about Evie as he was. Well almost. "There's nothing going on. It's just that she wanted to check in with me. Ria asked if she wanted to go to the bakery for lunch, and she wanted to ask if I thought that was okay."

Davin smirked at him.

"What? What are you looking at me like that for?"

"That sure sounds like progress to me."

Adam couldn't help smiling back at him. "It feels like progress to me, too. But it's not like she was calling to ask my permission or anything. She just... She values my opinion, I guess."

Davin nodded. "Yeah, she values your opinion. She's a smart lady; she's going to listen to you because she knows you can help her. But I'd guess that it's more than that. She cares. She cares about what you think, and she cares about you."

Adam's smile grew bigger. "She does. She's admitted as much."

Davin grinned back at him. "Happy for you, man."

"Don't get too carried away yet. I'm trying not to. She's admitted that she's catching feelings for me. But she's not convinced that once Anatoly is taken care of, there'll be anything left between us."

Davin gave him a puzzled look. "And you see that as a problem? I can't see it being much of a problem to make her see that you want to do more than just protect her."

"I'm trying not to see it as a problem, but I can't help thinking that perhaps she just wants to let me down gently. I mean, I've been thinking about it; her whole life is up there in Chicago. I know she left it behind. But that was because she had no choice, she had to run from it to stay safe. But is it realistic for me to go thinking that when she does have a choice, she'll walk away from it just for me?"

Davin shrugged. "I don't see why not. But what do I know?" He shot Adam a grin. "You know, I'm sure there are plenty of folks who need protection and security in a city like that."

Adam held his gaze for a long moment. He knew what his friend was saying, and he loved him for it. He loved that Davin would be prepared to walk away from Summer Lake if he wanted to go to Chicago, but he didn't want to. At least, he didn't want to go right now. He couldn't imagine leaving Clay, couldn't imagine leaving the lake. But he had a feeling that might change if Evie decided that she wanted to go back to her life in Chicago and that she wanted him to go with her.

"I think we're getting ahead of ourselves, don't you? The first thing I need to do is get Anatoly off her back."

"You mean the first thing *we* need to do," said Davin with a smile. "And where are we up to with that? That was going to be the first thing I asked you when you arrived this morning but then we got busy."

"That Dalton guy gave me a call over the weekend. He has someone on the inside of Anatoly's organization."

Davin let out a low whistle. "And who is this Dalton guy again?"

"Remember Jason Stone?"

Davin's brow furrowed. "Stone? Oh, wait, he was the team leader for…"

Adam nodded. "Yep. That's right. The SEAL team we worked with a couple times. I talked to Jason, and he put me in touch with Dalton. He told me that Dalton is someone he'd trust with his little sister's life. That's good enough for me. Dalton was on a different team but he's a good friend of Jason's."

"Okay," said Davin. "So, we know that we can trust Dalton. What's his man on the inside telling him?"

"Not much yet. Dalton's tasked him with finding out anything he can about Anatoly's plans for Evie. The guy did report that Anatoly has a new woman at the moment. From what I understand, that's buying Evie some time. But I don't know how much. By all accounts, he takes a shine to a new woman every couple of months, and when he tires of them…" Adam shrugged, not wanting to spell out or even think about what happened to the women that Anatoly discarded.

Davin scowled. "We need to take this bastard down before he can get anywhere near Evie. And I've got to be honest with you, I hate thinking about this other poor woman and what she's going through. We need to step this up, Adam."

Adam nodded grimly. "I know. Obviously, Evie is my top priority, but we're going to do everything we can to save this other woman, too."

"And what are we doing about that?"

"Both Dalton and Stone have feelers out and from what Stone told me, there are a couple of ongoing official investigations that might bring Anatoly down."

"Forgive my cynicism, but I don't think official investigations are going to move as fast as we need them to."

"I know. From what Cal told me, there have been plenty of attempts to take him down over the years, but that bastard is slippery as shit. Dalton's supposed to call me again tonight. Once we hear what he has to say, I'm thinking that you, me, Russ, Cal, Manny, and Ryan, should all meet up and kick some possibilities around."

Davin smiled. "Now that I like the sound of. What do you reckon, should I give the guys a call, too?"

Adam thought about it. The guys from the team had gone their separate ways over the last few years. They kept in touch but…

"In fact, scratch that," said Davin. "I'm not asking you if I should give them a call. I'm telling you that I'm going to."

Adam smiled. He might not be keen to reach out to his former teammates for help in protecting his woman, but he knew that if the tables were turned, and Davin was the one who found himself in this situation, Adam wouldn't hesitate to call on them. Those guys weren't just friends, they weren't even just former teammates, they were brothers — family.

~ ~ ~

Evie set her fork down and smiled at Ria. "So, there you have it. Now you know who I really am and why I'm here. I'm sorry I didn't tell you before. It's not that I felt that I couldn't open up to you, it's just ... I honestly believed that everyone was safer if they didn't know who I was. But I hope you know that I am forever in your debt. That day that you and Russ followed me to the car was my lowest point." She let out a short, humorless laugh. "And that's saying something."

Ria reached across the table and patted her hand. "I'm just grateful that we saw you. I hate to think that you might have moved on if we hadn't talked that day." She smiled. "I barely knew Russ at that point. I was thrilled when he gave you his card and I'm even more thrilled now that meeting you like that turned into you taking the job at the gym and being able to stay here." Her elegant eyebrows lifted. "And that you staying here meant that you met Adam. Please tell me if I'm overstepping the mark, but it seems to me that you're thrilled about that too."

Evie couldn't hide her smile. "I am. I was thrilled when he asked me to stay at his house. You have no idea how good it felt to sleep in a bed and to be able to take a shower after all that time I spent..." She shuddered. She didn't want to remember the time she'd spent living in her car and she didn't particularly want to remind Ria of it either.

Ria gave her an understanding smile. "I want to say that I understand or even that I can imagine but the truth is I can't. I can't imagine what you went through. Then again, before you were in that situation you probably could never have imagined it either."

"You're right, I couldn't. My family was well-to-do. I don't come from… I don't have the kind of wealth that you do but I never would have imagined that I was someone who could end up homeless."

Ria shook her head. "You weren't exactly homeless. You were on the run."

Evie smiled. "That's what Adam said, too."

"And he's right. You weren't in a situation where you couldn't afford a place to stay. You were simply avoiding staying in one place for too long. And I have to tell you, I'm glad that when you settled on a place to stay, that it was here."

"Me too." Evie glanced out through the window; they'd been here for a while now and were still chatting even though they'd finished eating. She knew that Russ didn't have a problem with her being gone, but he'd given her the job out of the kindness of his heart, and she didn't want to take advantage of him.

She frowned as she watched a dark blue Cadillac roll down Main Street past the bakery. It gave her an uneasy feeling. There was something about it that seemed off, but what that was she didn't know. It could well be just her imagination.

She looked back at Ria, who had followed her gaze and was also tracking the Cadillac as it passed and moved on toward the square at the resort. When it disappeared from sight, Ria turned back to her.

"Am I just getting paranoid on your behalf or…?"

"If you are, then I am too. There was just something about that car that…" She shuddered. "I don't know, but it's probably time that we went back anyway."

Ria gathered her purse, and Evie did the same.

"Thanks for coming in, ladies!" called Renée. "See you again soon."

They both waved at her, and when they reached the door, Ria slipped her arm through Evie's and gave her a squeeze. When they were on the sidewalk, she walked on the outside, closest to the road. "I know it's probably silly, but I'm hanging onto you so that no one can try to take you. I know we're new friends, but you've already become a dear one."

Evie squeezed back, not daring to say anything because she wasn't sure if she'd be able to keep the tears away if she tried to speak.

Chapter Thirteen

Evie shot a worried look out the window when they heard a truck pulling up outside. Adam went straight to her and wrapped his arm around her shoulders.

"It's okay. It's nothing to worry about. It's Davin."

He felt his heart clench in his chest when she immediately relaxed against him. It made him feel ten feet tall that she trusted him to keep her safe.

He didn't feel so great when she worried at her bottom lip with her teeth. He caught her lip with his thumb and tugged it free as he looked down into her eyes. "What's wrong?"

"I… I feel bad. I know that normally you'd be spending all your time with Davin. I feel bad that I'm taking you away from your work and from your friend."

He kissed the tip of her nose and smiled. "You're not taking me away from anything. It's my choice. I would have thought that you might have figured it out by now; there's nowhere else I'd rather be."

He loved the way she smiled at that. But he didn't get the chance to say anything else before there was a knock at the front door.

"Do you want me to go upstairs? I could take my shower now so that you guys can have some time together."

He shook his head at her. "I don't want you to go upstairs." Then a thought hit him. "Unless you want to?"

"I'm not trying to hide, if that's what you mean. I like Davin, at least, what I know of him. I just don't want to hog all your time, and he might want to talk to you without me around."

Adam chuckled as he went to the front door. "He'd be disappointed if you weren't around. He's heard so much about you, I reckon it'd be good for the two of you to get to know each other better." He turned back and raised his eyebrows at her before he opened the door. "Is that cool with you?"

She smiled at him and nodded. "It's very cool with me."

They'd been discussing it for so long that another, louder, knock came at the door. Adam opened it with a laugh. "Give us a minute, would ya? I was almost here."

Davin scowled at him, but his expression gentled when he looked past him and saw Evie. He smiled at her. "I don't know how you put up with this guy. He's a pain in my ass!"

Evie chuckled and looked at Adam. "Aww, he's not so bad, and you know it. I'm sure you love him really."

Davin nodded and elbowed Adam out of his way as he came toward her. "Yeah, I guess he's all right, really. And I have to tell you, he's a good guy to have around when you need someone to watch your back. I can vouch for that."

Adam grinned at them both. "It occurred to me today that the two of you have never actually been introduced. I wanted to remedy that; I need my best friend and my lady to know each other and hopefully, to get along."

He loved the way Evie smiled and nodded and held her hand out to shake with Davin. "He's right, although I've seen you in the gym and we've chatted, we've never been formally introduced."

Davin smiled. "I don't think we need the formal part, do you?" He leaned in and wrapped Evie in a hug. "This guy is as good as, probably better than, a brother to me, so as his lady, that must make us family."

Adam narrowed his eyes at his friend as he hugged on Evie and grinned at him over her shoulder. It was crazy, he'd never been the jealous type, and even if he were, he trusted Davin with his life. Still, he couldn't help grabbing Evie's hand as soon as Davin let her go. He pulled her into his side with a smile as Davin gave him a knowing smirk. He wasn't jealous of his friend, it was just that as far as he was concerned, Evie was his. And it hit him in that moment that he'd never be comfortable seeing her in another man's arms.

"Would you like a drink?" asked Evie.

Adam loved that she felt comfortable enough here to offer, that she wasn't looking at him to be the host. He loved the idea of them as a couple welcoming his friend — who would hopefully become *their* friend — into their home. And yes, he knew that this wasn't her home, but a guy could hope.

"I'd love one, thanks," said Davin.

"Jack Daniels?" asked Adam.

"Please."

Evie started toward the kitchen, but Adam put his hand on her arm. "It's okay, sweetheart. I can get them. Do you want one?"

She smiled. "Please."

Adam made a face to himself when he heard Davin talking to her while he fixed the drinks.

"I can't believe that he has you staying in this place and hasn't finished fixing it up yet. He doesn't even have furniture."

Adam couldn't help smiling to himself when he heard Evie defend him. "No, he hasn't had the time. It's so good of him to let me stay here. And I think you already know that even staying in a house that isn't quite finished yet is a heck of a lot better for me than what I was doing before."

Adam was glad that she felt comfortable enough with Davin to talk about it. It had bothered him when she'd said that she was ashamed about being homeless. He was relieved that it wasn't something she was too embarrassed to bring up. Obviously, he wouldn't expect her to go talking about it to just anyone, but Davin wasn't just anyone. If Evie was going to be a part of his life, and he sure hoped that she was, then Davin would become one of her closest friends too, he hoped.

"This is better than what you were doing before, but I still think we can make it better for you," Davin said.

Adam took the drinks back through to where they were standing. When they each had a glass, he raised an eyebrow at Davin. "Are you offering to finish renovating this place for me?"

Davin laughed. "Hell, yeah, I am. I say we get a work party together just as soon as we can. It was okay for you to camp out here, but a lady like Evie needs better."

"Honestly, I'm fine. I love this place."

Adam loved hearing that. He knew that she appreciated that he'd given her a place to stay, a roof over her head, but he'd imagined that she saw it as not much more than a hovel – because in its current state, that's pretty much what it was.

"It could be a good home," said Davin. "But it'll take some work before it becomes one. I wasn't joking, I'm going to see what I can do about that work party. And in the meantime, I have something in the truck that I wanted to deliver to you guys."

Adam's eyebrows drew together. It wasn't often that Davin surprised him; they were usually on the same page. And besides, they usually told each other everything. It was hard for one of them to do something without the other one knowing given that in the normal run of things they were together pretty much twenty-four seven.

Davin laughed. "Don't look at me like that." He turned to smile at Evie. "Wouldn't you think that after all these years the guy would trust me? I bet you do, don't you?"

Evie chuckled. "I do. I trust you. I don't know what you're up to, but I trust you anyway." As she looked up into Adam's eyes, he loved the way that hers sparkled. "And I think that Adam trusts you too. It's just that I suspect that he knows you might mess with him, whereas I don't believe that you'd mess with me."

Both men laughed, and Davin met Adam's gaze and gave him a slight nod. "She's a smart one. You're going to have to watch yourself, buddy. She's way smarter than you are."

Adam had to laugh with him. "I hate to admit it, but you're probably right."

Evie waved a hand at them. "I'm not that smart. I haven't figured out what this gift might be. Are you going to show us?"

Davin grinned. "I am. In fact, I think you should make yourself comfortable. At least, as comfortable as you can be on that rickety dining set that he has in the kitchen, while Adam gives me a hand to bring your gift inside."

Adam gave her a puzzled look before he followed Davin outside. "What are you playing at?"

Davin led him around the side of the truck and pointed. "I reckon that poor woman is probably sick of having to sit in the kitchen all the time."

Adam only just managed to stop himself from saying that they spent more time sitting on the bed than in the kitchen. He knew how that would sound and he didn't want Davin to start joking about it. That was a surprise, or at least, it was something new. It didn't surprise him that he wanted to be respectful of Evie or that he needed the same from Davin. But it was new territory for him to have a woman's feelings be so important to him.

Evelyn sat at the kitchen table and took a sip of her drink. She was glad that Davin had come over. She already knew that she liked him, and she could see that what he'd said about him and Adam being brothers was true. She knew that they were close, and the way Davin was teasing Adam reminded her of siblings. She loved that Adam had such a close friend.

Her smile faded at that thought. It made her think about Taryn, she thought of her as the sister she'd never had, and she missed her. She couldn't wait to have her back in her life. But even that thought didn't sit well. Of course, she'd love to be able to go back to her life. To spend her days working on design projects for her clients and her evenings hanging out at the restaurant with Taryn. But if she went back to that, it'd mean leaving Adam behind.

She blew out a sigh. She didn't think of herself as a greedy person, but right now, she was wishing that she could have it all. She pulled herself together. Going back to Chicago wasn't a given yet, anyway. Until something happened, until Anatoly was somehow dissuaded from his interest in her, it was all a moot point.

For now, her life was here in Summer Lake, and she might as well make the most of it.

She looked up in surprise when the front door opened, and she heard a grunt. "What the heck?"

She hurried out to the hallway to see Adam and Davin carrying a sofa between them. Davin winked at her. "I couldn't believe it when this guy told me that he still didn't have any furniture. I've had all of mine in storage since we moved up here. So ..." He pushed the end of the sofa he was carrying, and Adam stumbled forward, taking his end into the living room where he set it down.

Evie was touched. She knew that Adam wasn't worried about furnishing the place, and although she'd offered, he'd said that he rather she didn't use any of her accounts. She understood that and hadn't wanted to push him to start buying furniture just because she was there. She knew he planned to, but she also knew he'd had a lot on his plate between looking after her, finding out what he could about Anatoly, and his own job. "Thank you."

Davin grinned at her. "You're welcome. And if you find that you need anything else, you're welcome to come over to the storage unit with me and take a look around. You can have anything that's in there, for as long as you need." He made a face at Adam. "I'm hoping that at some point this guy will get his act together, but until he does, you can count on me."

Adam whacked him none too gently across the back of his head. "I have my act together! It's just that everything's been so up in the air that …" He glanced at Evie and shrugged. "Sorry."

"No!" She went and slipped her arms around his waist before she even thought about it. He'd done so much for her. She didn't want him to feel bad about not providing furniture on top of everything else he was doing for her. "There's nothing to apologize for."

Adam wrapped his arm around her shoulders and nodded at Davin. "See, you can try and land me in it, but I'm doing okay."

Davin laughed. "I wasn't trying to land you in it. I'm trying to help." He smiled at Evie. "He's crazy about you, but he's a bit rough around the edges. I swear I wasn't trying to show him up. I'm trying to help him out. I'll do whatever I can to make sure that you're comfortable here." He hesitated, and his expression grew serious as he added, "Comfortable enough to stay."

Evie nodded. Knowing that Adam wanted her to stay here at the lake was one thing. When it was just the two of them, she could keep trying to look at it as a little bubble that was removed from reality – both her reality and his. But with his friend now saying that *he* wanted her to stay, too, it was becoming more real. And it wasn't just Davin. Ria had told her that she hoped she'd stay. Teresa had texted her a couple of times already and had been open about wanting her to stick around.

Adam tensed beside her, and she knew why. He thought that Davin might have pushed it too far. She wanted to reassure them both.

"Thanks, Davin. I am comfortable here." She looked at Adam. "I'm comfortable in your house and I'm comfortable with you." She turned to smile at Davin. "And even though it surprises me a little, I'm comfortable with you, too."

Davin cocked his head to one side. "That surprises you?"

She laughed. "Yeah. I kind of worried that you might not like me because … this probably sounds silly, but I expected you to be suspicious of the woman who's been taking up so much of your friend's time."

"Nah. You've got no worries there. If there were any reason to be suspicious of you, Adam would know it, and I'd have picked up on it from him. Like I said, and I don't mind repeating it, he's crazy about you. That tells me all I need to know. Seeing the way that he's been since you arrived, made me hopeful. Seeing the way that you guys are together, I …" He chuckled. "I'm more than hopeful. I'm in your corner. You need anything – anything from a nightstand to advice on how to handle this guy, I'm your man."

His smile was so genuine it belied his joking tone. Evie knew that he meant every word he said, and she appreciated it. She looked up at Adam, hoping that he wouldn't mind his friend offering to give her advice about him. She needn't have worried. He held her gaze and nodded before turning back to Davin with a smile.

"He's right. I'd like to think that there won't be anything you need advice about. I'm an open book, but if I mess up, honestly, Davin knows me as well as I know myself. He might be able to help you."

It touched Evie deeply that these two big, strong men were being so open. She wasn't used to men being honest about their feelings, certainly not to them admitting that they might screw up. She'd loved Tom dearly, but he was kind of old-school in that respect. He would have been mortified if one of his friends had offered to be a sounding board for her about how to handle him. Although, she also knew that none of them would be able to offer their help. Those guys didn't like to admit that they had feelings, let alone talk about them.

Chapter Fourteen

Adam closed his laptop and blew out a sigh. "Are you sure about this?" he asked Clay.

"Sure, I'm sure. We're good, right?" Clay directed his question to Davin.

"Yep. Alec's already here." He gave Adam a reassuring smile. "I can handle anything that comes up here, don't worry about it. Well, I know you will worry about it, but you don't need to. You know what Alec's like; he's always checking in, seeing if we need him." He chuckled. "I think he's bored. The way things have been going with Evie, I thought it'd be good to have him around."

Clay nodded. "And I'm comfortable with him. He's a good guy. We should have brought in a third man earlier. And once I have any more concrete plans than just hanging out here, we'll bring him in and do the usual meeting, right Davin?"

Davin nodded.

Adam blew out a sigh. "I know we've got all the angles covered. I wouldn't even consider staying behind if I didn't. But it still feels … I can't even say wrong because what would be wrong would be leaving Evie here by herself."

"Exactly," said Clay. "I'd be pissed if you tried to do that. So, I'm not going to say don't worry about it, because I know better, but I will reassure you that I'm good with it." He smiled. "In fact, more than that. I'm happy about it."

Adam raised an eyebrow. He wasn't sure that he liked hearing that Clay was happy to be going over his arrangements for the next month and not including Adam in them – especially if he was going to be traveling.

Clay laughed. "Of course, I'll be happier when things are back to normal and you're working with me again." His smile faded. "And I'm not happy that Evie needs you the way she does. But I'm glad that you've found her."

Adam nodded. He was, too, but he didn't particularly want to get into discussing his personal life in any more detail than they already had.

Marianne popped her head around the open door and smiled at them. "Is the work talk over?"

"It is, darlin'." Adam loved the way Clay smiled at her. It was obvious that Marianne was perfect for him in every way. Adam had believed that from the first time Clay had met her. It might have taken them a long time before they got their act together, but once they did, Marianne had brought so much to Clay's life.

She grinned at Adam as she came in to join them. She sat down on the sofa beside Clay, and he wrapped his arm around her shoulders, pressing a kiss to her temple. She looked up into his eyes, and Adam felt a rush of warmth in his chest – there was no missing the love in the look the two of them exchanged. He'd been aware of what they shared ever since they'd gotten together, but it wasn't something he'd thought that he wanted for himself – not until he met Evie.

Marianne turned her smile on him. "I've been trying to be good. I've been patient, but I can't anymore. When do I get to meet her? You know I'm not one to spend my time in the gym, but I'm getting desperate enough that I've been thinking about signing up for a class just so that I'll have an excuse to go in and meet her."

Adam chuckled. He adored Marianne and he had a feeling that Evie would, too. They were similar in some ways. At least, he could see Evie being more comfortable with Marianne than she was with Teresa. Teresa was good people, he liked her a lot, but she was more outgoing.

He glanced at Clay. He didn't have any point of reference on how to handle this. He hadn't needed to figure out how to mesh his work life with his personal life before. It'd been easy to keep them separate. His work life was his life, and his personal life had only ever been ... secondary. The women he'd been with in the past had been people he'd spent some of his free time with – entertainment on the side. It was strange to realize that if anything, his personal life was now more important to him than his work life.

Clay smiled at him. "It's up to you. This is new territory for me as well. I want to meet her. I want to invite you both over, but just as I imagine you're wondering about what lines might get crossed, I'm doing the same. I don't want to stand on your toes. I don't want you to feel like, if I ask you, you have to bring her. Your personal life is your own. Just because you work for me doesn't mean ... But by the same token, you don't just work for me." He looked at him, then at Davin. "I consider you guys to be two of my closest friends. You don't just work for me. We spend most of our time together. You have my back, and I hope you both know that I have yours in all the ways I can. Shit. I don't know how to say it because I'm not sure what I mean. I …

Marianne laughed and put her hand on his arm. "Men! There's no hope for any of you. You're all as bad as each other. I know what you mean, both of you. I'm not sure if you're too dumb to see it, or too afraid to say it. So, I'll say it for all of us. We all live in the same home. We spend more time with each other than we do with anyone else. We all get along and we all care about each other. I'll say the word even though the three of you would probably deny it. I don't care. We all love each other. And in my mind, and in the minds of most people – people who aren't big, tough men who are afraid to admit it – that makes us family."

She smiled around at them with her eyebrows raised, as if asking if anyone wanted to disagree.

Adam had to swallow around the emotions that burned in his throat. She was right. Right on both counts; they were as good as family, and there was no way that he, Davin, or Clay was going to admit it out loud. Though, judging by the look on their faces, they felt the same way.

After a few moments of silence, Marianne laughed. "Okay. So, that's settled." She turned to Adam. "So, you and your Evie decide when you want to come over and hang out with us. You," she looked at Davin, "will be here anyway. We'll have dinner and hang out. Welcome her to the family."

Adam swallowed again, wondering what Evie would think if she heard Marianne say that.

Clay smiled at him. "I'd start prepping her if I were you, bud. It'll probably be easier on her to come over here than to have to face Marianne, and no doubt Chris, in the gym."

Adam had to laugh. Marianne's sister, Chris, was a lot like Teresa. She was more outgoing and outspoken. She was an amazing lady, but he didn't think Evie would appreciate being interrogated by her while she was at work.

"I'll talk to her."

He frowned when his phone buzzed in his pocket and pulled it out to check. It was a text from Dalton.

He got to his feet. "Sorry, guys. I need to take this."

Dalton: Call me ASAP

He already had his phone to his ear as he strode through the kitchen and out of the house, heading back to the guest house. Davin was close on his heels.

"You need to lock your woman down," Dalton answered without preamble.

Adam's whole body stiffened as he froze with his hand on the door handle. "On it," he replied and changed direction, heading straight for his truck. "Talk to me."

"Give me a minute. I've got more coming in."

Davin didn't even question him, he just followed. Adam frowned. He appreciated his partner wanting to help, but he had to stay – even though everything was quiet around here, Clay's safety was their responsibility.

Davin shrugged as he went to the passenger side and climbed into Adam's truck. "Alec's here; he's perfectly capable of keeping Clay safe." He jerked his chin at Adam's phone. "I take it that's Dalton. Put him on speaker and hand it over."

Adam gave him the phone and started the truck. "It'll hook up to the speakers now."

Davin took out his own phone. "Alec? We're out of here …
Going to secure Adam's woman. You're in charge here … Yep
… Will do … Okay … Later."

He turned to Adam. "He's aware. He's going to go up to the
house and let them know we're off-site."

Adam nodded, grateful to Davin, but impatient for Dalton to
come back on the line.

"You there?" Dalton asked a second later.

"Affirmative. What's happening?"

Dalton blew out a sigh. "Chicago PD pulled a body out of
the river this morning."

Bile rose in Adam's throat. He didn't need Dalton to tell
him who that body was. He knew. Shit. He should have been
able to do something sooner. Just because that woman wasn't
Evie …

"Anatoly's latest woman?" Davin asked.

"Yeah. Who …?" Dalton didn't sound thrilled to hear
someone else speaking.

"Davin Brookes. I …"

"Teammate, right?"

"Yeah."

"Okay."

"Talk to me," Adam growled. He needed more information.

"Okay, breathe. I told you to lock your woman down
because this asshole doesn't waste time. Once he's done with
his latest distraction, he wants his next one lined up. My guy
on the inside said that they grabbed this last woman to calm
him down – because he was so pissed that yours got away."

"Evie," Adam ground out between clenched teeth. "Her
name is Evie." And that other woman had a name too. Shit.

"Yeah. Right." Dalton didn't seem put out that he was pissed. Or he just didn't care. "My guy also reported that there were men out looking for her. One went to Florida. I don't know why."

Adam did – it was thanks to the phone Dan had given Evie that made it look like she was calling from there.

"Another went to Philadelphia. But when he started asking about it, he found out that another guy's already in California."

"Fuck!"

"Yeah," Dalton agreed. "He didn't get anything more; didn't find out where in California, but …"

"But we're not taking any chances. Thanks, man."

"Of course. And listen, if you need backup down there, I'll be there."

"Thanks. We've got a few good men. I think we've got it covered. Appreciate the offer, though."

"Any time. I have another call coming in. I'll let you know as soon as I have anything else for you."

"Thanks. Later."

As soon as the call ended, his phone rang again. Davin looked at it and frowned. "It's Evie."

Adam's heart thundered in his chest, and he hit the button on the steering wheel to answer.

"Evie, are you okay?"

While Adam had been talking to Dalton, Evie had received a call of her own. She'd been relaxed as she worked on updating Russ's billing system for the gym members. She enjoyed doing the accounting work. She used to do it for Tom before he got sick – and she couldn't help thinking that she should have kept up with it after Glenn took over. Though she wouldn't allow herself to question whether this whole business could have been avoided if she had. If she'd caught onto what Glenn was doing early enough, perhaps … but no. There was no point in playing the *what if* and *if only* game.

She'd frozen when her cellphone had rung. Taryn had the number for it now, but it still sent chills down her spine. The only other time she'd received a call since she'd fled from Chicago had been from Anatoly.

She let out a sigh of relief when she saw Taryn's number on the display, but the feeling hadn't lasted long.

"Hey, Taryn. Is everything okay?"

"No, Evie. It's not. Shit. I'm sorry, I know I said I wouldn't call you, that I'd wait for you to call me, but this is important."

Evie could hear her pulse pounding in her ears. "What?"

"That … that woman." Taryn gasped in a big breath. "I think she might be dead. And they're looking for you."

Evie had closed her eyes and felt herself start to tremble all over. "What's happened?"

"I … I was in the restaurant and two men came in –"

"Oh, my god! They came in there? I thought … I thought Anatoly knew to leave you alone."

"So, did I. But … that's not the point. These two goons were asking where you were. You know me, I was all mouthy. I asked why it mattered since everyone's seen Anatoly out with that woman. They just laughed, Evie. They said that she wasn't any use to him anymore and that she'd only been a stop-gap until he had you. They said he's getting impatient and …" She blew out a shaky breath. "And they said that I can have until tonight, then they'll be back and if I need help to jog my memory, they'll be happy to help."

"Oh, Taryn. I'm so sorry. I ..."

"It's not your fault, is it? I'm not calling you because I'm worried about myself. I'm calling because of what they said on the way out. You know I don't speak Russian, but Alina, my cleaner, was there when they came in. They were talking to each other, laughing as they left. After they'd gone, I asked her what they said. She said that they were making a bet with each other. One said that the man who'd gone to Florida would find you first. The other one bet him that the one who'd gone to California would be the one to find you and bring you back. But they laughed that whichever one found you they were still going to come back and have some fun with me."

"Taryn! You have to get out of there!"

"I already have."

"Did you go to Jonny?"

"No. If Anatoly sent his men into the restaurant, that means he doesn't care what Jonny will do. I don't want to be the spark that causes a war."

"What are you going to do?"

"Same thing you did. First, I'm going to pick up a phone. I'll call you back when I get it."

"Please be careful. And please call me as soon as you can, okay? I'm going to call Adam right now. He has some friends up there; he can get them to help. They'll be able to hide you. Maybe they can get you here."

"We'll see. I'll call you back once I've grabbed my things and bought myself a phone."

"Please hurry. Stay safe. I love you."

"Love you, too, girl. We'll be fine. Bye."

As soon as the call had ended, Evie had dialed Adam with shaking hands. She'd grown to love his deep voice, and she'd never been so happy to hear it as she was when he answered.

"Evie, are you okay?"

"I am. But Taryn isn't."

"Shit. What's happened?"

"Two of Anatoly's men went into the restaurant. They said she has until tonight to tell them where I am. She's gone to get some of her things and she's going to call me back after she buys herself a phone. Do you think your friend up there might be able to help her?"

"I'll call him as soon as we're done."

"Please, Adam, call him now. I'm scared for her."

"I know, sweetheart, and I will. But first, where are you?"

"I'm still at the gym. Why?"

"Where in the gym, Evie?"

"In the office. Why? What's happening? What …?"

"Just stay there, okay. Don't let anyone in. I'll be there in two minutes."

"Oh, crap! Are they here? Taryn said that someone had come to California looking for me and someone else had gone to Florida." Her hands were shaking even harder.

"Just hang in there, sweetheart. I'm pulling up outside now."

She couldn't stop trembling and almost dropped the phone before she set it down on the desk. A moment later, there was a knock on the door.

"It's me. I'm coming in."

Adam crossed the room in two strides and wrapped his arms around her. She clung to him, reassured by his solid presence, but still scared for her friend.

"Taryn …"

"I know." He smoothed his hand over her hair. "She's going to be okay. We'll get Dalton to pick her up. Davin's on the phone with him now." He jerked his chin to the door, where Davin had appeared behind him.

Davin came in and closed the door. He gave Evie a reassuring smile. "What's your friend's number? Dalton will call her and …"

She shook her head rapidly. "She was going to ditch her phone after we talked. She said she'll call me back when she gets a new one."

Davin frowned and repeated that information into his phone. Then he looked back at her. "Where's the restaurant?"

Evie told him and he nodded. Her phone rang again, and Adam grabbed it from the desk. He checked it and scowled. "It's not a Chicago number – it's Denver."

"Hopefully, that means it's her and she picked a number no one would associate with her?"

"Hello?" Adam answered.

"Put it on speaker," Evie told him. "She doesn't know you. She might not say anything if she thinks –"

"Evie, it's me," Taryn's voice filled the room.

"It's okay," Evie told her. "That's Adam."

"Well, thank … something for that! I thought they must have found you and got your phone, I was about to hang up."

"She's safe." Adam's voice sounded low and dangerous.

"Well, damn!" said Taryn. "I believe it now that I've heard you. You're ready to kick ass and take names to make sure she stays that way, aren't you?"

The hint of a smile crossed his face before he answered. It wasn't the most pertinent thing to be thinking right now, but Evie knew that Adam and Taryn would get along.

"I am, and to keep you safe, too. Listen, Taryn, there's a friend of mine on another line waiting for us to give him your number. He's going to call you and once you tell him where you are, he'll come to get you and keep you safe."

"I'm not sure I like the sound of that," said Taryn. "Do you know this guy, Evie?"

"No." She shot Adam an apologetic look. "But he's a friend of Adam's, so that means he's one of the good guys, and he'll be able to keep you safe."

"Maybe. But I'm not sure I want to meet up with some guy I don't know. I mean, how will I even know if he's the right guy?"

Evie looked at Adam. Taryn had a point.

Davin stepped forward and set his phone on the desk next to Evie's. "Hi, Taryn. I'm Davin. Adam's partner. I'm here with them and I have Dalton, the guy who's going to help you, on the line. I'm putting him on speaker, too, so that we can all talk."

"Okay."

"This is Dalton, can you hear me?"

"Loud and clear," Taryn replied.

"Okay, ma'am. If you can –"

"Nu-uh. Hold it there, soldier. I can't do a damn thing until you stop calling me ma'am. It's Taryn. Got it?"

Evie glanced at Adam, and she was relieved to see that both he and Davin were smirking. Trust Taryn to be able to make everyone smile, even under these circumstances. Evie waited, hoping that this Dalton person would find it amusing, too.

When he spoke again, it seemed that he did. "How about we make a deal then, Taryn. You calling me soldier pisses me off about as much as me calling you ma'am pisses you off."

Taryn let out a short laugh. "Okay, but I don't see why it bothers you. You're a military man. I could hear it the minute you spoke. Go on, tell me I'm wrong."

"You're not wrong."

"So, why does it bother you if I call you soldier?"

Evie shook her head at Adam, but he was smiling as he listened to the exchange.

"Because I'm a goddam Navy SEAL, *ma'am*."

Evie felt her eyebrows shoot up. Though perhaps it shouldn't surprise her that Adam knew a Navy SEAL.

"Oh." Taryn sounded as shocked as Evie felt, but she recovered quickly. "Okay. Well, now that we've got that sorted. Would you rather I call you, sailor? SEAL?"

"Just Dalton will do fine."

Adam and Davin exchanged a smile. Evie was glad that they didn't seem to mind Taryn giving their friend a hard time.

A few minutes later, after Taryn and Dalton had exchanged numbers, and Dalton had described himself in detail so that Taryn would know him when she saw him, they took both phones off speaker, and Evie spoke to Taryn while Adam talked to Dalton.

"Are you going to be okay?" Evie asked.

"I'll be fine. That Dalton guy sounds like he knows what he's doing. It's you I'm worried about. What are you going to do?"

"I don't know. I'm going to talk to Adam now and see."

"I like the sound of him. You deserve a good man."

Evie smiled. "Thanks. You do, too."

"Yeah. Maybe one day. I doubt it, though. You're a sweetheart. I can see why Adam wants to take care of you. I'm a pain in the ass, and we both know it." Taryn laughed. "And

Mr. Goddam stick-up-his-ass Navy SEAL Dalton is about to find that out, too."

Evie chuckled. "I think you already gave him fair warning."

"Yeah. But just because I have to hide from Anatoly's assholes, doesn't mean I'm going to let some other asshole start pushing me around in the name of keeping me safe."

"He's only trying to help."

"I know. And I'll try to be good. But …" she laughed, "he'll probably want to hand me over to Anatoly himself after the first half hour."

Evie closed her eyes. It had felt good to joke with her friend for a minute, but Taryn's words brought her back to reality with a bump. "Just be careful, okay?"

"Yeah. You too."

Chapter Fifteen

When they got back to the house, Adam looked around with a scowl. If someone was coming looking for Evie, his place wasn't what he'd choose to keep her safe. But he was having difficulty coming up with a place that would work. He didn't want to put anyone else in danger. Clay's place was a better bet. It was walled and rigged with top-of-the-line security systems and cameras – he knew it because he'd upgraded the whole system himself, and personally installed it, with Davin's help.

Davin cleared his throat, reminding Adam that he'd need to take him back to Clay's place. "Sorry, man. I came here without thinking; we'll take you back now."

"Like hell you will," said Davin. "I'm not going anywhere. At least, not until we figure out where you're going. Alec's fine with Clay. You know that as well as I do. What we need is a plan. Where's Evie going to be safest? Because it's not here."

"I know, but what options do we have?"

Davin took his phone out. "I'll call Austin and find out."

"Austin?"

"Yeah. We've advised him on the installation of enough security systems on properties he has for sale. And I can think of three of them that are standing empty. The market's cooled off and nothing's selling. He'll let us use one of them."

Adam nodded. It made sense. He should have thought of it, but it seemed that he was off his game. He was too worried about Evie, and about her friend, too, now. "Thanks, man." He didn't need to say more than that. He and Davin had worked as a team for most of their adult lives. This might be new territory – he'd never needed help in his personal life before – but they were still a team. Davin had his back just like he always had, and whenever he needed it, Adam would have his.

He went to wrap his arms around Evie when he saw that she was standing there wringing her hands together.

"I didn't think they'd come here. I certainly didn't think that they'd go after Taryn. Something must have changed. Taryn said that she didn't even want to go to Johnny for protection because she doesn't want to start a war between them."

"She sounds like a smart lady. She's probably right. Do you want to go upstairs and pack your things? I'll come up to get mine after Davin gets off the phone."

"Okay. Where are we going?"

"I don't know yet, but I want to be somewhere with better security. Davin's seeing what he can find us."

She sucked in a deep breath and blew it out slowly. "Okay. I'll go and pack. Do you want me to throw your things in your bag as well?"

He pressed a kiss to her forehead, loving that she was trying to be brave, and was able to be practical. She was still shaking, but she wasn't letting it stop her from doing what she needed to. "Yeah, thanks. My duffel bag's up there. Just throw in whatever you can find. Leave the bags up there. I'll carry them down."

Her eyes looked softer when her gaze met his and she nodded. "Okay."

~ ~ ~

Evie stared around the kitchen. It could be perfect. She couldn't believe that in her current circumstances all her mind could focus on was how much potential there was in this house. If she'd been offered this place as a project to work on, she would have been in heaven. It had great bones and there was so much she'd love to do to it. But that was so not what she should be thinking about right now.

Right now, she wasn't an interior designer, she was a woman in hiding from dangerous men. Dangerous men who were out to find her and bring her back to Chicago, to Anatoly, and … she shuddered … to her death. This house wasn't a job that she'd get to work on. It was a place where Adam and Davin had brought her to keep her safe.

She blew out a sigh and straightened her shoulders. It was all too much, but she couldn't let it be too much. She had to be strong. She had to make herself useful. Adam and Davin were doing everything they could for her. She was going to do what she could for them. And although it didn't seem like nearly enough, all she could do right now was make them dinner.

She went to the fridge and shook her head in wonder at how well stocked it was. Clay's lady had sent another man, Alec, over with more groceries than they'd need if they stayed here for a month. Adam had told Evie that Marianne had wanted to help. She'd gone grocery shopping, but he – and she didn't doubt Clay, too – had said that she shouldn't come to the house. Evie was glad of it. It was bad enough that Adam and Davin and their friends were all going out of their way for her – putting themselves in danger for her. She didn't want Marianne or anyone else coming anywhere near her until this was all over.

She jumped when Adam appeared in the doorway.

"I'm sorry, sweetheart. I didn't mean to startle you."

He came and closed his arms around her and pressed a kiss to her forehead.

"You didn't. At least, you shouldn't have. I was lost in my head. That's all. You didn't scare me."

He looked down into her eyes and pressed a kiss to her lips. "Good."

His big brown eyes looked wary as they looked into hers. She wanted to reassure him, and she needed him to understand. "You could never scare me, Adam. You make me feel safe. Even in the middle of all this craziness. When you put your arms around me?" She gave him a small smile. "It makes me feel like everything's right with the world. Even though it isn't."

He kissed her again, and when he pulled back so that he could see her, his eyes were filled with tenderness. "I know I'm not supposed to be pressuring you. But I have to tell you; once all this is behind us, Evie, I want to be able to make sure that everything is right in your world. Every day."

A rush of warmth spread through her chest. She wanted that, too. And the more he talked that way, the more she believed him. It didn't matter that she was a couple of years older than him. It didn't matter that they came from different worlds – that he'd been some military superhero while she'd been a wife who lived a mundane, if content, little life in Chicago. None of that made any difference. What mattered was how they felt about each other, and there was no denying that they had a real connection. Her breath caught in her chest when she realized that somewhere in the middle of all the craziness that had become her life, she'd started to fall for the wonderful man who stood before her.

"It doesn't feel like pressure, Adam. It feels like hope. I'd like to think that maybe I'll bring something good into your world, too."

That smile. She knew how happy he was when one side of his mouth lifted higher than the other. "You already have brought something wonderful into my life, Evie. What I want is to be able to keep you."

She nodded; she already knew that she wanted to keep him, and she was starting to believe that staying here with him might just be the best move – for both of them.

"Hey, Adam. Shit, sorry!" Davin stopped dead in the doorway when he saw them standing there with their arms around each other.

Evie kept one arm around Adam's waist and waved Davin to come in with the other. "Don't be," she told him. "If anyone should be sorry it's me, for holding him up in here when I know the two of you are checking the security system. But …" she shrugged and gave them both a smile, "I'm really not sorry." She reached up and pressed a kiss to Adam's lips before stepping away from him. "I am thinking about making us all some dinner, though. That sound good?"

Davin grinned at her and nodded. "Sounds great, thanks."

"Do you need any help?" asked Adam.

She laughed. "No, this is my way of helping. You go back to doing what you do, and I'll be in here if you need me." Her smile faded, and she looked at Davin. "Have you heard anything more from your friend yet?"

"Yeah. I should have told you, sorry. He picked Taryn up, and one of his men has eyes on the restaurant."

"Thanks."

"She's going to be okay," Adam reassured her.

She nodded, hoping that he was right, but still feeling guilty that her problems had affected her friend this way.

Adam leaned his head against the back of the sofa and looked up at the ceiling. He needed a minute to catch up with himself, which surprised him. He was used to things happening quickly and to having to adjust on the fly. That had been the way of life back when he was in the unit. It was the same with security work, too. When there was work to be done, decisions had to be made in the moment and acted on immediately. Between missions, there was only waiting and preparing, studying information, and formulating plans. This situation had been different in that there hadn't been enough information available to study. He still had plans, though. He knew where he planned to take Evie if they had to run. He didn't see it coming down to that, but it was his fallback option.

This afternoon, this house hadn't even been on his radar, but now it was their safe house. He and Davin knew the place well. They'd worked with the local realtor, Austin, on several properties over the last year or so. Homeowners who were looking to sell higher-end properties had started asking for state-of-the-art security systems to be installed. Not that security was much of an issue in Summer Lake, but since Clay, the granddaddy of country music, had bought property here, sellers were hoping that others like him might move here – and that they might be looking for the same kind of security.

Adam had liked this house the first time he saw it. It was on the water, on the quieter end of Main Street. It wasn't as big as some of its neighbors, but it had a quiet elegance about it that appealed to him. It was just grand enough to be something special, but it still had a warmth that made it feel like a home, even though it had stood empty for a long while. It needed work, but only superficial stuff. It wasn't a fixer-upper in the same way that his place was, it just needed some TLC from someone with an eye for design. He smiled. Someone like the woman sitting beside him.

Evie turned and smiled at him. He knew that he should snap out of his thoughts and back into the conversation that was going on around them. Then again, Cal and Ryan were deep in discussion with each other, Manny was talking on his phone, and Dan, Russ, and Davin were huddled together over by the island that separated the den from the kitchen.

He smiled back at Evie. "If you had your way with this place, what would you do with that island?"

She chuckled. "Sometimes I think you can read my mind. Is that part of your Special Forces training? You can just look at someone and know what they're thinking?"

"No. I think it's just that we're in tune with each other. I didn't know you were thinking about it, but I guessed that you might have some ideas of what you'd like to do to this house."

"I do. It's a lovely house. I was thinking earlier that it has so much potential. If it were a project of mine, I'd …" She stopped when she saw Davin coming toward them with his phone to his ear.

"Yeah, hang on a minute. I'll give you to her now."

Adam watched him hand the phone over and loved the look of relief that crossed Evie's face.

"Taryn. Are you okay? Where – in fact, no. I'm not going to ask, and you don't need to tell."

Davin smiled at Adam. They were both glad that she was thinking – that she knew that talking openly on the phone wasn't wise. He figured that it wouldn't be a problem since Dalton would have had Taryn call from his phone – a phone that Adam had no doubt was secure.

He got up and left her to talk to her friend when Cal caught his eye and jerked his chin for him and Davin to come to join them.

"I appreciate you guys all coming over like this," he began when he reached them.

Cal nodded. "Not a problem. You know we've all got your back whenever you need us. But we want to make this official."

Adam frowned, not understanding.

Dan stepped forward with a smile. "You know we've had delay after delay with getting all our approvals and contracts in place. Well, I got word today that we're finally good to go. We won't have any official contracts coming in until at least next week. When I heard what's going on with Evie, I decided that Prometheus Security should kick off operations with a pro bono case."

Adam was stunned. He knew these guys would all be happy to help. But the kind of security operation that Dan had mounted – the kind that had bid on, and by the sounds of it had secured, some major government contracts – could charge the kind of rates that he could only imagine.

He was grateful, more than he could say but … he looked around at them, all standing there grinning at him.

Before he had the chance to speak, Ryan winked at him and said, "And before you even think about mentioning money, you should know that Dan has more money than God. It's no skin off his nose. Right, Dan?"

Dan nodded and rolled his eyes at Adam. "Don't worry about Ryan talking about me like that. He still calls me Nerd, and Boy-Wonder most of the time."

Adam had to laugh. He knew those two had a lot of history, but he couldn't see how anyone could think of Dan as a boy. He was a man who Adam was proud to know. Though, maybe there was some merit to the nerd thing.

Ryan grinned at Dan and continued, unperturbed. "We'd all do it because we want to help. But Dan says this is official business. So, you have us, and the cyber team back at HQ at your command. The way we'll work with our clients is that we'll tell them what to do, but this is you; you tell us what you want, and we'll make it happen."

Adam had to swallow a couple of times before he dared to speak. "Thanks, guys. I … this means more than you know."

He looked around and met each man's eye before he continued. Every single one of them was someone he was proud to know and not just happy, but grateful to work with.

"How about we set up a command center in the dining room?"

Cal laughed. "Thank you! I've been itching to do just that, but you're the man in charge."

"No. We work this as a team. You all have strengths and I want to use them. No egos here."

Cal nodded. "Okay, so I'm manning the desk and we'll work the rest out from there."

Davin grasped Adam's shoulder and shook it as they walked to the dining room. "I wish the mission were different, but it kind of feels like old times, huh?"

Adam nodded. It did, but until the mission of making Evie safe was accomplished, he wouldn't be able to enjoy even the camaraderie with these guys.

Chapter Sixteen

Evie stared up at the ceiling. She was tired but she couldn't sleep. Her mind was racing. She felt terrible that her troubles had landed at Taryn's doorstep. Well, they'd gone beyond the doorstep and barged right into Taryn's life. Evie hated to think about those two big, scary men who'd come to her apartment with Glenn going into the restaurant and threatening her friend. But that's exactly what they'd done. She blew out a sigh.

Adam rolled onto his side and smoothed his hand over her hair. "You okay?"

She turned to face him. "Sorry, I thought you were asleep."

He smiled. "Nope, I've been lying here listening to you think."

She smiled back at him. "I was thinking that loud?"

"Pretty much. Want to talk about it?"

She shrugged. "You know it all already. I feel so bad about Taryn. I've been worrying about the gyms as well. I know I shouldn't have left Glenn in charge. That's stupid, but I didn't feel like I had any choice. I didn't dare to contact anyone else to ask them to take over. I … it's weird, but I haven't given them much thought since I left."

"You've had enough to think about. And from what you've told me, you've been hands-off with them for years."

"I have. I keep second-guessing myself about that, too. If I'd paid more attention, if I'd been doing the books myself ..."

He stroked her hair again and leaned in to press a kiss to her lips. "You couldn't have known, Evie. You were busy living your life. And I'd guess that for the first couple of years, you wouldn't have been able to face it anyway."

She nodded. He was right again. She loved that he understood about Tom. He seemed to understand how she felt and what she'd gone through after he died. "Did you lose someone you loved?" she asked before she even thought about it and felt bad once she had. "Sorry. I don't mean to pry. It's just that you understand so much. It made me wonder ..."

He shook his head. "It's okay. I don't mind you asking. I'd tell you if there was anything to tell, but there isn't. I mean, I lost my dad, almost twenty years ago. That was hard, and of course, it was harder on my mom. I tried to be there for her as much as I could. They were high school sweethearts; they'd been together since they were fifteen. It devastated her. I told you that she used to say that talking about him kept him around. It helped to know that. Left to my own devices, I would have tried to steer her thoughts away from him, would have tried to make her focus on the life she had after him, to make the most of what was. But she was right, it felt good to talk about him, to remember. That's why I imagine that it feels good for you to talk about Tom."

"It does." She cupped his cheek in her hand and pressed a kiss to his lips. "Is your mom still around?"

"No. She died seven years ago. She did okay after he died; she got involved in everything she could in town. Any committee or fundraiser, she was right there." He smiled his lopsided smile. "She enjoyed herself. She made the most of her time and did a lot of good. But she wasn't the same person after he died. She said that half her heart died with him." He looked into her eyes. "Do you feel that way – about Tom?"

She pressed her lips together as he held her gaze. Her heart pounded in her chest as she slowly shook her head. She wanted to feel bad, wanted to feel disloyal to the man who'd been a good husband and her best friend for most of her adult life, but she didn't. "No. It might sound strange, but I almost wish I did. Don't get me wrong. I loved him and I know he loved me. We were good together. But ..." She swallowed. "Maybe it's because we knew for so long that the end was coming. He talked to me so much about making the most of life after he was gone. My business wasn't much more than a hobby back then. He encouraged me to take it more seriously after he was gone. He wanted me to live my life. He made me promise him that I would." She chuckled. "He even made me promise that I'd travel. He hated to travel, and I always wanted to."

She loved that Adam smiled at that.

"And he told me not to be lonely when he'd gone. He wanted me to be happy. He made me promise that if I got the chance to love again, I'd take it."

Adam's eyes widened and she wanted to bite her tongue off. She shouldn't have told him that last part. He'd probably think that she was trying ... she didn't know what he'd think. Yes, she'd admitted to herself that she was falling for him. And from everything that he'd said, he might even be open to that. But ...

He leaned in and pressed his lips to hers. This time, he didn't pull away after a brief peck. He closed his arm around her and drew her to him. Once she was pressed against his warm, hard body, her breasts touching his muscular chest, making it hard to hold on to coherent thoughts, he nipped at her lips, and she opened up for him.

They'd done a lot of kissing over the last few weeks. He'd kissed her softly and slowly; the kind of kisses that gave her reassurance. He'd kissed her deep and hard; the kind of kisses that made her weak at the knees and eager for more of him. He'd given her friendly kisses and tempting kisses. But there was something new about this kiss.

His tongue slid against hers. His heart pounded in his chest, synchronizing with her own heartbeat. His arm held her close, and his hot, hard length pressed against her hip, promising where the kiss would lead. She clung to him and kissed him back, feeling like this might be the most memorable kiss of her life.

When he finally lifted his head, he leaned back to look into her eyes. "That's something else that Tom and I have in common."

It took her a moment to come back to her senses and remember what they'd been talking about.

He pressed a kiss to the tip of her nose. "I don't want you to be lonely." He brushed his lips over her forehead. "I want you to be happy." He held her gaze for a long moment and then claimed her mouth in another deep, sweet kiss. "And I want you to take a chance on love again."

Her breath caught in her chest as he held her gaze. "What I'm saying is that … I'm falling for you. I didn't plan to. I didn't plan to fall for anyone. I'm not that guy. At least, I never was before I met you but … shit … I have to say it. I'm not just falling. I've already fallen. I love you, Evie."

Her heart leaped into her mouth. She'd hoped that he might get there, but …

The crinkles around his eyes deepened, and he stroked her hair. "Sorry. I shouldn't have said it, not yet. But you need to know, it's not just words, Evie. Words aren't enough to …"

A rush of warmth filled her chest as he muttered away, trying to backpedal his way out of it. But she didn't want him to. She pressed a finger to his lips and his eyes widened. "Shush. It's okay that you said it. I'm glad that you did. I know it's not just words, Adam. Words are never enough, but they're all we have. I've been thinking those words and trying to talk myself out of saying them — thinking that you wouldn't want to hear them and …"

His hand came up to cover hers, and he pulled her finger away from his lips. His eyes shone with something she didn't quite understand until he spoke. "Say them, Evie. If they're true, I need to hear them."

"I love you, Adam." Her heart felt as though it melted in her chest when he smiled.

"You do?"

"I do."

He kissed her fast and hard before pulling back with a smile. "Since we both agree that words aren't enough, do you want me to show you?"

She had to laugh, even as he rolled her onto her back. "I do."

Adam's heart was still pounding in his chest as he got rid of his boxers and then tugged her panties down. When he'd been with women in the past, he left them to undress themselves while he shed his clothes before joining them in their bed. It was different with Evie. She lifted her hips, and he felt his cock start to throb as he dragged the scrap of cotton down her long, shapely legs. Every time he did that, it turned him on big time.

Once she'd kicked her ankles free, he looked up at her with her a smile, but froze when he saw the look on her face. "What's wrong?"

"Nothing. I don't want to spoil the moment, I just … the way you were looking at my panties … I'd guess that … I know they're not exactly sexy."

He crawled back up beside her and pressed a kiss to her lips. "They are to me because they're yours. I wasn't thinking about them, I was thinking how much I love dragging them down your legs and off."

He reached for her hand and let out a low growl when he curled her fingers around his aching cock. "That's what you do to me. You, Evie, not your panties."

Her eyelids drooped, and he loved the look of lust in her eyes as she touched him. "I wanted to tell you that I only bought those cotton things while I was on the road, that they're not what I normally wear, and that I hope you'll like it when you get to meet my lingerie collection."

His cock twitched in her hand at the word lingerie. He didn't think he'd known another woman to use that word, and when she did … damn! He trailed his fingers up over her ribcage. "I'm sure I'll love it. I'll look forward to it. But you need to know, it's not your panties that do it for me, it's what's inside them – you."

Her fingers tightened around him, and she began to pump her fist slowly. It felt so damned good – too good. He propped himself up on one elbow so that he could look down into her eyes and let his free hand roam over her. She was so damn responsive, he loved it. Her nipples drew into taut peaks when his fingers circled. She moaned when he ducked his head and worshipped first one breast then the other with his lips and tongue. His fingers walked their way down over her stomach and a low growl escaped his lips when he found how wet and ready for him she was.

He traced her opening and her hips bucked up to meet him. He was planning to taste her, but her fingers tightened around him, and he looked into her eyes.

"I love it when you go down there, you know I do. I love it when you touch me and when you taste me. I love everything we do together. But right now, you said that you're going to show me that what we said isn't just words. And to me that means …

He smiled when he understood what she meant. "You're right, Evie. I'm going to make love to you."

He loved the shiver that rocked her body at his words. He loved the way she looked up into his eyes even more. He knew that she expected him to position himself above her and give her what she wanted. Instead, he took hold of her hips and rolled, taking her with him so that he was on his back, and she was sitting astride him.

He lifted her hips and she guided him to her entrance. It felt so damn right, watching himself disappear inside her, listening to the little moan she made when he pulled her down to take all of him. He reached up and cupped her breasts, circling her peaked nipples with his thumbs. "I love you, Evie."

She'd never looked more beautiful than she did in that moment, her hair falling around her shoulders, her face and neck flushed with desire, her eyes shining as she nodded and breathed. "I love you, Adam."

Damn! He'd thought that he was afraid to hear a woman tell him those three words, but when Evie said them, it sent a rush of heat through his veins. His heart clenched in his chest as he gripped her hips and began to move with her. The way her breasts bounced as she rode him made him pull her down so that he could taste them. She was so responsive that every play of his lips and tongue on the taut peaks was rewarded by her inner muscles tightening around him. She was amazing.

He felt her getting closer, as she gripped him tighter. He could see it, as her eyes drifted closed, and she let her head fall back. "Come for me, Evie."

He wanted to go with her, but he held himself back. "Adam!" She gasped as she let herself go, grinding her hips against him, taking him deep as she gripped him tight and convulsed around him.

"I love you, Evie," he told her. "You're mine now, mine for as long as you want me. And I'm yours, forever."

She slumped down on his shoulder and breathed, "I'm yours forever, Adam. I love you. I wouldn't say it, couldn't feel it, if it wasn't forever."

He felt the smile spread across his face as he tightened his arms around her and rolled them back over so that she was under him again. He was still so hard for her, that it was easy not to break their connection. He started to move, slowly at first, pulling all the way out then thrusting back in. He wasn't going to last long, but he needed to get her there again before he allowed himself to give her everything.

Her arms came up around his shoulders and she pressed her face into his neck, sending electric currents shooting down his spine. Her legs came up around his back, and he felt her lock her ankles together.

"Adam! I didn't know I could. I didn't … you're going to … I'm going to …."

He smiled as he drove harder and faster, loving that she was tightening around him again already.

"Go with me, Adam. I need you to … Oh, God, Adam! I love you!"

As she gripped him tight, he chased her orgasm, thrusting two more times and then holding deep as his balls drew up tight, and he let go. Wave after wave of pleasure crashed over him, through him, and into her. She milked him for all he had to give, and he gave it willingly. When they finally stilled, he nuzzled his face into her neck and breathed, "I love you."

Her hand came up to cup his face and she planted a sweet kiss on his lips. Then she chuckled and said, "I love you, too. And it seems that now that we've said those words, we might be in danger of wearing them out. I love hearing them, I love saying them, but I think that I like the way you show me the best."

He laughed with her and when he did, they lost the connection, but it was okay. With her, everything was okay. He loved the way she could do that; that she could joke and make him laugh after such an intense moment. He'd thought that any talk of love was supposed to be serious and intense – that was one of many reasons why he'd never had much interest in going there. With Evie, it didn't feel that way. Yeah, it was huge, and it was important, the most important thing he'd ever had in his life, but it was light and fun, and it felt natural. He didn't feel the need to try to be anything but himself for her, and he knew that she felt the same way.

He dropped a kiss on her lips. "I like that part the best, too, I —" The sound of his phone ringing cut off the words he'd been about to say. He rolled off her and grabbed his phone from the nightstand. Even as he worried what news he was about to hear, he knew he didn't need to worry about Evie. He hated it when women got pissed at him when his work interrupted their time. With Evie, she knew that in this case, his work was all about keeping her safe. But even when it came to his work with Clay, she was always trying to make sure that she wasn't getting in the way. She encouraged him to put his work first, not set it aside for her.

"Dalton. Talk to me," he answered with a frown. This couldn't be good; it was almost one in the morning, and Dalton had said he'd call with an update tomorrow.

Chapter Seventeen

Evie looked up from her spot on the sofa when Russ appeared. She'd heard the doorbell ring a little while ago, but she'd thought it was one more of the guys coming over. Adam had called Cal about an hour ago – even though it was only six-thirty now – and they'd all arrived at the house shortly afterward.

Adam had explained to her that all the guys who worked for Dan Benson were going to be helping them, that Dan had taken her on as his company's first case. She was more grateful than she could express. Not that she didn't think Adam couldn't handle it, but she liked that he didn't have to handle it by himself. She liked knowing that if someone showed up here in town looking for her, Adam wouldn't have to face them alone. Well, she knew that Davin would have his back, but it was even better knowing that Cal, Manny, and Ryan, and their whole team would have their backs as well.

She pulled herself together when she realized that she was sitting there staring at Russ, and he was giving her a worried look in return. She knew he wanted to do whatever he could to help as well, but at this time in the morning, he should be at the gym, opening up.

He took a few steps toward the sofa before he stopped. "Are you okay? Ria sends her love and wanted me to ask if you need anything. She wanted to come over with me, but I didn't think … I can go get her if you like?"

Evie shook her head slowly. She was still in shock. She couldn't believe what had happened last night. She sure as hell didn't want to drag any more of her friends into the mess that her life had become. "No," she managed to say eventually. "She needs to stay away from me, Russ. So do you. I quit. I … if you need me to do any computer work, I'll do it from here, but I'm not coming into the gym again."

Russ blew out a sigh and came to sit beside her on the sofa. He wrapped his arm around her shoulders and said, "It's not your fault, Evie."

She sniffed and shook her head. "It's all my fault. They only went after Taryn because she's my friend. Ria's my friend, too. Give her my love back, and tell her I'm sorry, but she shouldn't be my friend anymore. She needs to keep her distance. Tell Teresa, too."

Adam looked up from the dining room table where he'd been talking to Cal. He frowned and came to join them, sitting on Evie's other side and hauling her against his chest.

"What's up?" he asked Russ.

"I was just trying to tell Evie that she doesn't need to worry about Ria or about the gym."

Evie sat up straighter. "But I do, Russ! Look what happened last night! Taryn … thank God she wasn't there, that she was with Dalton. But the restaurant's gone! Burned to the ground! That place isn't just her business, it's her life. Just like you with the gym. I don't want them burning down the gym or threatening Ria, or anyone else because of me."

Adam tightened his arm around her shoulders. "It's not your fault, Evie. None of it. It's that asshole, Anatoly, and the idiots who work for him. They're going to pay for what they've done. And believe me, they're not going to get the chance to do anything like that here."

Evie felt the tears rolling down her face. It was all too much. Adam brushed the tears away with his thumb. "It's all going to be okay."

She nodded numbly. They all kept saying that, but they couldn't see that it couldn't be okay. Taryn had lost the restaurant because of her. Glenn had lost his life because of her. He was dead.

Adam gave her a gentle shake. "You still with me?"

She looked up at him. "I should have gone and paid them myself."

"You can't take it on yourself, Evie. It's not your fault, any of it."

She shrugged. She knew there was no point in arguing with him. He wanted to make her feel better, but she knew better.

Russ gave her a sad smile. "Just give it a bit of time, you'll see."

She stared at him, thinking about Ria. Ria was lucky to have him. He was a good man. He was lucky to have her, she ... she frowned as a memory flashed in her mind. A memory of sitting in the bakery with Ria, watching that car drive by, the car that had given them both the creeps. She tensed, and Adam met her gaze.

"What? What did you just think?"

There he went again, seemingly able to read her mind. "I'm sorry. I should have told you sooner. I just … I guess I forgot. When Ria and I went to the bakery for lunch, we saw a blue Cadillac driving down Main Street. It was … it didn't do anything strange, but it gave us both the creeps. I didn't think much of it at the time. We joked about it, and Ria kept hold of my arm on the way back to the gym but …"

Adam looked so intense it was almost scary, but she'd told him the truth; she couldn't ever feel scared of him.

"What do you remember about it?"

She shrugged. "It was a blue Cadillac, a sedan not an SUV. It was a newer model; you know, with the more modern-looking front grill. I didn't get the plate number, but it was a California plate – I did think to check if it was a Chicago plate." She felt stupid now, she should have taken a note of the plate number and told Adam about it immediately. Maybe she was too stupid to live, after all. As soon as that thought crossed her mind, it was like someone had poured a bucket of ice water over her.

She was better than that! Things might be bad right now, she might be feeling sorry for herself, but Taryn wasn't hurt, even though the restaurant was gone. Glenn was dead, but she knew full well that had been a likely outcome of all of this anyway. And that certainly wasn't her fault. She might have been able to do things differently than she had, but the whole thing was down to his poor choices – and his gambling addiction.

Adam pressed a kiss to her temple, and she turned to look at him, wiping the dampness from her face as she did. "Sorry I didn't tell you sooner, but I'm going to do better now. I'm going to go upstairs and take a shower. What time do you think Dalton will get here with Taryn?"

"I don't know, sweetheart. I'll let you know when I hear from him again. I don't know how he's getting here, but I know he's being careful."

"Okay." She got to her feet and both men joined her.

Russ put a hand on her shoulder. "You're going to be okay, Evie."

She smiled back at him. "I know, and it's all thanks to you."

He shot a look at Adam. "I'll do what I can, but it's this guy ..."

She leaned against Adam. "I know, I'm not taking anything away from him, but if you and Ria hadn't followed me that day ... If you hadn't offered me a job, I wouldn't have stayed here. And you know, it was the name of the gym that swung it. I sat there with your card in my hand, debating whether I should call or just take the money you'd given me and move on since I'd already been around here for a few days. It was the longest I'd stopped in one area since I left Chicago. I thought I should move on and try to find a job for a couple of weeks in the next town. But it was your card, the name of the gym on it, that convinced me to stick around. Guardian Fitness. It felt like a sign." She smiled at them both, even though tears were rolling down her cheeks again. "And it was. I found my guardian right here."

Adam hugged her into his side. "Just don't go calling me a guardian angel. I love you, sweetheart, but I'll never be an angel."

Evie didn't miss the flash of surprise that registered on Russ's face, but it was quickly replaced with a smile. He was happy for them, no question about it.

"I wouldn't want you to be," she told Adam. "I love you just the way you are." She looked back at Russ. "I'm sorry I freaked out on you. I will come back to work if you still want me when it's safe. And if you want me to do anything in the meantime, I'll do whatever I can from the computer here." She gave him a wry smile. "I could use the distraction."

"I'm sure I'll be able to find something for you." He looked to the dining room, where all the other guys were now seated. "I'm going to check in with them before I head to the gym. Let me know if I can do anything for either of you, okay? It looks like those guys have you covered, but I'm happy doing grocery runs or bringing takeout or whatever else you need."

Evie surprised herself and Russ by stepping forward and giving him a hug. He'd been so good to her, yet she'd always held back. She didn't think she'd ever hugged him before, and she needed him to know how much she appreciated him.

She only got to wrap one arm around him, though. Adam didn't let go of her other hand, even when she tugged.

After Russ had gone to the dining room, Adam closed his arms around her and rested his chin on top of her head. "This will all be over soon."

"I know." She had to ask. "Did you have a problem with me hugging Russ?"

He stiffened, and she looked up at him in surprise.

He gave her a shamefaced smile. "You noticed?"

"I noticed."

He shrugged his shoulders, looking for all the world like a kid who'd been caught with his hand in the cookie jar. "I … I'll figure it out if it pisses you off." He frowned. "Actually, that may be a lie. I'm not sure if I can."

"If you can what, Adam?" She wasn't sure if she should be amused or if she should be worried that he might turn out to be overly possessive. She didn't think she'd be able to handle that.

"If I can stand to see you in another guy's arms."

She frowned. "I wasn't in his arms. I was just giving him a hug. He's a friend. He's ... I'd never. He'd never."

Adam scrubbed his hand over his face. "I know, Evie. And I'm sorry. I'll try to do better. I promise. It's just ... I love you. I know I have no right to ... anything. Jesus, I'm sorry."

She reached up to touch his cheek. "It's okay. I like that you care so much. But ... you're not seriously jealous, are you?"

His face relaxed. "I'm not jealous at all. It's not about Russ, or about any other guy that you might want to hug on. I'll do better, okay? It wasn't a rational response. I'm not the jealous kind. I ..." He shrugged again, looking ashamed of himself. "It's nothing to worry about, I promise you."

She felt the tension leave her shoulders. She knew it wasn't. She might have panicked for a moment, but that was all. Adam wasn't that kind of man, and she knew it. "Okay. Now, I really am going to go up for a shower."

"Okay, sweetheart. I'll make you some fresh coffee for when you come down."

"Thanks."

~ ~ ~

Later that afternoon, Adam walked back into the kitchen and sat down on one of the stools at the island with a sigh.

"You okay?" asked Davin.

He nodded. "How's Evie?"

She said she was going to take a nap. "I peeked in on her a little while ago ... for fuck's sake, Adam! Don't look at me like that! I wanted to make sure she was okay. She bucked up for most of the day, but it's hard on her. With you gone, I just wanted her to know that she's not all by herself. That I was there if she wanted to talk. I thought she might be sitting up there fretting. She was asleep."

Adam scrubbed his hand over his face. "Sorry. I need to get a lid on that. I just … I appreciate you looking in on her. I'm not stupid. I know you're looking out for her and for me. I didn't think for one minute …"

Davin smiled. "I know you didn't. I know what's going on with you, even if you don't."

"Can you tell me then? Because I don't have a freaking clue!"

"You're in love. It's new. You're not used to it. And you are used to being overly protective of those in your charge. Up until now, you've spent your life protecting people professionally. Now, for the first time, it's personal – it's as personal as it gets. Evie's not just in your mind, she's in your heart, and your heart wants to protect her the same way the rest of you does. But you can't; you'll blow it if you don't get a lid on it. In my experience, women like to know that their man cares, but they don't like it if he starts to care too much." He gave Adam a wry smile. "If he starts pulling shit like you did with Russ, not letting go of her so she could hug him."

"I know, you're right. I didn't mean to. I'll figure it out. I'll be better once this shit is over."

"What's happening out there?"

Adam had been over to Dan's building. Even though all the guys had been here at the house most of the time, Dan's tech team worked out of the offices, and Adam had understood why when he saw the computer power they had over there.

"They hacked into the laptop of Anatoly's second-in-command and managed to track down the guy who went to

Florida. He's no threat, obviously, since he's following the wrong lead, but one of Ryan's old buddies is down there and he was happy to go and put a stop to him."

"That's good. Anything on the one who came here?"

Adam blew out a sigh. "Not yet. They're still working on that. Dalton called when I was on my way back here. He should be arriving in the morning with Taryn."

"That'll make Evie feel better."

"Yeah."

"You have a problem with it?"

"Hell no! I just feel bad that she got caught up in it. She's lost her livelihood too, now. Just like Evie."

Davin shrugged. "Maybe she'll want to stay. Evie's going to stay, right?"

"I hope so." Adam couldn't believe that she'd ever want to go back to Chicago after everything that had happened.

"I just keep wishing that I'd gone up there myself as soon as I knew what was going on. I could have gone up there, taken Anatoly out, and that would have been it – end of story."

Davin shook his head. "Nope. We're not in the unit anymore, bud. We're civilians on American soil. And when one civilian goes out and kills another in cold blood, even if he kills someone like Anatoly, even when the world would be better off for it, it's still called murder, and it could still land your ass in jail for the rest of your life. I understand. I've had the same urge myself. But our hands are tied way more than they used to be. We have to stay within the lines."

Adam blew out a sigh. "I know, but it doesn't stop me from wishing. And I tell you now; if I'm the first one to get to the guy they sent out here to look for her, you can call it whatever you like, but I *will* take him down."

Davin nodded. "And if you do, then in one way or another it will work out to be self-defense."

"Yeah."

Davin grasped his shoulder. "It will. I talked to Don."

"The sheriff?"

"Yeah. I wanted to bring him into the loop. He's a good guy, and he's more likely to be understanding about whatever goes down if he's already in the loop."

"Thanks, man." Adam knew that Davin was right. He should have talked to Don himself before now.

"So, what now?"

"Now, we wait." Adam hated his answer, but it was the only one he had. "We wait for the guys to figure out who the asshole who came out here is – and if he even came here to the lake. All we know so far is what Taryn said – that someone came to California. We wait for Dalton to arrive with Taryn tomorrow, and we wait for Dalton's team up there in Chicago to give us anything they can on Anatoly. I wish that bastard would come down here himself. He wouldn't get anywhere near Evie, and I'd make sure he didn't make it out of town again."

"I'm with you, but that's not likely to happen. Are you going to go up to see Evie?"

"Not if she's sleeping. She needs the rest. She didn't sleep much last night." He pulled his laptop toward him. "I'm going to do some more digging. I keep feeling that maybe there's something I can find, something I can dig up that'll help me put an end to Anatoly. If we could take him down, the goons would all go home, and Evie wouldn't even be on their radar anymore."

"If anyone can find a thread to pull, you can. I know that."

"Yeah. Are you okay to stay here again tonight?"

Davin smiled. "I'm going nowhere. You should know better than to ask."

Chapter Eighteen

Evie let herself out onto the patio and took a seat at the table. The view of the lake from here was beautiful. She didn't know how she could even think about it with everything that was going on, but she was falling in love with this house. Yes, it had great bones, and could be something special, but even apart from everything she could do to it, it just had a feel to it.

Every house had a feel to it. Some were grand and aloof waiting to be admired, others were waiting for their family to come in and fill them with life, and others still were ready to party and host good times. This house felt like a sanctuary. Of course, it felt that way to her right now because that's what it was. But it was more than that, too. It was a two-story Mediterranean, nowhere near as big as some of its neighbors – there were some grand estates along this stretch of Main Street. Evie knew that Clay McAdam lived a little farther down the road, and Zack, one of Clay's pilots who came in the gym every day when he was in town, lived close, too.

This house wasn't on the same scale as theirs, but it had a character, and an elegance, that she just loved. She blew out a sigh and took a sip of coffee. She stared out at the lake and wondered what it would be like here if she'd just come on vacation. She loved the town; she loved the lake. She loved that this house had a boat dock. If she and Taryn had come here on vacation, they would have rented a boat, maybe even rented this house, and …

She pulled herself together. She wasn't on vacation, and there was no point in trying to distract herself with that kind of thinking. She was here because Anatoly Petrov wanted to use her as his woman until he got bored of her, and then he would want her dead. She shuddered at the thought.

"Are you cold?" She hadn't heard Adam come out after her.

She was about to tell him that no, she wasn't cold, but he came and wrapped his jacket around her shoulders, so she kept quiet. The gesture warmed her heart more than the jacket warmed her body. He leaned in and pressed a kiss to her forehead.

"I just heard from Dalton. He said that they'll be here within the hour."

"Thank, God." She couldn't wait for Taryn to get here – to know that she was safe. "Did he say how Taryn was?"

Adam smiled through pursed lips. "She's fine."

Evie raised her eyebrows. "What does that mean?"

His smile faded. "Honestly, she's okay. You don't need to worry about her."

She had to chuckle. "It's not so much that I'm worried about her – not now that she's almost here. It's … I'm guessing from the way you answered my question that Dalton had something to say about her, but you went with, she's fine."

Adam's eyes shone with amusement as he nodded.

"Come on. You have to tell me, she's my best friend. I know what she's like. I imagine that as soon as Dalton gets her here safely, he'll want to turn straight around and run back to Chicago – or anywhere – to get away from her."

Adam couldn't keep his laugh in any longer. "Okay. I should have realized that you'd know what to expect. Dalton said that she's holding up well, so well that she's been a pain in his ass from the second he met her."

Evie shook her head with a smile. "Good. That means she really is okay."

"It sounds that way."

"And is there any other news?"

Adam shook his head. "Nothing we can act on yet. Dan's cyber team has been making progress getting into Anatoly's systems."

"Okay." She wasn't sure how that was going to help.

Adam rested his hand on her shoulder and leaned in to kiss her again. "It's almost over, sweetheart."

Her heart felt as though it melted in her chest – it did every time he called her sweetheart.

"I hope so."

"I know so."

She looked up into his eyes, and he nodded. She didn't see how anything would be resolved any time soon. Well, they might find and stop the man who'd come to California. But that wouldn't stop Anatoly. He'd just send someone else. But even with that knowledge, she couldn't help believing Adam. If he said it would be over soon, it would be over soon.

"Do you want coffee?" asked Adam.

Dalton held his gaze for a moment and then nodded sharply and followed Adam to the kitchen.

Dalton and Taryn had arrived fifteen minutes ago. Of course, Evie was Adam's main concern, but once he'd assured himself that her tears were tears of relief, he'd been happy to watch her disappear upstairs with her friend. She needed that. He was sure that Taryn must, too.

Dalton took the mug of coffee and leaned back against the kitchen counter. "I could do with something a hell of a lot stronger than this right now." He took a sip before he looked back at Adam. "But given that it's before noon, and ..." he glanced up the stairs, "…I can finally get more than three feet away from *her* …"

Adam cringed. "I take it it wasn't an easy trip?"

Dalton scowled and shook his head. "Damn woman."

"Sorry."

Dalton shrugged. "Not your fault, is it? You've never even met her until now, have you?"

"Nope."

Dalton chuckled; well, it might have been a chuckle. His broad shoulders shook, and his lips twisted into something that looked like amusement, but it could have been pain.

"What?" Adam was almost afraid of the answer.

"You'll see. The woman's a piece of work. I mean, I get loyalty to her friend; I can respect that. I get that she's madder than a wet hen about her restaurant being burned down but damn, the trip out here with her is the longest one I've taken in my life. Still, I'm better off than you are. I'm the guy who helped her get away from Chicago and to her friend. You're the guy who's taking her friend away from her."

Adam frowned. He didn't want to take Evie away from her friend, but then … he wanted nothing more than for her to stay here – with him. "What did she say?" He had to wonder what she knew. He knew that Evie had spoken to her since Dan had given them the phone, but he didn't know how much she would have told her about him.

Dalton laughed. "What didn't she say? She's uttered every imaginable threat – and a few unimaginable ones – since I first picked her up."

Adam sucked in a deep breath. Taryn hadn't seemed hostile toward him when she arrived here at the house, but she'd barely greeted him before she and Evie had launched themselves at each other and gotten lost in their hugs and tears and chatter.

Dalton gave him a wry smile. "The rest of the time she was waxing lyrical about how you could be just what Evie needs.

I've heard all about Evie and how amazing she is and how she is the best friend and was the best wife in the whole world. One way or another, whether Taryn decides to love you or hate you, you're going to have to put up with more than any man should have to take from that one."

Adam nodded. He could take as much as he had to if it meant that he'd win Evie's best friend over to his side. Of course, he hoped that she'd decide that she liked him, and he hoped that he'd like her – for Evie's sake more than their own.

"Anyway," Dalton continued. "Now that I can breathe again without her in my ear, now that I can think straight, let's sit down and update each other. One of my guys called just as we were getting into town."

Adam led him to the big dining room table that Cal had set up as his command center. Cal had gone over to the office with Manny and Ryan to catch up with Dan and the cyber guys, but Adam was expecting them back soon. He could bring Dalton up to speed while they waited for them to return.

He looked up when the kitchen door opened and nodded when Davin came in.

After Adam had introduced them, Davin poured himself a coffee and sat at the table with them.

"I was just at the resort. Brayden called me. There's a blue Cadillac out at one of the bigger cabins. He was worried that even though the name associated with both rentals is Russian, it might just be a regular tourist – a coincidence."

Adam frowned. It didn't make sense to him that one of Anatoly's men would be staying at the resort. If he was in town to grab Evie, it'd make more sense for him to lay low – not rent a car from the airport and then rent a cabin as if he were a regular tourist.

Dalton set his mug down with a scowl. "What's your take? You went by to check, right?"

"Yeah." Davin shook his head. "It doesn't feel right. The cabin is one of the bigger ones, it sits on its own cove, and it has a boat dock. It's the kind of place you'd expect a big family or a group to rent, but the Cadillac is the only vehicle there. There's no sign of life."

Adam blew out a sigh. "Can we spare anyone to watch the place?"

"When they get done at the office, Ryan and Manny are going up there. Cal's coming back here and bringing Donovan with him."

"Okay."

"Can they still access Dmitriev's laptop?" asked Dalton.

"Yeah," said Davin. "Brayden's been digging around in there the whole time." He looked at Adam. "The kid's good."

Adam nodded.

"He's going to let us know immediately about any emails or anything else that comes in. I just wish we had the same kind of access to his phone."

"Yeah."

Dalton stopped with his mug halfway to his lips. "I may be able to help there."

"How?"

"I know someone. She's good. She can't always get access when the target's on the move, but in this case, we know exactly where Anatoly and Dmitriev are. She might be able to access their phones."

Davin's eyebrows drew together. "Why do we need that when we already know where they are?"

"I don't mean locate their phones; I mean access them – listen in and read incoming and outgoing messages."

Adam's heart started to beat faster. He knew it was possible to do that kind of thing, but he also knew it required a warrant – especially when the target was on US soil. He looked at Dalton, but Dalton just shrugged.

"I know what you're thinking. And if you don't want to go that route, we won't. Nothing that she can find out that way would stand up in court – in fact, we'd all end up in court if it came out. But we're not trying to build a case against Anatoly, are we?"

"No," Adam agreed. "We only want to take him down."

They all looked up when Cal came in and stopped short. "We're not trying to build a case against Petrov? Why?"

Adam scowled at him. "Because our priority is to get him off Evie's case."

Cal came and sat down at the table. "Obviously. But in the process of doing that, we can maybe build a case against him that would take him down – stop him from taking another woman – stop everything else that he's doing. I get that Evie's the priority, but …" He held Adam's gaze … "We could do a lot more good, as well."

Adam closed his eyes. Cal was right. But …

Dalton got to his feet and pulled his phone out. "Callahan's right. I'm going to call Amelia. Like I said, she's good. Let's see what she can do, and then we can decide …"

Cal frowned. "Good to see you, Dalton. You know as well as I do that if we use illegal means against him, Anatoly Petrov's lawyers will get him off without question."

Dalton paused with his hand on the door. "I do. But if I know Amelia, she'll be able to work this so that the means used to collect the information will never come to light." He looked at Adam. "You good with that?"

Adam's heart thundered in his chest. "Yeah."

Dalton looked at Cal. "Do you trust me?"

A little pulse ticked in Cal's jaw, and he narrowed his eyes, but after a moment, he gave a curt nod. "No one's ever managed to take him down by going through official channels. Let's try coloring outside the lines."

Dalton nodded and brought his phone up to his ear as he went outside. "Amelia? Dalton. Yeah, darlin'. I'm good."

After he'd gone, Adam sat there looking at Davin and Cal, hoping that bringing this Amelia woman in wasn't a mistake.

~ ~ ~

As soon as they made it to the bedroom, Evie closed her eyes and blew out a big sigh.

Taryn was by her side immediately, wrapping her arms around her. "What?"

She shook her head. "That was just a sigh of relief that you're here."

Taryn laughed. "Glad I can do that for you. Dalton had the same reaction as soon as we arrived here, and Adam opened the door, though I don't think it was the same kind of relief."

"Only you," Evie said with a smile.

"Only me what?" Taryn's eyebrows shot up. "If you're going to tell me that only I would drive that man crazy, then I have to say that you're wrong. Anyone – any human being – would annoy him. He's a grouch."

Evie laughed. "Maybe, but that wasn't what I was going to say. I meant that only you would be more bothered about the man who brought you here than the reason that you're here."

Taryn shrugged. "I learned when I was little, you've got to roll with the punches. Life's a bitch and she'll try to knock you down."

"I'd say she has knocked you down, Taryn. The restaurant …" Evie sucked in a deep breath "… It's gone."

Taryn shrugged again. "I know. But … you're not. I'm not. We're both still breathing, Evie. That's all that really matters."

She had to smile at her friend. "You're right. I know you are, I just … I feel so guilty. It's all my fault."

Taryn waved a hand at her. "That's bullshit, and you know it. It's Glenn's fault for bringing Anatoly into your life, for putting you on his radar. It's Anatoly's fault for being the biggest asshole known to man. Stop blaming yourself and start counting your blessings."

"I don't – "

"Ha!" Taryn grinned. "Don't you dare tell me that you don't have any blessings to count. If you do, I'll remind you about that man downstairs … Adam! In fact, I'm going to remind you about him anyway. This whole thing might be a shitshow, but damn, girl, if he's your reward for going through all of this, then I'd say it was worth it. Come on, you have to tell me all about him."

Evie let out a short laugh. "God, I love you! You've just lost the restaurant. Everything that you've spent the last ten years working for went up in flames. You've been threatened by Anatoly's men, and you're not mad at me. Instead, you want to hear about Adam."

Taryn tugged her hand and went to sit on the bed, taking Evie with her. "I also just spent a couple of days on the road with the grouchiest man on Earth, don't forget that, but none of it matters. I'll build another restaurant or buy one. The threat's behind me now, and I'm alive to tell the tale. And your man – possibly assisted by The Grouch – is going to make sure that Anatoly doesn't threaten you or me ever again. So, why dwell on the bad stuff?"

"You're right. Maybe I'll be able to look at it that way when Anatoly's behind bars or at least, prepared to leave me alone."

Taryn pursed her lips. "If I've judged your man right, and The Grouch, then I don't think Anatoly will live long enough to get behind bars. But you're right. For me, the worst has already happened. The restaurant's gone. What was my life is gone." She held her hand up when Evie started to speak. "And I'm fine with that. Sure, it sucks. But it is what it is, and my momma didn't raise a whiner. I'll buckle down to whatever comes next and make it good. But, for you, the threat's still there. But it won't be for long. Your man will see to that. I know it as sure as I know my name's Taryn. You found yourself a good 'un. There's no doubt about it. And fine, too!" She batted her eyelashes and fanned her hand in front of her face, making Evie laugh.

"So, come on. Tell me all about it. I want to know everything."

She wriggled farther onto the bed and once she'd piled up the pillows and leaned back against them, she patted the space next to her for Evie to join her.

Evie sat beside her friend and nodded. There was nothing else she could do right now but sit here and tell Taryn all about Adam. And it felt fitting that her friend had done the same thing he did so often. She'd climbed up and made herself comfortable as if it were the most natural thing in the world to sit on the bed and talk.

"Before you start, can I ask you one question?" Taryn's eyes sparkled as she spoke.

"You can ask me anything; you know that."

"Do you love him?"

Evie's breath caught in her chest, and she'd been wondering how Taryn would feel when she told her that. Taryn had been close to Tom, after all. Still, she didn't hesitate to answer honestly. "I do."

"Oh, my God, Evie! That's awesome! And has he told you that he loves you? I'm not asking if he does because it's obvious – he does. But has he told you?"

"He has."

"Are we staying here, then?"

Evie gave her a puzzled look.

"Are we moving here?" Taryn clarified.

Evie didn't know what to say.

"Just saying. I'm up for it. The restaurant's gone. I have nothing to go back for. The gyms ..." For the first time since she'd arrived, Taryn's energy dropped, and she hung her head before she looked up again and met Evie's gaze. "It's sad about Glenn, but he brought it all on himself."

She nodded.

"And you could sell the gyms, you know. I reckon Tom would want you to do that."

She pressed her lips together and closed her eyes. It didn't stop tears from leaking out between her lashes. "I should have done that a couple of years ago. He told me that he didn't want me to keep them just because of him. He wanted me to sell and have the money so that I could do whatever I wanted." She wiped the tears away. "But I didn't want anything. I wanted him back and I couldn't have him. Other than that, I had everything I needed. I had you and I had the business and …"

Taryn took hold of her hand and squeezed it. "You still have me. Your business is gone, but I'd say that selling the gyms would be like letting Tom take care of you one last time. You know he wanted you to be happy. He told me so many times that if you had a chance at love again, I should help you, encourage you."

Evie had to wipe her eyes again. "But you don't even know Adam yet."

Taryn smiled. "I know, that's why you're going to tell me all about him. But even though I don't know him, I know that he's the guy for you."

"How?"

"You were on the road for how long before you came here to Summer Lake? How many people tried to help you? How many people did you let in? How many did you tell what was going on with you?"

Evie didn't answer, she knew they were rhetorical questions.

"You told Adam, you let him help you. And not only is the guy helping but he's also put together his own little army, including Mr. Grumpy Pants downstairs. He's one of the good guys, Evie. And even in the few minutes that I've spent with him, there's no missing the fact that he's in love with you."

"Yeah."

"Okay, so start at the beginning and tell me your love story."

"Okay, but first tell me if you're after one of your own."

"My own what?"

"Love story! Don't think I haven't noticed that Dalton's gotten under your skin."

Taryn shrugged. "I told you, he's a grouch. He may be the most disagreeable man on the planet. He'd get under anyone's skin – like chiggers."

Evie laughed but kept her friend on track. "But you like him."

Taryn laughed. "Of course, I do! Have you seen him?" She fanned her face again. "He's hot! But even if I wanted a love story, I wouldn't be looking at him in that way. What about Adam's friend, what was his name … Davin?"

"Yes."

"He's hot, too. Is he nice?"

"He is. He's a good man. But honestly, Taryn, it feels surreal to me that we're sitting here discussing men after everything that's happened – to both of us – and everything that might still happen."

Taryn's expression sobered. "I know, but what else are we going to do? Neither of us is big on the whole weeping and wailing and gnashing of teeth thing, so …" She shrugged. "And I think you're wrong that anything else still might happen. I don't think Adam will let anything happen. But thinking about it is too scary; I'd rather talk about hot men. So, for the last time, would you, *please,* tell me about Adam?"

Chapter Nineteen

"Where are you going?"

Adam paused at the edge of the bed. He'd been trying to get out without waking Evie, but she reached out and curled her fingers around his wrist, giving him a sleepy smile that made him want to get back under the covers with her.

"I'm going with Davin to do some scouting. We shouldn't be long."

"Okay."

"Go back to sleep, sweetheart. It's early."

She nodded. "I'll try."

He got ready and thought that she was sleeping as he left the room, but just as he reached the door, she opened her eyes again.

"Adam?"

"Yeah?"

"Do you … Would you mind …"

She sounded so hesitant that he had to go back to her. He knew that Davin would be waiting downstairs, but he needed to know what was bothering her. He wanted to reassure her before he left.

He sat on the side of the bed and took her hand in his. "Tell me."

She sucked in a deep breath. "I'm being dumb, and I know it, but I think I need to hear you say it before I believe it."

He chuckled. "If you give me a clue what you mean, I'd love to help."

"Oh. Sorry. I …" She sucked in another big breath and then rushed out the words on the exhale. "Would you be happy if I stayed here? I want to. Taryn said she'll stay, too. She could buy or build a new restaurant. I could maybe find some work. I know they're starting another phase of the development over at Four Mile Creek, maybe they'll want an interior designer. And … I … this is going to sound crazy, but I think I want to buy this house."

Adam gripped her hands tighter. He could hear the blood rushing in his ears.

She started to pull her hand back. "Of course, I'll understand if you say no … if …"

He leaned in and closed his arms around her, pulling her off the bed and hauling her against his chest. "Evie, sweetheart, I'd be more than happy if you stay. I want you to stay. If you want to. I'll go to Chicago if that's what you want. Honestly, I'd rather you move here. But where we live is secondary. What matters most is that we're together. I haven't wanted to push until all this is behind us. But, when I say I love you, I mean I want to spend the rest of my life with you. I want to wake up next to you every morning and go to sleep with you every night."

Her hazel eyes brimmed with tears as she nodded along with him. "That's what I want, too. I love that you'd go to Chicago for me, but I don't want to be there anymore. I want to be here, with you."

"Then let's make that happen."

She nodded.

His heart rate was starting to return to normal. He didn't know if he'd ever felt as happy as he did in that moment. He let everything she'd said sink in and warm his heart, until one thing she'd said struck him.

"You want to buy this house?"

She nodded. "It's beautiful. At least, it can be. I'd love to make it beautiful."

"Yeah."

"What?"

He chuckled. "I guess I didn't do a great job of providing a beautiful home for you, did I?"

She squeezed his hand. "You did better than that, you gave me a safe place. You gave me your home and you gave me your heart."

He pressed a kiss to the tip of her nose. "I hope you'll always think of my heart as your safe place. It's yours. If you want this house then you should have it, but can I be the one to buy it?"

She held his gaze for a long moment. "I ... don't want you to be the provider, Adam. You're already the protector. I need to feel like I'm bringing something of value to ..."

"You are. You're the most valuable thing in the world."

She shook her head with a smile. "You know what I mean."

"I do, and I think you know what I mean, too. But, Evie, if you're giving up your life to move here to be with me, I want to be able to give you a home that you'll love."

She pursed her lips, and he knew that she wasn't convinced. "How about we start as we mean to go on? Do you want to buy it between us?"

He nodded slowly as he thought about it.

Her smile faded. "I know that could make life difficult if ... if we decide not to ... that we don't want to ... but we could sell it or one of us could buy the other out if ..."

He gave her a stern look and pressed a kiss to her lips to stop her from talking. "Not happening, Evie. I'm not worried about getting out of joint ownership. I don't plan to get out of anything that we go into together. Not our house not …" He didn't hesitate more than a second before he said the word that he'd spent at least thirty years thinking he didn't want. "… our marriage."

Her eyes widened, but he just smiled and nodded. "Yes, I said that. Yes, I know it's not romantic, but that wasn't me asking you; that was me planting the seed in your mind, letting you know that's what I want. I know you might not want it. So, I'm putting it out there now to give you the chance to think it over. What I'm saying is, let's buy the house together, and let's spend the rest of our lives together. Sound good?"

Her eyes brimmed with tears, and she nodded rapidly. "That sounds wonderful."

"Good." He leaned in and kissed her fast and hard. He wanted to stay and share so much more than a quick kiss, but he could hear Davin moving around downstairs. "I'll be back as soon as I can. Dalton's here; you'll be safe with him."

She let out a short laugh. "I believe that, but I'm not so sure that he'll be safe with Taryn."

He laughed with her. "Yeah. There are definitely sparks flying there, but I don't know what they mean. She might love him; she might hate him."

"With Taryn, it could go either way. And it's not just her; he's as bad."

"They'll figure it out one way or another. In the meantime, try to stop them from killing each other, and if you can't do that, take cover!"

She chuckled. "I will. I'll see you later."

He brushed his lips over hers one last time, then headed downstairs to find an impatient Davin waiting for him.

Evie paused on her way down the stairs. Adam had left a while ago, but it was still early, so she was surprised to hear voices in the kitchen. She'd expected Taryn to sleep in; it'd been a long drive to get here from Chicago.

"Would you move over, you big lug?"

"Dammit, woman. Can you keep your elbows to yourself? I was trying to pour you a mug."

"I can get my own, thank you very much."

Evie smiled to herself. Taryn and Dalton had continued to snip at each other ever since they arrived. Taryn was always up for a laugh and a joke. She took no prisoners with her sense of humor, and she didn't suffer fools. She didn't take kindly to bossy men, either. Dalton had been perfectly polite to Evie, but there was no denying that he treated Taryn differently. Evie knew that her friend could get under people's skin – if she took a dislike to them. But she also tended to keep her distance from people who irritated her.

She'd have to talk to her later and see what was going on. Taryn dated sometimes, but if she liked a guy, she was usually flirty and fun. Her banter was usually upbeat, not snarky. Whatever was going on, she needed coffee before she'd be able to figure it out. She just hoped that her presence in the kitchen might inspire a truce.

"Morning," she called.

"Morning." Taryn greeted her with a smile.

"Morning." Dalton nodded and reached for the coffee pot. "Do you – "

"I'll get her one." Taryn rudely elbowed him out of the way.

Dalton's eyes closed briefly. When he opened them again, he caught Evie watching him and shrugged. "I'll be in the dining room."

Once he'd gone, Evie went to take the mug that Taryn offered and proceeded to add lots of cream and sugar. Her days of going without those particular luxuries were over.

"What's with you and him?" she asked Taryn in a low voice.
Her friend shrugged. "Wish I could tell you. He rubs me the
wrong way. Come on, let's take these outside. The sun's on the
patio, and if we're out there, *he* won't be able to listen in."

Evie followed her to the kitchen door.

"Where …?" Dalton stood in the doorway from the dining
room with a scowl on his face.

"Oh, stand down, would you?" Taryn glared at him. "We're
going to drink our coffee outside. You can see us through the
window. You just can't hear us. No need to get your panties in
a wad!"

She flounced out the door, and Evie gave him an apologetic
smile before she followed.

"Taryn!" she reprimanded once they were outside. "That
man rescued you and brought you here. You could at least …"

"I know. I'm sorry. I'm being an ass, but I just can't help it.
You have no idea. Ever since I met up with him, in fact no,
right from when I spoke to him on the phone with you he just
… I don't know. *I'm a goddam Navy SEAL, ma'am.* He just
pissed me off! And every half hour or so, I convince myself
that I should apologize for being such a bitch to him, and I
open my mouth to do it, but then he goes and does something
else." She rolled her eyes. "The sooner he goes home, the
better. I'll send him an apology note and a decent bottle of
whiskey or something and call it good."

Evie watched her for a moment as she sipped her coffee. She
still couldn't figure out if Taryn's dislike for the man was
genuine or if she was having a very different reaction to him
and trying to hide it – knowing Taryn, hide it from herself.

"Anyway. Enough about him. How are you this morning?
How's Adam? What's happening?"

"He and Davin have gone out to …they have a lead on the
man who came to California looking for me."

"I hope so. I hope they can take him down and ..." Taryn shrugged. "And I don't know what else they can do. Anatoly's not going to give up just because one of his men doesn't succeed." She met Evie's gaze. "You're not going to be safe until Anatoly's gone."

"I know." She hated to admit it, but unless Anatoly was locked up – or gone, in a more permanent way – she'd always be looking over her shoulder.

"The Grouch said that he has someone – some woman – who's a computer genius and might be able to gather enough evidence to send Anatoly to prison. But even then ..."

Evie nodded, even then, even if Anatoly were behind bars, that wouldn't mean he couldn't get to her somehow. She blew out a sigh.

"Damn. I'm sorry. Let's talk about something else. Tell me more about this restaurant. I can't wait to go once this is all over. Giuseppe's; do you know if that's a family name? It's not what I'd name a restaurant, but ..."

Glad to change the subject, Evie stood. "I'll go and get you their menu. I don't know if it's a family name. The guy who owns the place is Tino. He's lovely."

"Hm." Taryn cocked her head to the side. "I wonder what that's short for. Could be Agostino, Martino. Wait, no, Valentino." She smiled. "I hope it's Valentino."

Evie shook her head and went inside for the menu, happy to have diverted her friend's attention.

Dalton looked up when she came in the door. "Everything okay?" he asked.

"Fine, thanks. I'm just getting a menu for Taryn."

He glanced out through the window at her. "She's hungry?"

"No. It's just so she can see what the Italian restaurant here offers."

"Ah. Right." He glanced out the window again. "She doing okay?"

"She is. Are you?"

Dalton's attention snapped back to her. "I'm good, thanks. I'll let you get back to her."

As Evie went back outside, she couldn't help hoping that the animosity between those two was just a cover for attraction. Dalton seemed like a good guy. He was certainly easy on the eyes. And there was no disputing the fact that he was a big, tough guy. If Taryn were to find herself a man, he'd need to be tough.

~ ~ ~

Adam braced his hands against the desk in the conference room and let his head hang as he listened.

Amelia's voice filled the room and every word she spoke made it more difficult for him to breathe. His heart pounded and his chest burned. He wanted to hope that Amelia was wrong, but he knew she wasn't. She was good – the best at what she did. Even Dan was in awe of her. All the techy guys referred to Dan as a legend. He had joked with Amelia when she came on the line that his legend paled beside hers. Adam was grateful to have her working with them, but he hated hearing what she had to say.

Davin stood to attention beside him, playing the same role he had for years. When one of them needed a moment – whether because of an injury or simply to take a leak – the other stood watch. had his back, in both the literal and the figurative sense.

"So," Amelia summed up what she'd found out. "Getting my program into Dmitriev's phone was easier than I expected. From there I'll be able to pull details on every operation that he's running. It looks like he's grown complacent. He's been with Anatoly for over twenty years and for the last seven years or so, the organization has gotten stronger, and their competition has gotten weaker. They've gotten, not sloppy, but their security isn't as tight as it should be. I've already seen enough to know that once I collect what I can and land it anonymously with every office in the Chicago PD and District Attorney's office, there's no question they'll be able to build a case – and make it stick."

Cal scowled at the whiteboard on the wall. "What makes you think you can make it stick?"

"Callahan, right?" Amelia asked.

"That's right."

"No disrespect. I admire your work. But things have changed in the last few years. I have access to tools that you didn't. I'll be able to give the DA's office everything they need."

"But you operate outside the law?"

Adam ground his teeth together. He understood that they had to think about the big picture. Evie was his priority, but he wanted to see Anatoly's operation blown apart, as much as Cal did. He just wished that they could get back to the urgent part of what Amelia had told them. The part about Anatoly flying out here – to Summer Lake.

"All you need to know is that the authorities in Chicago will be able to use whatever information I provide them with – legally. It'll stand up in court. Now, if we're done with that?"

"We're done," said Cal. He didn't look happy about it, but he turned to Adam and nodded.

Adam looked around the room. He hated speaking to disembodied voices; he wished Amelia were on a video call so that he could get a better feel for who she was – how good she was – but that wasn't an option. Apparently, that was one of her rules of engagement; no one got to see her, no one could identify her.

"Where is he right now?" Adam asked.

Amelia sighed. "That I can't tell you, not until either he or one of his men mentions it. I told you, they're using the same kind of technology that Dan put on Evie's phone. They're bouncing the signal around constantly. I can't locate them that way – not quickly enough, anyway. What I have is direct access to everything they say or send. The program I sent to Dmitriev's phone installed itself as soon as he clicked on the link in the email. I can now listen in on every call and ..." Her voice drifted away, and Adam scowled as he waited for her to continue. "No, I was just checking, and I don't yet, but soon, I'll have access to his camera, too. I'll be able to look out through it. That's rarely as useful as it sounds, mostly I get to the see the inside of pockets, or a ceiling if the phone's placed on a desk but ... sorry."

Adam was glad that she stopped spouting unnecessary details. He needed her to tell him ...

"Wait!"

He glanced at Davin and then around at the others. Cal, Manny, and Ryan were all scowling as they listened. Dan looked puzzled. Brayden and Donovan were looking at each other wide eyed. Davin stood beside Adam, staring out the window. They all waited for the rustling on Amelia's end of the line to stop.

When it did, two male voices filled the room. Adam cursed when he realized that they were speaking Russian.

Then Amelia spoke again. "That's Anatoly, he's asking Dmitriev how long until they reach the ... cabin. Are there cabins there?"

"Yes." Adam's heart was thundering in his chest. He wanted to run for the door, for his truck. Wanted to haul ass to the cabin and ...

"Oh, my God!" Amelia breathed over the voices of the two men, who were still speaking. "Dmitriev just said that they're ten minutes out and that by the time they get there, Sergei will be back with the woman. He's gone to get her."

Adam pulled his keys and phone out of his pocket as he ran for his truck. Davin snatched his keys from his hand as he passed. "I'm driving; you get Dalton on the phone."

"We're behind you, I'll get Amelia on the line and keep you updated," he heard Manny call in the moment before he pulled the passenger door shut and the tires of his truck screeched as Davin pulled out of the lot.

Chapter Twenty

Evie opened her eyes but had to close them again against the bright sunlight. Why was the sun so high in the sky? She must have drifted back to sleep after Adam left but she was surprised that it had gotten so late. Her mind went to their conversation before he went out. He wanted to get married! She did, too. She might have felt like she didn't know much of anything over the last few months, but she knew that she loved Adam. And she knew how to be a wife; she'd been a good one to Tom and she would be to Adam, too. It felt right. She smiled but then winced. That didn't feel right – it hurt! The whole side of her face and her head hurt, too, now that she thought about it. She brought her hand up to touch her cheek, but her hand wouldn't come.

She started to panic. Her hands were tied behind her back. She struggled to move, but her feet were bound together, too. That was when it all came flooding back.

She and Taryn had been sitting out on the patio talking over their coffee. Dalton had come out to see if they wanted refills, and Taryn had snapped at him, telling him to go inside and give them some privacy. Dalton was much like the other guys from what Evie had seen of him – he was serious, professional, a bit gruff. Except when it came to Taryn. She brought out the worst in him, just as he did with her.

Instead of going inside, he'd said that he was supposed to be keeping an eye on them and had stood just outside the kitchen door, arms folded across his chest as he glowered at Taryn.

Of course, Taryn refused to be outdone, so she'd taken Evie's arm and led her away. They'd gone to sit on the bench on the dock. After a while, Evie heard Dalton's phone ring and he'd gone inside. Taryn had laughed, saying that she'd won that battle, but then her expression changed. A man had emerged from the water, grabbed Taryn, and threw her in.

Evie didn't have time to process what was happening before he grabbed her, too. She braced herself, expecting him to throw her into the lake. She'd been so focused on gulping in a big breath of air before she hit the water, that it had been easy for him. He brought a cloth up to her face, and even though she struggled to push it away, her vision was already fading. She breathed in whatever was on the cloth and everything had faded.

She squeezed her eyes shut as her mind searched for more, but that was all she could remember.

Her heart and head were pounding now. What had happened to Taryn? It didn't make sense that the man had just thrown her into the water. Why hadn't he …? But the answer hit her all too clearly. He'd gotten Taryn out of the way. He hadn't needed to drug her or take her – because he wasn't there for her. He was there for Evie.

And now Evie was here – wherever here was. Her whole body started to tremble. One of Anatoly's men had come for her. He'd taken her. Her only hope was that he now had to get her to Chicago – and she was not going to make that easy for him.

She looked around wildly. How long had she been unconscious? Where was she? She was lying on a bed in what seemed to be a cabin. Not a rustic cabin, more like a vacation home. Looking out through the window, she knew she was still in Summer Lake. She couldn't see much, but she could see pine trees and mountains in the distance.

A warm hope spread through her chest. If she was still in Summer Lake, Adam would find her. She knew he would. But the warmth turned to ice and slid down her spine. He'd find her; but if anything happened to him, she'd wish that he hadn't.

~ ~ ~

Adam's phone rang in his hand before he had the chance to dial Dalton's number. When Dalton's name came up on the display, Adam's breath caught in his lungs. He wanted with every fiber of his being to hear Dalton tell him that someone had been to the house, someone had tried to take Evie, but he'd stopped them.

He knew that wasn't the case the second he answered the call. "Fuck, Adam. I'm sorry. They got her."

"How?" he roared.

Davin glanced at him and hit the button so that Dalton's next words filled the cab of the truck.

"In a boat. Evie and Taryn were sitting on the dock – and that's my fault. I took a call and …"

"Let me talk to him."

Adam closed his eyes when he heard Taryn's voice. They hadn't taken her. Just Evie.

"Adam! I'm so damned sorry. It's all my fault. I made her go down to the dock with me. We were sitting on the bench and this guy just launched himself up out of the water. He grabbed me and threw me in. Then he grabbed Evie and he put something over her face – chloroform maybe? Whatever it was, he held a cloth to her face, and she passed out. I tried to get out of the water, to get to them. But he pulled a dingy out from under the dock. I had no idea it was there. He must have been there waiting the whole time. He pulled it out, threw her in, started the engine, and took off."

Adam screwed his eyes tight shut. He couldn't allow himself to think about Evie, not about what she was going through and what she would go through if he didn't get to her fast. He blew out a big breath then sucked another one in to clear his mind. When he spoke again, his voice was calm, and his mind was clear. He was back in the zone. He thought he'd left it behind after he left the unit. But he needed it one more time.

"How long ago, and which direction did the boat go?"

"Are … are you okay?" Taryn was no doubt surprised by the change in his voice.

Dalton wasn't. "Three minutes tops," he answered. "I ran down to the dock as soon as I heard the motor kick up. I couldn't get a shot. Sorry. I couldn't see where he went past the headland, but he was headed in the direction of the resort."

"Thanks."

"You going to the cabin?" Dalton asked.

"Yes."

"I'll meet you there."

"No. Meet me in the square. We're going to have to go in quietly. Anatoly's on his way to the cabin now."

"Shit," Dalton muttered.

"Anatoly's here?" Taryn gasped.

Adam didn't bother to answer. "Park in the square by The Boathouse and we'll meet you around the back by the dumpsters. Cal, Manny, and Ryan are behind me; we need to coordinate before we go in."

"Copy that. Hate to ask you this, but are we waiting until Anatoly's there before we go in?"

Adam hissed out his anger. "Yes. But only because he'll probably be there by the time we arrive."

"See you there."

~ ~ ~

Evie had managed to sit herself up, but she couldn't manage to work her hands or her feet free. She froze when she heard a door open and close. Then, she heard voices; it sounded like three men. She didn't know what they were saying because they were speaking in Russian.

She let out a whimper when she recognized one of the voices. That was Anatoly. She knew it. She'd never be able to forget his voice. It had etched itself into her mind the night she and Glenn had gone to his house. She'd heard it in her nightmares ever since she left Chicago. She looked around the room, searching for somewhere to hide. There was no point, and she knew it, but she was dreading the moment the door would open and she'd see that man again.

Her whole body shook as she watched the doorknob turn. Here it came …

It wasn't Anatoly who stood there but another man, one she hadn't seen before. He wasn't the one who'd thrown Taryn into the water.

The man smiled, which made Evie's blood run cold.

"It's good to see you, finally."

She just stared at him. How could he talk like she was someone he'd just been introduced to at a social gathering?

"You've made my life difficult, Evelyn. I intend to do the same to you."

It took her a moment to understand. He was still smiling, and his tone didn't match his words. But she started to shake even harder when his meaning got through.

"What do you mean?"

"I mean," the smile evaporated, and he glared at her with cold, hard eyes, "that I've had to waste time and manpower hunting you down, bitch. If you'd come when Anatoly asked you, you would have enjoyed a few months of being treated as his lady — before you died. But no, you made my life difficult. You hurt Anatoly's feelings when you rejected him. Now, you will not enjoy the next few nights. Then you'll die anyway."

Evie just stared at him. She wasn't going to give him the satisfaction of seeing how scared she was. He'd enjoy it — she could see it in his eyes.

His eyes narrowed and he came a step closer. "You're not going to cry and beg me for your life?"

She shook her head slowly. She wasn't. Even if Adam couldn't get to her in time, even if she was going to die, she'd do it with as much dignity as she could.

To her surprise, he laughed. "You might beg me for your death before we're finished. Anatoly came all this way for you. I think he deserves some alone time with you."

He came into the room, and she cowered back as he ran his hand over her hair. "Usually, I let the men take care of business once Anatoly is done. You … I think I'll take care of you myself."

"Dmitriev?"

The man stepped away from her quickly. Anatoly's voice scared him too, it seemed.

Evie wanted to scream when Anatoly appeared in the doorway. He'd played the role of a charming businessman the first time she met him. But there was no trace of that character now. He glared at Dmitriev, and then at her. "We have to move."

"But you wanted …"

"Yes. I wanted!" He glared at Evie. "I wanted this one so badly that I got stubborn." When he met her gaze, his eyes were cold. "Don't flatter yourself. I didn't go to all this trouble for you. I did it for me. I did it because I am a man of my word. I said I'd have you. So I will."

He turned back to Dmitriev. "But not here, not now. We'll take her back."

"But you wanted to leave her body here afterward."

"I did. But Andrei sent a message. We need to get back." He glared at Evie again. "And we need to get away from here."

"I'll bring her." Dmitriev's fingers dug into Evie's arm as he pulled her to her feet.

Anatoly grabbed her other arm, pulling her toward him. "You go out first. I'll bring her."

Dmitriev's eyes narrowed. He looked from Anatoly to Evie and back again, but didn't say anything as he headed for the door.

Evie cowered when Anatoly wrapped his arm around her. Finally coming to her senses, she screamed and tried to pull away from him. If they were leaving, she'd only have a few moments before they put her in a vehicle. She had to make as much noise and disturbance as she could and hope to get someone's attention.

Anatoly easily pulled her back to him, and her head jerked back when he hit her. "Be quiet."

When they left the bedroom, Dmitriev nodded at another man – he was the one from the dock. "Go and bring the car. We're leaving."

"I thought –"

"Don't question me, Sergei. Go."

Evie watched him get into the blue Cadillac and pull it closer to the cabin. He couldn't come much closer though. They'd still have to walk down the path to get to the car. Evie's heart felt as though it was trying to beat right out of her chest; she was terrified. But she had to start making noise as soon as they were outside. She didn't know how close the other cabins were, but she had to try.

Once they were down the porch steps, she drew in a big breath and tried to wrench her arm away from Anatoly.

The scream came out louder since his fingers bit into her arm, and he dragged her forward. His other hand flew through the air, and Evie saw stars. She heard the impact of his hand against her cheek, but she heard other noises, as well. Two loud bangs that could only be gunfire.

Anatoly moved behind her and wrapped his arms around her, pulling her back against his chest. By the time she'd recovered enough to look around, Dmitriev and Sergei were both lying on the ground.

She couldn't see anyone else, though. She didn't get it. Dmitriev and Sergei had been shot. She'd heard it, but there was no one else in sight.

She closed her eyes when she felt cold steel press against the side of her head.

Anatoly laughed as he held her tighter. "She's coming with me," he shouted. "One way or another. You let me drive away with her, I'll turn her loose later. You shoot me, I'll take her down with me."

Evie closed her eyes. With her feet and hands bound, there wasn't much she could do. She wanted to help. She knew Adam was out there. In the trees, or where, she didn't know. But he was here somewhere. She wished she could get herself away from Anatoly so that Adam or one his friends could shoot him. But she knew that he wouldn't risk what Anatoly was threatening – if they tried to shoot him, he'd shoot her.

Still, she had to try. "Shoot him!" she shouted.

Anatoly's arm tightened so hard around her chest that it felt as though her ribs cracked. "Shut up!" he screamed at her.

"Put the gun down." That was Manny's voice.

"Back off!" Anatoly returned. "I'm going to walk her to the car."

"He doesn't have the keys!" Evie shouted. She wasn't sure how that information might be useful, but she'd be damned if she'd just stand here and shake while she waited to die.

"He doesn't need them, Evie. He's not going anywhere." That was Ryan's voice.

The gang was here, then, but the voice she needed to hear was Adam's.

She swallowed, hard, as Anatoly started shuffling her toward the car. She wanted to hear Adam's voice because she loved him. Because she believed that he'd be able to get her out of this – alive. But if she was going to die, she wanted to hear his voice, see his handsome face one last time.

~ ~ ~

Adam held two fingers up and Davin stopped beside him. His mind was clear, he had the target in sight. This was going as smoothly as any mission he'd been on – it had to; it was the most important mission of his life. He pushed that thought away. This wasn't the time for emotions to creep in. This was the time for quiet professionalism.

When they'd met behind The Boathouse, they'd agreed that Cal, Manny, and Ryan would approach the cabin from the front, while Adam, Davin, and Dalton came in from behind. They'd rounded the sides of the building silently while Anatoly was focused on his, now deceased, companions.

Adam's gut roiled when he saw Anatoly's gun pressed into Evie's temple. He was in the perfect position to take the shot that would take the bastard down. But he couldn't risk it. He couldn't guarantee that Anatoly's finger wouldn't squeeze the trigger as a bullet went through his brain. It wasn't a risk Adam was prepared to take. He knew that the others wouldn't either.

He peered at the trees beyond the parking area, knowing that Cal, Manny, and Ryan were out there, but unable to see them. He needed them to keep talking. Needed them to keep Anatoly's attention on them so that he could make his move.

Manny must have heard his silent plea. He shouted, "Let her go, Petrov. We all know that if you let her go now, and we take you in, your lawyers will get you off. But if you harm her, there's only one way this ends."

Adam winced. He couldn't think about Evie being harmed. He gritted his teeth when he saw Anatoly's arm tighten around her. He'd had enough trouble seeing Russ, his friend, put his arms around her in a friendly hug. He hadn't even liked it when Davin had hugged her. There was no way he could stand to see what was happening before him. He knew the move he had to make. He glanced at Davin; Davin nodded back. They'd pulled this move off before, they could do it again.

As soon as he moved forward, Manny started shouting again. Adam didn't even process what he was saying. It didn't matter. All he was doing was making noise to keep Anatoly's attention focused on the trees in front of him – and away from what was happening behind him.

What was happening behind him was that Adam was getting closer and closer, Davin moving in sync with him to his right.

When he couldn't wait any longer, he nodded, Davin nodded back, and they rushed.

~ ~ ~

Anatoly's arm jerked forward. The cold metal was no longer pressing into Evie's temple. His other arm tightened around her, and then loosened. He fell backward, and she tried to keep her balance, but she fell, too. No sooner had she landed on top of him than Adam was there, hauling her away.

He picked her up and then he was running toward the trees, carrying her as though she was a bride, and he was a groom desperately seeking a threshold he could step over. She closed her eyes. Maybe Anatoly had shot her? Maybe she was dead, and this was her version of crossing the rainbow bridge. There was no bright light to walk toward, just Adam picking her up and carrying her away.

When they reached the trees, he stopped. He let go of her legs and let her stand, but he kept his arms wrapped tightly around her as he pressed his forehead to hers and looked deep into her eyes.

"Are you okay? Are you hurt?"

She shook her head as she slowly took inventory. Her ribs ached. Her head ached. She felt as though the side of her face was swelling, maybe her eye as well – she'd probably end up with a black eye and a split lip, but she wasn't hurt in a bad way. Anatoly no longer had hold of her. He was … she didn't know where. She didn't know what had happened to him. All she needed to know was that Adam was right there in front of her.

"I'm okay," she breathed. "I knew you'd come."

He sucked in a deep breath and closed his eyes. When he opened them again, he looked deep into hers.

"Are you okay?"

He pressed a kiss to her lips. "I am now."

"Clear!"

She looked up. That was Davin shouting.

"He had to make sure that there wasn't anyone else still inside the cabin," Adam explained.

"I only saw the three of them. Sergei, the one who grabbed me. Dmitriev, who seemed to be the second-in-command, and Anatoly." She tried to turn to look back at the cabin. "What happened to him?"

Adam made her face him, not letting her see. "He's gone, Evie. They're all gone. You don't ever have to worry about him again."

"Gone?" She didn't understand. "Someone shot Dmitriev and Sergei. I know that. I saw them." She shuddered at the realization that the two men were most likely dead.

Adam held her tighter.

"But Anatoly. There were no shots. His arm just moved away and then … then he fell down." She looked up into Adam's eyes, needing to know. "What happened to him, Adam?"

His jaw clenched as his eyes searched her face. "I did."

"You did what?"

"I happened to him."

"I don't understand."

"You don't need to." He turned when Davin called out from closer this time.

"Is Evie okay? It's clear back there, you can bring her out."

"Yeah."

Davin came closer and gave her a reassuring smile before he pulled a set of keys out of his pocket. She watched as he flipped open a penknife on his keychain. Then he carefully and gently slit the zip ties that bound her wrists and ankles together.

"There you go."

"Thank you." She rubbed her hands together and rolled her shoulders, trying to get some feeling back into them.

"Ready to go home?" Adam asked.

"Yes, please."

He smiled and picked her up again.

"I can walk. I'm okay."

Davin grinned at her. "You might as well relax and enjoy the ride. I think carrying you is as much about making him feel better as it is about you not having to walk."

Adam's big, brown eyes shone as they looked down into hers, and he smiled. "He's right."

She reached her arms up around his neck and hung on. She wasn't going to argue with that.

Chapter Twenty-One

Adam leaned back against the headboard, and Evie leaned back against him. She turned to look at him when he chuckled.

"What are you laughing about?"

"It just struck me as funny that even though we have a fully furnished house, we're still sitting on the bed to talk."

She relaxed back against him as she said, "It seems to have become our tradition."

"I love that – that we already have a tradition. I want us to create lots of them."

"I do, too."

His smile faded. "Do you still want to create them in this house?"

She was bearing up well after everything she'd gone through the day before. She'd been taken, and drugged, tied up, and slapped around, held at gunpoint, and seen two men shot in front of her. Anatoly had died while he had hold of her – Adam wasn't sure if she'd even realized that part yet, and he didn't look forward to telling her about it. Maybe she wouldn't ask, and that'd be fine with him.

Yesterday morning, she'd said that she wanted to buy this house, but he didn't know if she'd still feel that way, considering it was where she'd been taken from. He'd understand if she didn't feel safe here anymore.

"I do. If you do. I know Sergei grabbed me down on the dock right here, but …" She was quiet for a moment before she continued. "If that bothers me, it bothers me for Taryn, not for myself. The scariest thing was seeing her thrown into the water. I didn't know much of anything after that."

Adam clenched his jaw. He couldn't let himself think about Sergei taking her. He calmed his mind before he spoke again. "She doesn't seem traumatized by what happened. She's more upset that she feels like it was her fault." He couldn't allow himself to think about that either.

Taryn felt guilty. Dalton felt guilty. The two women should never have been down on the dock. But if anyone was to blame, he was. He should have made clear from the outset that Evie shouldn't go down to the dock. He knew if he'd told her that she wouldn't have gone – no matter what stupid game Taryn and Dalton were playing.

Evie leaned her head back so that she could look into his eyes. "You don't blame her do you – or Dalton? I don't."

"I don't."

"Good. Are they okay down there?"

"Yeah. They're staying out of each other's way. They're not blaming each other either, which is good."

"It is. It was just one of those things, Adam."

"It was and –"

A knock on the door interrupted him. He wasn't sure that he wanted to face anyone. He just wanted Evie to himself right now. They'd spent a couple of hours with the sheriff, Don, and his deputy, Colt. The guys had all been over here for that and for their own debrief afterward. The whole thing was wrapped up. Now, he just wanted to be with Evie, to hold her and talk to her, and quietly give thanks that she was still here.

"It's only me," called Davin.

Evie smiled. "Come in."

He came in and closed the door behind him, smiling at them as he leaned back against it. "Sorry, I hate to disturb you guys. I just wanted to let you know that I'm heading out. Alec's been on his own with Clay and Marianne for too long. He's doing great," he assured Adam before he could ask. "But he needs a break. And you guys don't need me here anymore."

"Thanks, brother." There weren't enough words for Adam to express his gratitude, but he didn't need them anyway. Davin knew.

"Yes, thank you, Davin." Evie held her arms out to him. "Can I give you a hug before you go? And would it be okay if I call you brother, too? I always wanted a brother, and ..."

Adam had to swallow the emotions that burned in his throat as Davin approached the bed.

He leaned in and gave Evie a hug. "It'd be an honor."

"Do you mind if I ask you something before you go?"

"Anything."

"I know I've thanked you a dozen times for saving me. I didn't register it at the time, but you were the one who pushed Anatoly's arm forward so that he couldn't shoot me, weren't you?"

Davin glanced at Adam before he nodded. "It was a team effort."

Adam felt her suck in a deep breath before she pushed on. "Tell me what happened to him? I know he's dead but ... how? I need to know."

Davin held Adam's gaze, waiting for him to speak. He'd hoped that she wouldn't ask, that she wouldn't have to know. But if she needed it ...

"Are you sure you want to know, Evie?" he asked.

She looked back at him. "I don't think I want to, but I need to. It's been going around and around in my head. I couldn't get away from him. I could feel the gun pressing into my temple ..." She shuddered. "It felt so cold. But then his arm flew forward, and then he fell backward, and then you were pulling me up and ..." Her words trailed away. "You?"

Adam swallowed. It wasn't the first time he'd taken a life. There had been plenty over the course of his career. He didn't feel even the tiniest hint of remorse over Anatoly. He'd do it again in a heartbeat. But he didn't know what Evie would think. Would it change how she felt – would she see him as a killer? He sucked in a deep breath, feeling as though his next words were about to decide his fate. "Yes, Evie. It was me."

Her eyes grew wide. "How? There were no shots. You didn't have a weapon – did you?"

He shrugged. She didn't need to hear the details. He'd rather she never knew.

She was still staring at him. "Did you snap his neck – like they do in the movies?"

He stared back at her. That was another thing that Hollywood so often got wrong. They made it look easy to twist a victim's head to the side. They used the sound effect of snapping a stick of celery to complete the illusion, and most people never questioned the plausibility – most people never needed to.

Davin cleared his throat. "Evie?"

She turned to look at him, her eyes still wide.

His smile was gentle as he touched her arm. "As your newly appointed brother, I'm going to give you some advice – forget about it. Don't let your mind go there. All you need to know is that Adam saved you. Anatoly's gone, and you don't have to worry about him anymore."

She held Davin's gaze for a long moment before she looked back at Adam. Then she nodded. "You're right. I don't want to know. I know the important stuff. He's gone. It's over. And you guys gave me my life back."

Adam felt the tension leave his shoulders and he shot Davin a grateful smile.

"I'm glad the two of you are such a good team."

He tightened his arm around her. He was, too.

~ ~ ~

Evie hugged Taryn tighter. "Are you sure you don't want to wait?"

Taryn let out a short laugh. "I'm positive. I have to go and deal with the insurance company and the mess that was the restaurant. I'm going to put my house on the market and …"

Evie nodded. She knew that Taryn had a lot to deal with. But she also knew that wasn't the reason she was in such a hurry to leave. She felt guilty. And she had no need to. Evie had known even as they walked down to the dock that it would be safer to stay close to the house.

She squeezed Taryn's arm. "Why don't you wait a while? Hang around here, get used to Summer Lake. We'll go to Giuseppe's, and I'll introduce you to Tino."

Taryn shook her head. "I need to go, Evie. I …" She glanced at Adam, who was standing in the dining room with Cal and Dalton. Cal had given them a couple of days – everyone had – to just relax at home without intrusions. Even Taryn and Dalton had taken rooms at the resort. Evie felt bad about that, but she'd still been grateful to be alone with Adam. "I want to give you and Adam time to decide if you even want me around after … after what happened."

Evie scowled. "It wasn't your fault!"

Taryn shrugged. "You keep saying that. I'm trying to believe it. But I'm not sure that Adam does. He's your future, Evie. He's good for you. I'm not going to screw it up for you. If he doesn't want me –"

"He does! What will screw my future up is if my best friend doesn't move out here with me like she said she would. Seriously, Taryn. You're a huge part of why I haven't second-guessed myself about going back to Chicago. This is fast, and it might seem crazy to move across the country for a man. But it doesn't feel crazy. It feels right. But it won't be right if you're not coming with me."

Taryn's gaze dropped to the floor. "I want to come. I can't imagine not having you in my life every day. The whole time you were on the run I was worried sick about you, of course, but I missed you so much. I just …" She glanced at Adam again. "I don't want to mess things up for you. Adam must –"

"Adam?"

He came straight over when Evie called him and wrapped his arm around her shoulders.

"Would you please tell Taryn that I need her to come back?"

He frowned. "You are coming back, right? Just as soon as you deal with the restaurant and put your house up for sale?"

Taryn blew out a sigh. "I don't want …"

Evie loved Adam even more when he let go of her and wrapped Taryn in a hug. "I thought we talked about this? I told you. I don't blame you. We're good." He stepped back. "But we won't be good if you don't get your ass back here in a hurry. You know that what I want most in life now is to make Evie happy. She's not going to be happy if you're not here. I need you to help me out." He raised his eyebrows and waited.

Evie was relieved when Taryn finally smiled. "Okay. If you're sure. I do want to be here. I just don't want …"

Adam waved a hand at her. "We've talked it to death. Get over it."

Taryn smiled through pursed lips, and Evie knew that her friend was going to be okay when she put her hands on her hips and said, "If I'm going to move up here, you'd better start talking to me a bit nicer than that."

Adam laughed. "There she is, that's the Taryn I've come to know and love. Now stop moping and get your stuff together. Dalton's almost ready to go."

Taryn looked into the dining room, where Dalton was shaking hands with Cal. She blew out a sigh. "He might not make it to Chicago. I might strangle him before we get there."

Evie had to laugh. That was the first time she'd joked about Dalton since everything had happened.

Adam shot Evie a mischievous smile before he told Taryn, "You're not allowed to strangle him on the way there or on the way back. Cal needs him."

Taryn gasped. "What? What are you talking about?"

"I thought he would have told you. Dan asked him if he wanted to join the team, and he said yes."

Taryn's eyes flashed, and Evie didn't miss the smile that crossed her face before she put her hands on her hips and pursed her lips.

"Damn! I can see why you made me agree to come back before you told me about that!"

Evie laughed. "Yeah, because you hate the idea of spending more time with him, don't you?"

Taryn shrugged and didn't manage to hide her smile this time. "I guess he's okay, really."

"I'll see you guys," Cal called before letting himself out.

Dalton came to join them where they were standing in the kitchen. "How long do you need before we can hit the road?" he asked Taryn.

"I think I'm good." She leaned in and gave Evie another hug. Then she scowled at Dalton. "And the sooner we get on the road, the sooner you can start explaining to me why in the hell you think it's a good idea to take a job here."

Dalton rolled his eyes and shook Adam's hand before leaning in to kiss Evie's cheek. "I'll see you guys soon."

Evie reached up to give him a hug, but she only managed to do it with one arm. Adam wouldn't let go of her other hand. "Thank you."

He stepped back and nodded. "I'm sorry. I …"

She shook her head, but Adam spoke before she could. "I've told you. It worked out for the best. If they hadn't been able to take Evie in a surprise attack, who knows what they would have been prepared to do to get her?"

Evie shuddered. Adam was right. She was glad that she'd been dragged off in a boat if it meant that Anatoly's men hadn't come in shooting. Her friends could have been injured or worse if she'd been taken by force.

Dalton nodded. She wasn't sure that he felt any less guilty, but she hoped so.

After they'd gone out to wave Taryn and Dalton off, Adam took her hand and led her back inside. Once he closed the door, he closed his arms around her and rested his chin on top of her head. She loved the way he did that.

"So, what do you think, sweetheart? Is it time for me to call Austin and make an offer on this house?"

She leaned back so that she could see up into his eyes. "I do, as long as it's us making the offer and not just you."

He smiled his lopsided smile and nodded. "It is. From now on, it's us and not just me in everything."

She rolled up on her toes to press a kiss to his lips but winced when pain seared through her ribs.

"Are you okay? How bad does it still hurt?"

She smiled. "I'm fine. It doesn't hurt a bit."

He raised his eyebrows, and she chuckled. "It doesn't! I know you've been avoiding making love to me because you don't want to hurt me. Well, I'm telling you that whatever physical pain I'm in doesn't hurt nearly as much as thinking that you don't want −" She didn't get to finish. Adam had lifted her off her feet and was already on his way up the stairs.

~ ~ ~

A few hours later, Adam lay watching Evie sleep. It was finally settling in his chest that the danger was past − behind them. Ever since he'd met her, Evie had been scared − afraid for her life, and with good reason. He stroked her hair, hoping that she'd relax into being the woman he'd only seen glimpses of. He wanted to give her a life that she could relax into. He wanted to share his friends and his town with her. She'd been here for a while, but she'd been so busy hiding that she hadn't been able to make friends or have much of a life. Of course, she'd had her job at the gym, but she needed more than that.

He smiled to himself. He was going to make sure that she got everything she needed. He knew he couldn't *give* her everything; she didn't need him for that. She had to do it for herself, but he'd be there at her back, smoothing the way for her as much as he could, as much as she'd let him. He couldn't wait.

There was so much about life with her that he couldn't wait to get started on. He wanted to talk to Austin about buying this house. Part of him still wanted to buy it *for* her, and he could. But that was something he was going to have to learn. He was used to having Davin as his teammate, but that wasn't something he'd shared with a woman before. With Evie, he'd learn.

If she wanted them to buy the house together, that's what they'd do. And soon, just as soon as he could make it happen, he was going to make her his wife. He hadn't thought he wanted a wife – hadn't thought he was cut out for marriage. But he'd been wrong. He stared out of the bedroom window at the moonlight reflecting off the lake and sent a silent thank you to Tom. He knew that if the guy were still alive, Evie would never have come into his life. He was sad for them that Tom had passed. But he'd loved her well, that was clear in the way she talked about him, and in the fact that she wasn't afraid to love again. Tom had wanted her to have a good life after him, and lying there in the darkness, Adam silently promised him that he'd do everything he could to care for her and make her happy.

Chapter Twenty-Two

Three weeks later

Evie looked up from her computer at the front desk and smiled when she saw Manny and Ryan coming into the gym.

Manny slapped the back of Ryan's head as they came through the door. "Would you quit with the old man shit?"

She had to laugh. Those two were always fighting and bickering.

"Hey, Evie!" Ryan greeted her. "Are you all ready for the big weekend?"

She frowned. Big weekend? Oh, he must mean because Taryn was coming back, though how he knew that … well, of course, he'd know that because Dalton was coming, too.

Manny slapped the back of Ryan's head again, harder this time.

She had to laugh. "I am. I'm excited to get Taryn back here. I imagine you guys are looking forward to having Dalton on your team, too. I was talking to Cal when he was in this morning, and he said that you guys are busy now that you're officially open for business."

"We are," said Manny. "Busy and looking forward to having Dalton on board. How about you, though? Nina wanted me to ask you if you're going to lunch with all the ladies tomorrow."

"Oh, I forgot about that. I … I'd like to, but I'll have to check with Taryn. Would you tell Nina I'll call her?"

"Sure thing."

She watched the two of them head to the locker room to get changed. Russ came out of the back office a few minutes later. He greeted her with a distracted nod as he checked his watch.

"Everything okay?" she asked.

"Yeah. Sorry, Evie. I'm just expecting Ria. Have you heard from her?"

Evie laughed. "Yes, and I was going to give you the message as soon as you rejoined the planet. She called and asked me to tell you that she's not going to make it over here. You should go straight home."

He frowned. "Did she say why?"

"Yes. She didn't want to disturb you because she knew you were busy in the office. And she's not going to make it over here because she's busy getting the spare room ready for Alyssa."

Russ shook his head but couldn't hide his smile. "She won't have it, but Alyssa's not going to stay with us. She booked a room at the resort."

Evie laughed. "I know that, you know that, but Ria's feeling bad that she'd already offered the spare room to Bentley. Of course, Bentley said he'll stay at the resort and let Alyssa have the spare room. So, Ria's making up a bed for the weekend for nothing."

Russ chuckled. "Yeah. I suppose I should be grateful that they're being so considerate and each saying the other can have the guest room. It beats them fighting over who gets it." His smile faded. "But I guess they'd have to be real brother and sister before they were fighting."

"I'm sure they'll feel like family soon enough," Evie reassured him. She loved that his daughter and Ria's son were both going to be in town this weekend. She knew that he was eager for his daughter and Ria's kids to get to know each other. From what Ria had told her, her daughters were eager to meet Alyssa. She hadn't said much about her son, Bentley, though. It must be strange to all of a sudden have a stepsibling in your thirties.

"Anyway." Russ smiled at her. "I'm sure my weekend will work out fine. The kids will take care of themselves tomorrow night." His smile grew bigger. "While we're at Giuseppe's with you guys."

Evie nodded. She didn't get why everyone was making such a big deal about tomorrow night. She loved that all her friends thought that Taryn's return — and Dalton's — was such a noteworthy occasion, but she wasn't sure why.

"Yeah. I hope I get to meet the kids over the weekend."

"I'm sure you will." He checked his watch again. "Do you want to get going?"

"I will, if you don't mind." She chuckled. "It's weird. I'd gotten so used to waiting for Adam to come to get me that I forget I can just take myself now that I have my car back."

Russ laughed. "I'm glad he got it back for you, but it wouldn't surprise me if he's back to bringing you himself soon."

Evie laughed with him. "I know! He thinks I don't realize that he drives past at least four times a day."

"Yeah. Don't give him a hard time, though. He's just checking on you. I imagine it'll be a while before he can relax and accept that you're safe."

"I know. I wouldn't give him a hard time. I love it."

"And how long do we get to keep you here? I love having you, but I thought you were going to tell me you weren't coming back to work."

She blew out a sigh. "I'll give you my notice at some point. I know you don't need me desperately. And I don't need you to pay me anymore."

Russ started to protest, but she held her hand up to stop him. "I don't, really. Now that I'm not scared to access my accounts anymore, I don't need to work if I don't want to. I'm still coming into work because I want to. I want to help you out, and I … well, I enjoy being here."

Russ smiled at her. "I enjoy having you here. You can do whatever suits you, as far as I'm concerned."

"Thanks."

"And would I be right to guess that once your gyms sell, you won't have to work anywhere ever again if you don't want to?"

"Yeah. And there's someone who's interested in buying. I talked to one of Tom's old friends and apparently, this guy has been waiting and hoping that I might decide to sell someday."

"You happy about that?"

"I am. Taryn said that selling the gyms – the money it'll give me – is like Tom taking care of me one last time. Helping set me up for the next chapter of my life."

Russ smiled. "I like that. Of course, I didn't know Tom, but I believe that he'd like Adam. He'd … approve."

Evie had to swallow before she could answer. "I believe that, too." She sniffed. "Anyway, I'm going to go now before I cry."

"Shit. I'm sorry, I …"

She smiled as she grabbed her purse. "Happy tears, Russ. It's okay."

"Ah." He chuckled. "Okay. Alyssa tried to teach me about those."

Evie laughed as she headed for the door. "I'm sure that between Alyssa and Ria, you're familiar with them by now."

He laughed with her. "Call me on my bullshit, why don't you?!"

As she walked toward her car ready to head home, Evie inhaled deeply. She felt good. Not only was she free and out of hiding, she was happy – happy with her new life, her new friends, and most of all with her new man. Life was good.

~ ~ ~

Adam cut the engine on his truck and sat there for a moment, smiling at the house. He loved this place. He loved that Evie was going to enjoy herself redecorating it. He loved anything that made her happy.

He wiped his hands on his jeans. He was hoping that tonight he was going to make her happy. In fact, he knew he was. They'd talked about it a few times since everything had gone down with Anatoly. He knew that some men like to propose out of the blue, but he hadn't felt good about that. He'd needed to know that it was what she wanted. She'd been married to a good man for a long time. He would have understood if she didn't want to get married again. He would have understood, but it would have made him sad. He smiled. But she did want to. She'd told him that.

What he hadn't told her was that although they'd talked about it as something they'd like to do at some point, he couldn't wait. He'd had to wait until Taryn came back. Evie didn't have any blood family left, but Taryn was as good as family. He'd needed her to be here for Evie when he proposed.

Now, she was back. She and Dalton had rolled into town this morning. Evie had spent the day getting her friend settled into the house that she'd rented, while Adam had shown Dalton around his house. He'd been surprised when Dalton had asked about it. He'd imagined that he'd keep working on the place when he could and then sell it when it was finished. He had no need for it now that he and Evie had this place. But Dalton needed a place to live, and he'd said that he'd be happy

– more than happy – to have a project to work on. Adam was letting him stay there rent free, and in return he was going to finish the remodeling.

He reached for the door handle. He didn't need to be sitting out here in his truck. He needed to get his ass into the house and see Evie. Then, they needed to get over to Giuseppe's to meet up with all their friends. The excuse was that everyone was going to be there to welcome Taryn and Dalton back to town. The reality was that Adam had asked them all to come tonight because he wanted Evie to be surrounded by people who cared about her when he asked her to marry him.

She'd been in town for a while now, but it was only over the last few weeks that she'd been able to live a normal life. He wanted her to feel like it was a good life. A life in which she had friends and was a part of the community.

He let himself into the house and called her name when he didn't find her in the kitchen.

"Up here!"

He took the stairs two at a time on his way up. He pushed the bedroom door open and stopped dead when he saw her standing there naked but for a towel wrapped around her.

He prowled across the room and closed his arms around her, dropping his head to lick the drops of water from her shoulders.

She laughed, and he loved the way her body shook in his arms. It was a far cry from the sobs that had wracked her that first night he'd gone to see her at his house and Anatoly had called her.

"Hello, yourself," she said.

"Oh. Yeah. Hi." He nibbled her shoulder before trailing his nose up her neck until his lips were under her ear. "I love you, Evie."

"Aww, Adam. I love you, too."

He pressed a kiss to her lips. "It's not just words, you know."

She chuckled. "I know, but if you plan on showing me, you might have to wait until we get home later. I said we'd pick Taryn up on our way to Giuseppe's and …"

He pressed another kiss to her lips. He hadn't meant that he was about to show her that he loved her in the way she was thinking. He was going to show her tonight that he loved her in a way that meant he wanted to commit the rest of his life to her – in a way that meant so much more than words, more than making love. But he couldn't explain, not without spoiling it. So, he just smiled and nodded. "I think by the time we get home, you'll understand."

Her eyes widened. "I like the sound of that."

~ ~ ~

Evie clung to Adam's hand as he led her through the restaurant. She hadn't realized how many of their friends would be here. It was lovely that they all wanted to welcome Taryn to town.

She glanced back over her shoulder and rolled her eyes when she saw that Taryn and Dalton were bickering again. Oh well. At least neither of them was feeling out of place in a new town. She doubted they even cared what town they were in – they were too busy bickering to notice.

She was happy when she finally got to introduce Taryn to Tino. She had a feeling that the two of them would get along well – and it was obvious that they did from the minute they started talking. Taryn even went in the back with him to see the kitchen.

Evie nudged Adam's arm when she saw the look on Dalton's face as he watched Taryn walk away. That wasn't the look of a man who was concerned about providing security for a woman or who was relieved to get a few minutes peace from her. Adam grinned when he saw what she meant.

Davin chuckled and waggled his eyebrows before Dalton's attention came back to the table and he looked around.

Even Russ had noticed what was going on. He smiled at Dalton. "I'm guessing that we'll be seeing you in the gym now that you're here?"

"Yeah." Dalton smiled at him. "You can sign me up for a membership."

Ria smiled at him. "Do you have family?"

Evie loved Ria. From what she'd said, she hadn't been close with her own family for a long time, but now that she'd learned to chill out – now that she was with Russ – she wanted everyone to know the joy of family.

Oops. It didn't look like Dalton found much joy in that subject. He shook his head with a scowl. To his credit, he recovered quickly and smiled back at Ria. "I hear you have family in town this weekend – your kids, right?"

"Just my son this weekend. I'm hoping my girls will come soon. But Russ's daughter's here."

"She's here already?" Evie asked. "You could have brought her out."

Russ laughed. "Don't you start. I've accepted that our weekend with the kids begins tomorrow morning. Between the mix-up over who got to stay at the house meaning that neither of them did, and then them not wanting to come out with us *old folks* tonight …" He shook his head, but he was grinning, obviously thrilled that they were both here. "They both decided that they were going to do their own thing tonight. The official introductions will have to wait until they come over for breakfast in the morning."

Evie frowned. "I thought all your kids met when you guys got engaged."

"Alyssa couldn't be here – not in person, remember?"

"But I talked to her," said Evie.

Russ chuckled. "Yeah, you talked to her because Tino had her on a video call and took her around to say hi to everyone. She met Ria's daughters that way, too. But she didn't get to meet Bentley because he had his dad and Gabriel on his phone, and he was taking them around so they could feel like they were here, too."

Evie smiled at Ria. She loved that her ex-husband was still a good friend to her, and to their children. "Well, I hope they get along and that you all have a great time."

"We will."

Evie looked over to check on Taryn; she was back at the table and chatting happily with Clay and his lady, Marianne. She'd been thrilled when she heard that not only did Clay McAdam live in town, but that Adam worked for him.

Evie already loved Marianne and Clay. They'd come to the house the day after everything happened with Anatoly, and Marianne had been a frequent visitor since. She was even talking about getting Evie to work on Clay's house. It was only a little way down Main Street from them. Which was perfect for Adam, too. He hadn't spent a night at Clay's guest house since they'd gotten together, but he was only two minutes away if he was needed.

She took a sip of her wine, thinking that this was one of the best nights she'd ever had. It was certainly the best since Tom died. She pressed her napkin to her mouth and blinked away tears. He'd be happy for her; she knew he would.

Davin caught her gaze from across the table and gave her a concerned look. She loved him. He was becoming a brother to her. She smiled and nodded, hoping to reassure him, but he got to his feet and came around the table to her.

Crouching down on the other side of her from Adam, he rested his hand on the back of her chair and asked quietly, "Are you okay?"

She put her hand on his arm. "I am, thanks, Davin. I'm happy. Those were happy tears."

"Okay." He held her gaze for a moment. "You deserve to be happy, Evie. And it's only going to get better from here."

Adam turned to look at them. He wrapped his arm around Evie's shoulders and narrowed his eyes at Davin. "Are you making a move on my lady?"

Davin laughed. "Nope! I'm checking on my sister."

Warmth spread through Evie's chest as she watched the two men smile at each other.

Then Davin's expression sobered. "I reckon it's time."

"For what?" asked Evie.

Adam dropped a kiss on her lips and then looked around at everyone. A hush fell over the table when he spoke. "It's time, folks."

Evie's breath caught in her chest when everyone turned to look at her. She didn't know what was going on. Until Adam got down on one knee and took hold of her hand.

Her free hand came up to cover her mouth and tears pricked her eyes as happiness bubbled up in her chest.

~ ~ ~

"Evie." Adam cleared his throat and tried again. He wasn't nervous, he was just so full of emotion that he felt like it might overflow.

He looked up into her eyes and a sense of peace washed over him.

"Evie, you know I'm not a romantic kind of guy. But I need you to know that I've waited my whole life for this, for you. I love you and I want to spend the rest of my days with you, making you happy." He smiled. "Being a team with you."

She was already nodding, tears rolling down her face.

"I kept hoping that when the moment came, some flowery words would flow out." He lifted her hand to his lips and kissed her knuckles. "But I've got nothing, sweetheart. Words could never be enough to tell you how much I love you, how much I hope that you'll spend the rest of your days with me. Will you marry me, Evie? Let me spend the rest of my life showing, you not just telling you."

She grasped hold of his hands and leaned in to kiss him. "Yes, Adam. I want to marry you. I want to spend the rest of my life loving you right back."

He slid the ring on her finger and got to his feet, drawing her to him so that he could kiss her.

When they finally came up for air, he rested his forehead against hers and looked deep into her eyes. She pressed a kiss to the corner of his mouth and nodded. He loved that they didn't need words to say it.

It was a long while before they got a quiet moment with each other after all the congratulations and hugs and backslaps. He loved that their friends were all there to share their happiness. But he needed her to himself for a minute.

He led her out to the back patio of the restaurant, grabbing two flutes of champagne from Tino as they went.

Once they were outside, he handed her a glass. She took it with a smile.

"I wanted to do a toast just for us. The only words I could think of were the words that you and Tom used to share." He smiled. "I want a new tradition just for you and me. I racked my brain trying to come up with the right words." He held his glass up to her and she clinked hers against it.

She laughed. "Go on, whatever it is, say it. I can tell you're pleased with whatever you came up with."

He chuckled and pressed a kiss to her lips. "I am. Let's do it again."

She clinked her glass against his for a second time with her eyebrows raised expectantly.

"Here's to no words."

She looked puzzled for a moment and then laughed. "Perfect! Because words are not enough."

He pressed another kiss to her lips. "That's right. And because instead of telling you, I plan to show you. I'll show you just as soon as we can ditch this party and go home, and I'll show you every day for the rest of our lives.";

;

A Note from SJ

I hope you enjoyed Adam and Evie's story.

Next up, we're going back to MacFarland Ranch for Deacon and Candy in The Sheriff's Irresistible Love. They are the first 'older' couple in the MacFarlands series. I decided not to separate the 'silver' characters into their own series this time. Roughly half of the books will feature the MacFarland brothers and sisters, and the other half will focus on the eldest brother, Cash's, friends.

Deacon is the Sheriff in Paradise Valley, and Candy – who we met in The Cowgirl's Unmistakable Love – was a foster mom to Rocket and Spider when they were young. She's come to Paradise Valley to help them out at the bakery, and to get away from some problems she was facing after her husband's death in California. That trouble is about to come looking for her in Montana, but since she's staying in Deacon's upstairs apartment, trouble is going to have to get past the Sheriff before it gets to her.

Deacon's still not sure how he ended up with that woman living upstairs. He'd like to get her out of there and get his life back to normal, but he can't get her out of his mind, there's no way he'd throw her out of his apartment, and before long he can't imagine letting her out of his life.

Then it's back to The Hamiltons and Napa for Bentley and Alyssa in Bourbon and Bluebells. Even though this will be book seven in the Hamiltons series, these two meet in Summer Lake. They've both gone to visit their parents – Alyssa has gone to see her dad, Russ, and Bentley's there to see his mom, Ria. Neither of them sees a problem in hooking up with the hot stranger they meet at The Boathouse, but the next day when they go off to meet up with their parents they each discover that their one-night stand is also their soon-to-be step-sibling.

Please let your friends know about the books if you feel they would enjoy them as well. It would be wonderful if you would leave me a review, I'd very much appreciate it.

Check out the "Also By" page to see if any of my other series appeal to you – I have the occasional ebook freebie series starters, too, so you can take them for a test drive.

There are a few options to keep up with me and my imaginary friends:

The best way is to Sign up for my Newsletter at my website www.SJMcCoy.com. Don't worry I won't bombard you! I'll let you know about upcoming releases, share a sneak peek or two and keep you in the loop for a couple of fun giveaways I have coming up :0)

You can join my readers group to chat about the books or like my Facebook Page www.facebook.com/authorsjmccoy

I occasionally attempt to say something in 140 characters or less(!) on Twitter

I love to hear from readers, so feel free to email me at SJ@SJMcCoy.com if you'd like. I'm better at that! :0)

I hope our paths will cross again soon. Until then, take care, and thanks for your support—you are the reason I write!

Love

SJ

PS Project Semicolon

You may have noticed that the final sentence of the story closed with a semi-colon. It isn't a typo. <u>Project Semi Colon</u> is a non-profit movement dedicated to presenting hope and love to those who are struggling with depression, suicide, addiction and self-injury. Project Semicolon exists to encourage, love and inspire. It's a movement I support with all my heart.

"A semicolon represents a sentence the author could have ended, but chose not to. The sentence is your life and the author is you." - Project Semicolon

This author started writing after her son was killed in a car crash. At the time I wanted my own story to be over, instead I chose to honour a promise to my son to write my 'silly stories' someday. I chose to escape into my fictional world. I know for many who struggle with depression, suicide can appear to be the only escape. The semicolon has become a symbol of support, and hopefully a reminder – Your story isn't over yet

Also by SJ McCoy

Summer Lake Silver

This series features couples in their fifties and older. Just because a few decades—or more—have skipped by since you were in your twenties it doesn't mean you can't find love, does it? Summer Lake Silver stories find happily-ever-afters for those who remember being thirty-something—vaguely.

Marianne and Clay in Like Some Old Country Song
Seymour and Chris in A Dream Too Far
Ted and Audrey in A Little Rain Must Fall
Diego and Izzy in Where the Rainbow Ends
Manny and Nina in Silhouettes Shadows and Sunsets
Teresa and Cal in More Than Sometimes
Russ and Ria in Like a Soft Sweet Breeze
Adam and Evelyn in When Words Are Not Enough
Coming Next
Dalton and Taryn in Can't Fight The Moonlight

Summer Lake Seasons
Angel and Luke in Take These Broken Wings
Zack and Maria in Too Much Love to Hide
Logan and Roxy in Sunshine Over Snow
Ivan and Abbie in Chase the Blues Away
Colt and Cassie in Forever Takes a While
Austin and Amber in Tell the Stars to Shine
Donovan and Elle in Please Don't Say Goodbye

Summer Lake Series

Emma and Jack in Love Like You've Never Been Hurt
Holly and Pete in Work Like You Don't Need the Money
Missy and Dan in Dance Like Nobody's Watching
Smoke and Laura in Fly Like You've Never Been Grounded
Michael and Megan in Laugh Like You've Never Cried
Kenzie and Chase in Sing Like Nobody's Listening
Gabe and Renée in Smile Like You Mean It
Missy and Dan's wedding in The Wedding Dance
Ben's backstory in Chasing Tomorrow
April and Eddie in Dream Like Nothing's Impossible
Nate and Lily in Ride Like You've Never Fallen
Ben's Story in Live Like There's No Tomorrow
Smoke and Laura's wedding in The Wedding Flight
Leanne and Ryan in Fight Like You've Never Lost

The Hamiltons
Cameron and Piper in Red Wine and Roses
Chelsea and Grant in Champagne and Daisies
Mary Ellen and Antonio in Marsala and Magnolias
Marcos and Molly in Prosecco and Peonies
Grady and Hannah in Milkshakes and Mistletoe
Jacob and Becca in Cognac and Cornflowers
Coming Next
Bentley and Alyssa in Bourbon and Bluebells
Slade and Willow in Whiskey and Willow
Xander and Tori in Vodka and Violets

Remington Ranch Series
Mason
Shane
Carter

Beau
Four Weddings and a Vendetta

A Chance and a Hope Trilogy
Chance Encounter
Finding Hope
Give Hope a Chance

MacFarland Ranch Series
Wade and Sierra in The Cowboy's Unexpected Love
Janey and Rocket in The Cowgirl's Unmistakable Love
Deacon and Candy in The Sheriff's Irresistible Love
Coming Next
Laney and Luke in The Cowgirl's Inevitable Love

The Davenports
Oscar
TJ
Reid
Spider

Love in Nashville
Autumn and Matt in Bring on the Night

Standalone Novella
Sully and Jess in If I Fall

About the Author

I'm SJ, a coffee addict, lover of chocolate and drinker of good red wines. I'm a lost soul and a hopeless romantic. Reading and writing are necessary parts of who I am. Though perhaps not as necessary as coffee! I can drink coffee without writing, but I can't write without coffee.

I grew up loving romance novels, my first boyfriends were book boyfriends, but life intervened, as it tends to do, and I wandered down the paths of non-fiction for many years. My life changed completely a few years ago and I returned to Romance to find my escape.

I write 'Sweet n Steamy' stories because to me there is enough angst and darkness in real life. My favorite romances are happy escapes with a focus on fun, friendships and happily-ever-afters, just like the ones I write.

These days I live in beautiful Montana, the last best place. If I'm not reading or writing, you'll find me just down the road in the park - Yellowstone. I have deer, eagles and the occasional bear for company, and I like it that way :0)

Printed in Great Britain
by Amazon